WHY DO 300 MILLION VIEWERS IN 57 COUNTRIES LOVE TO HATE J.R. . . . ?

"DALLAS is different . . . DALLAS offers adventure . . . DALLAS tells viewers that the rich really are different, they sin more spectacularly and suffer in style."

—Time

"DALLAS is the boldest, brassiest, most notorious series on TV . . . provides more treachery each week, more drink, criminal business dealings, adultery, panic, and different strands of love *faster* than anything else on the air."

—Gloria Emerson, Pulitzer prizewinner in *Vogue*

"The Ewings leave the Borgias at the post!"

—TV Guide

The Women of Dallas

A Novel by
BURT HIRSCHFELD

Based on the series created
by David Jacobs
Based on the series created by
David Jacobs and on the teleplays
written by Loraine Despres, D. C. Fontana,
Richard Fontana, Arthur Bernard Lewis
and Camille Marchetta

BANTAM BOOKS · TORONTO · NEW YORK

THE WOMEN OF DALLAS
A Bantam Book / February 1981

ISBN 0–553–14497–9

Published simultaneously in the United States and Canada

Bantam Books are published by Bantam Books, Inc. Its trade-
mark, consisting of the words "Bantam Books" and the por-
trayal of a bantam, is Registered in U.S. Patent and Trademark
Office and in other countries. Marca Registrada. Bantam
Books, Inc., 666 Fifth Avenue, New York, New York 10103.

PART 1

Miss Ellie

1

The heat wave spread across the southwest like a thick, poisonous cloud. In Texas the temperatures rose to well over a hundred, the air dry with dust, the sky faintly yellowed. On ranches and farms everywhere, cows and horses dehydrated and died. In chicken coops, farmers paced up and back in a vain attempt to keep their chickens from sinking into a lethargy from which there was no return. Rivers ran dry, and lakes and water holes were transformed into cracked, hard mud. Soon reports of human beings dying began to be heard, and people prayed for relief from the drought, for rain. But there was no rain and no relief.

On the morning of the twenty-first day of the heat wave, Ellie Ewing made up her mind. She had finished her morning toilet, had dressed, and now stared at herself in the mirror above her dressing table. The face that stared back at her seemed different, the face of a passer-by—vaguely familiar, reminding her of someone she had once known well but had not seen for a very long time. The soft lines were blurred, and faint creases added age and concern to the image in the glass. Oh, the hair was still that tawny yellow, and the eyes were still blue, if not quite as clear. But there was a pinch of worry in the expression, evidence of the fear that could no longer be contained, no longer concealed. Life, in its casual disregard for feelings and fantasies, had thrust itself cruelly upon her. She no longer was the lovely young woman she had once been. The years had penetrated every aspect of her being, warning her that time was running out. For the first time in easy memory, Miss Ellie was scared for herself.

She braced herself for what lay ahead and went downstairs to the den. It had always been one of her favorite rooms, rustic and rugged, with the rich scent of soft leathers and hard woods. Natural smells and looks. Here the imprint of her family was strong and lasting, assurance that the path she had chosen for herself so long ago had been a good one, sound, productive, laced with respect and affection. She shut the door behind her and picked up the phone. Hesitating only briefly, she dialed. A woman's voice answered.

"Doctor's office."

"This is Ellie Ewing. May I speak to Dr. Danvers, please?"

"Doctor isn't in yet. May I help you, Mrs. Ewing?"

"I think I'd like to come in and see Dr. Danvers."

"Yes, ma'am. Will Thursday morning be all right? Ten o'clock."

"I mean right away. Today."

"I see. Well, we do have a tight schedule."

"It's important."

The impersonal voice at the other end of the line didn't seem impressed. "Is this an emergency?"

Miss Ellie made no attempt to keep the annoyance out of her voice. "Young lady, I said it's important. I have been Dr. Danvers' patient for a considerable period of time. I want to see him this morning. Ten o'clock will be fine. Make the appointment, please."

The secretary understood that all her choices had been snatched away. Ellie Ewing was not a woman to argue with. "Ten o'clock, Mrs. Ewing. I've written you in."

Miss Ellie hung up just as her husband, Jock, entered the den. He was a tall, well-built man with a shock of white hair framing a rugged outdoorsman's face. In tooled black boots and blue ranch pants, he seemed fit enough to ride herd on a bunch of longhorns for the best part of the day. He took his wife's elbow.

"Been looking for you, Miss Ellie. Don't care to breakfast by my lonesome. How about some hotcakes and sausage?"

"I'm not hungry."

"Well, all right. Coffee then?"

She shook her head and disengaged herself from his grip.

4

He measured her narrowly. "You all right, Miss Ellie?"

"Just fine, Jock. Guess my head's elsewhere this morning. Got a dozen chores to do in town and all that juggling to do."

"Okay. Thought I'd go into the office later on. I'll ride you in."

"No," she said, trying to keep her voice natural. "Pam's going into Dallas. I'll catch a ride with her." Without another word she left the den. Jock, slightly perplexed by this wife of his, as he often had been over the four decades of their marriage, went after his breakfast.

Earlier that same morning, Ray Krebbs, foreman of Southfork, and Bobby Ewing drove up to the stable area in an old Ford pickup and unloaded a recently repaired tack and saddle.

Bobby mopped his brow. "This heat is getting to be too much for man and beast alike."

Ray agreed. "Don't know what's likely to happen if'n we don't get rain before long."

They strolled over to Bobby's car, parked nearby. "You comin' up to the house for some breakfast, Ray?"

"Believe I'll pass. Got a long day in front of me."

Bobby hesitated, then decided to plunge in. "You intend to see that lady of yours again?"

Ray considered his answer. "Not right away. But I talked to Donna the day of the rodeo. I told her all her letters came on through."

Bobby shook his head. "You are a case, man. I can't understand how you could let 'em just pile up like that, never read a one."

Ray tugged at his chin. "Well, Bobby, it's like this. When I heard Donna and old Sam Culver had reconciled, I had to figure—" He broke off and looked away.

"Had to figure what? That Donna was after you just for your beautiful body? Man, if the lady wants a roll in the hay, she don't have to beg for it from Ray Krebbs. I mean, she is one good-looking gal."

"I know, I know. My feelings for her go way beyond just a once-in-a-while diddlin'. I had no idea Sam Culver was dying."

5

"Which was why she went back to him. I tell you, you thought all wrong about Donna."

"A man's been burned as often as I have, he gets a little gun-shy." His eyes swung away, and Bobby followed his glance. A car went rolling past out on Braddock Road. "Pretty early in the day for Sue Ellen to be traipsing about, isn't it?"

"Maybe the shrink gave her an earlier appointment, trying to beat the heat."

Ray shook his head. "She left the same time yesterday. I saw her go past, out on the range. Well, I reckon that's her affair, and J.R.'s."

"I reckon. See you by 'n by, pardner."

Ray went back into the stable, and Bobby drove off in the direction of the big house, trying not to worry about his sister-in-law's comings and goings. He had his own life to consider, his own wife. . . .

Initially Jock was pleased to have the company of his granddaughter, Lucy, at breakfast. But he soon grew weary of her babbling about Alan Beam. The young lawyer was not one of Jock's favorite people, and his mind drifted to his own concerns, only to be brought rudely back to Lucy's high-pitched enthusiasm.

"I tell you Granddaddy, I think it is important for someone to stand up to J.R. once in a while." She flashed a brilliant smile toward Jock. "Not that I am saying even one solitary word against J.R., Granddaddy. But it was just fantastic the way Alan Beam faced him down at the rodeo. Just simply fantastic."

"Lucy—" Jock felt himself to be sinking into a sump hole of verbiage. He yearned for slow conversation or none at all. "Lucy," he said again.

"Yes, Granddaddy?"

"Don't you have to get yourself out to school this morning?"

She made a gesture of dismissal. "Oh, I have some time yet. I just love being alone with you, Granddaddy, conversing this way. I don't get much of a chance to spend time with you thisaway."

Jock patted her hand. "You're a good girl, Lucy."

"Thank you, Granddaddy."

"But I got to tell you straight out—I have heard about all I want to hear about Alan Beam for this morning, if you don't mind."

"Oh, I don't mind a bit."

"What's that you don't mind, pretty Lucy?" It was Bobby, striding in from outside, his faded denim shirt stained with sweat.

"Good morning, son," Jock said.

"Good morning, Bobby. I was just telling Granddaddy how highly I thought of the way Alan Beam confronted J.R. at the rodeo. Seems to me he—"

"Lucy," Jock said in warning.

Giggling, she stood up. She kissed Jock, then Bobby. "I guess it's time I did get on to school. Bye, y'all."

When she was gone, Bobby helped himself to a cup of coffee.

"Cooled down any?" Jock asked.

"Not a bit, Daddy. The land out there is baked dry. Some of those small ranchers goin' to be in bad trouble if we don't get some rain soon."

Jock rocked his head back and forth. "That's the thing about this country. Ain't a question of *if* we're goin' to get a drought. Just a question of when."

Bobby grunted his assent. "Brought your saddle back in this morning. Jed did a fine repair job on it."

"I'll have to thank the man."

"When you have the time, I'd like to run down those feed bills with you. They're beginning to look like the national debt."

"Maybe later."

Bobby put his coffee cup aside. "Something on your mind, Daddy? Last couple of weeks, you seemed preoccupied. Any trouble you got—well, your troubles are my troubles."

Jock considered his reply. "No, nothing amounts to a hill o' beans. I wanted to talk a few things over with J.R. this morning. Only thing is, he didn't come home last night."

"You reckon there's trouble again between him and Sue Ellen?"

"Seems likely. I thought things had changed now, with the baby and all. Guess I was mistaken."

"J.R.'s a grown man. He's going to have to work out his own problems."

Jock placed his hands flat on the table and pushed himself erect. "Seems like that holds for us all in this world. Maybe I can catch up with J.R. later on at the office. See you this evening, son."

Frowning, Bobby watched him go. It seemed to him that when a man attained Jock Ewing's station in life, his accomplishments, his age, he was entitled to a little peace. Life tended to dictate otherwise.

Kristin managed to look ravishing without lipstick or eye shadow. Wearing only panties and a bra, she returned to the darkened bedroom, a cup of coffee in each hand. J.R. sprawled comfortably on the bed, still deeply asleep. She spoke his name twice, louder the second time. He shifted positions, but did not awaken. She placed the coffee on the night table and stroked his broad back, nibbled at his ear. He moaned in protest.

"Wake up, J.R., and see what Kristin's brought you. Wake up, J.R., and see what you can have just by reachin' out and helpin' yourself."

He snored fitfully in answer, and she frowned.

"Wake up, J.R. The well was spudded in. You got yourself another real gusher."

"Huh? . . ."

"The core is all gray shale. We're cementing in the surface pipe, and I've called for the blowout preventer. Better git your butt up out of the sack and ramrod this strike through to the end."

One baleful blue eye rolled open. "What in God's name time is it?"

"Talk of a gusher and you can rouse any oilman worth the name."

J.R. sat up. "Dammit, girl! It is daylight! It is morning!"

"That's right, luv. Another day, another million dollars."

"You let me sleep through the night."

"Let you! Oh, man, you just rolled over and were out. I figured maybe I gave you a cardiac arrest."

"Not funny, Kristin."

"You complainin' about last night, lover?"

"No complaints. But I told you to get me out of here at a reasonable hour."

"I didn't have the heart. Besides, all the good lovin', I figured you were entitled to a long night's rest. Can I interest you in a little encore to start off the day?"

"I told you never to do that. You should've wakened me."

He rushed into the bathroom, and Kristin could hear the sound of the shower running. "Well, you sure did toss and turn all night long. You seemed exhausted."

His voice came over the sound of the shower. "You are an exciting young woman, sugar. Gets me all keyed up."

"That's got the Kristin stamp of approval." She picked a dress out of the closet and put it on. "Only thing is," she called, "sometimes you get keyed up over the wrong things."

"Where are my clothes?" he shouted.

"They're all messed up. I'll drop them at the cleaners. I put another suit behind the door for you."

She heard the sound of the shower cease and imagined him drying himself. It was a pleasant image, a pleasant fantasy. "You be comin' round this evening again, J.R.?"

"You are a sweet thing, only don't let's pull this kind of thing again."

He came out of the bathroom, buttoning his shirt.

"I do so enjoy waking up with you beside me, J.R."

"Sure you do." How many women had said that to him; how few had meant it. "But that's no excuse. I'm a married man."

"I know, to my sister."

"Remember it next time."

"J.R., I can really help you, if you'll permit me to."

"You're doing just fine."

"I mean, I know how worried you are."

He turned a cold glance her way. "Everything's under control."

"It's not really, not when everything the Ewings own is mortgaged, including Southfork."

"That," he said coolly, "is none of your concern."

"I know how concerned you are that Jock will find out."

"Leave my father out of this."

"Maybe if you'd just talk to me a bit more, it would help you relax."

9

"Well, darling, if you know and I know, then there's nothing to talk about, is there? Now if you really want me to relax, you'll hustle your pretty little tail out of here, drop my suit off at the cleaners, and get to the offices of Ewing Oil where you belong. That way you can be on the spot to greet me when I make my grand entrance."

Pouting, she strode out of the apartment. J.R. finished dressing and picked up his coffee cup. As he drank, he frowned. "Damn woman can't even make a decent cup of coffee."

2

$\mathcal{H}$arlan Danvers had the practiced, detached manner utilized by so many physicians to keep them distant from their patients' problems. Danvers had assured himself a thousand times that only thus could he apply his very great medical and scientific learning to the full benefit of those who needed it most. Yet he was—and always had been—a man with a deep sympathy for human beings in trouble. Each week he devoted a substantial amount of his working time to providing first-rate medical care for the working poor and the indigent, convinced that it was his duty as a doctor to see to the good health of the community at all its levels.

Now as he entered the examining room he carried an X-ray, which he snapped into place on a viewing screen. He switched on the light.

"Look here, Ellie, this is your X-ray mammogram. As you can see, there are no tumors."

She exhaled audibly. "Well, that's a relief."

He tapped the X-ray with one strong finger. "The mammogram does show what might be cysts."

"That's what I had the last time."

"Exactly. I went over it carefully with the radiologist. He agrees with me. There is no sign on the mammogram of a cancer in your breast."

She gave him a wan smile. "You must think I'm an awful ninny, Harlan. I'm beginning to feel like a hypochondriac. But I did feel a lump."

"Of course you did. But most lumps are not cancer, Ellie. When a woman examines herself she may discover a lumpy area that is persistent and recurring."

Her lips flattened out, white spots at each corner of her mouth. "Harlan," she said firmly, "what I felt was a distinct change."

He shook his head, then spoke deliberately. "Ellie, all the other tests are negative. I don't think we should rush you into surgery on that kind of evidence."

"You stand close watch on your own body, Ellie. As soon as I receive the results of the test, I'll inform you."

Ellie nodded and gave a small smile. "Which means everything is on hold until then?"

"Until we know for sure."

It was not the most encouraging of comments, she thought wryly. But it was one she would have to live with.

MITZI'S COFFEE SHOP—BRADDOCK, TEXAS: the sign outside read. Inside, the walls were lined with booths, and a few tables with checkered tablecloths filled the floor to the counter. Hand-painted signs on the walls called attention to breakfast and luncheon specials. The breakfast rush over, only a few customers were present at this hour: a couple of truckers at the counter, a farmer in the rear booth, two men in business suits near the door. And Sue Ellen, chic and lovely in a print dress from Neiman-Marcus, lingering over a cup of coffee and some uneaten toast. Her eyes kept focusing on the front door as if she were waiting for someone. The waitress moved over to her table.

"Anything else I can get you, Mrs. Ewing?"

"I don't think so. I'm fine—" She stiffened in place as a tall cowboy entered the restaurant. He turned in her direction, and she realized that he was no one she knew. She slumped back in disappointment. "Thank you," she said to the waitress. "Just the check, please. I have to get on in to Dallas."

The waitress presented the check. "Nice to have you in again, Mrs. Ewing. Don't often see any of the Ewings in here for breakfast."

Sue Ellen dropped a bill on the table. "Keep the change."

"See you again tomorrow, Mrs. Ewing?"

Sue Ellen hesitated, nodded quickly, and left.

Jock barged into the reception area of Ewing Enterprises and greeted the secretaries. "Good morning, ladies. J.R. in his office?"

"Good morning, Mr. Ewing," Connie said.

"Good morning, Uncle Jock," Kristin said. "J.R. isn't in yet."

Jock frowned. "Keeping banker's hours, is he? Hope he ain't missing any important business."

Connie answered evenly. "Loyal Hansen called in twice, seemed anxious to talk to J.R."

"Well—" Jock began.

Before he could go on, the door opened, and J.R. strode in, cheerful and smiling. "Good morning, Daddy. Ladies. Hope I didn't keep you folks waiting." He swept past them and into his office, scaling his white sombrero onto the long leather couch. Behind him, Jock followed, shutting the door.

"Didn't expect to see you down here this morning, Daddy. Ain't this heat something awful? Seems to me you'd be better off back at the ranch, cool and comfortable."

"I got something on my mind."

J.R. placed himself behind his desk, put his finger tips together to form a steeple, and addressed his father. "My time is your time, Daddy."

Jock put himself into a chair, swung his boots up to the edge of J.R.'s polished desk, almost as if establishing his own authority. "I was hoping to have a chance to talk to you last night. Privately."

"Had a long meeting with some of the boys," J.R. said smoothly. "First thing I knew it was too late to drive all the way back out to Southfork." He flipped the switch on the intercom. "Which one of you ladies made the coffee this morning?"

"I did, J.R.," Connie said.

J.R. was relieved. "Well, bring us a couple of cups, if you don't mind." He switched off. "Stayed at the Fairview, got me a good night's sleep. Still the best hotel in town by far, Daddy."

Jock scowled, started to speak, and broke off when Connie appeared with the coffee. He waited until she had gone before going on. "Didn't drive all the way in here to discuss where you spent the night or how you slept."

13

J.R. tried the coffee. It was hot, strong, satisfying; it made him forget the awful stuff Kristin had made earlier. "Well, fine. What's on your mind?"

The intercom buzzed. J.R. answered. "Yes?"

It was Kristin. "Loyal Hansen on the phone. Third time he's called."

"I'll get back to him." He switched off and turned back to Jock. "You were saying, Daddy?"

Jock hesitated. "That Loyal Hansen, he's a foreign oil expert, if I recollect right."

"He's been after me to make a small investment overseas."

"Overseas! What about the import quota? How's that goin' to affect our domestic operation?"

"Well, you know, Daddy, if you find it over there, you can sell it over there. World's a big place, Daddy, and the demand for oil is growing every day."

Jock started to respond, but he had other, more pressing matters on his mind. "J.R., where are the papers for me to sign?"

"Papers?"

"Yes, dammit! I told you to set up a trust fund for my ex-wife. That was weeks ago. What in hell you fiddle-faddling around for, boy?"

"Well, now, Daddy, when you told me to do that, you weren't feeling exactly tip-top, if you remember. All that's past. You're in super condition now. You've been sending checks for Amanda's care at that institution. Don't hardly see the need to alter things any."

Jock brought his feet back down to the floor, leaning forward, his seamed face firmed up, eyes glinting. "J.R., there's something you better understand straight out. Amanda was my first wife—even if you and me's the only ones who know about it. She was one of the women in my life and an important one at the time. I cared for her then, I still do. This is one Ewing who does for the women in his life, whatever needs doing. Do you hear me, boy?"

"I hear you, Daddy."

"Well, good. So you get Kristin to haul the accountants in here and my lawyer, Harv Smithfield. I want them on this right away. Looks like I got to handle this matter by my own self."

"Now, Daddy, I told you it was in the works."

"In the works! Then let's get a look-see at those papers."

J.R. considered his answer carefully. "Okay, Daddy, I got to admit it. I have lied to you, for the first time. The very first time."

"Lied? Why?"

"Because of Momma. Maybe it's none of my business that you were married before. But I can't help feeling as if I'm doing something behind Momma's back."

Jock froze in place. He had always fancied himself as a man of integrity, honest, a man who did things up front where everyone could see. But this—

"Keep talking," he said.

"Have you told Momma about this?"

"Can't say I have. Never did seem to be the right time."

"Well, Daddy, if you want me to go ahead with this and keep it hidden from Momma, I surely will do it, though I got to say it goes against the grain."

Jock stood up. "You're right, son. I'm not being square with Miss Ellie. I'll tell her about it tonight. You hold off till then." He marched out, shoulders high and stiff, back straight.

J.R. breathed a sigh of relief. He'd bought some time, time to figure out how to deal conclusively with this matter, how to use it to his own eventual benefit.

3

The Joshua Tree was a Mexican restaurant only blocks from the Ewing Building. There among brightly hued murals of Mexican life in a large room under a skylight surrounded by potted plants and fresh-cut flowers, Pam Ewing, Bobby's wife, was having lunch with Miss Ellie. They began with Margaritas, followed by guacamole and chile rellenos. By the time the coffee came, Miss Ellie had finished revealing the details of her visit to Dr. Danvers.

Pam, a frown creasing her ordinarily open face, took her mother-in-law's hand in hers. "What happens next?"

"I keep up the self-examinations and have frequent check-ups."

"That doesn't sound so difficult." The words gave no indication of the depth of her concern. Since her marriage to Bobby, Pam had come to know Miss Ellie for the strong and courageous woman she was, reliable in a crisis, always loving, with a profound and ongoing respect for other people. She had come to admire and envy her and her down-to-earth approach to life. The thought of Miss Ellie being ill had never crossed her mind. Vigor and energy, a powerful life force were the qualities that distinguished the older woman. The possibility that she might be brought low by cancer, that she might indeed die, was so stunning and terrifying a thought as to encase her mind in a dark, oppressive cover. Her voice broke when she spoke again. "Everything's going to be all right."

Miss Ellie almost smiled. "We'll have to wait and see."

"I'm sure of it."

"I hope you're right. There's so much to live for. My children, my grandchildren, the grandchildren that you and Bobby will one day give us. . . ."

Pam struggled not to cry. "Does Jock know?"

"I don't want him to know."

"But he's your husband. Isn't he entitled to know? Wouldn't he want to know?"

"That man gets better looking as he gets older," she said with grim intensity. "Taller it seems, leaner, not an ounce of fat on him. I know how Jock admires beauty—in the land, the sky, in animals, and in women. That old reprobate—he still has a sharp eye for a good-looking woman. How can I tell him that I may need an operation, that I might be disfigured?"

"He loves you, Miss Ellie. It will be all right. It has to be."

"All right! Perhaps. Perhaps not. What if he turns away from me? The thought chills me to the core."

"No . . ."

"My big fear is that Jock will never be able to accept me again. Never be able to look at me again. Never love me again. I don't think I can face the possibility of losing him because of this."

Pam shuddered and held on to Miss Ellie's hand as if gaining strength from the other woman. "You told me once that your marriage to Jock was built on being honest with each other. Now, maybe more than ever before, you have to trust your love for each other, and that honesty."

Miss Ellie let her eyes flutter shut, and they stayed that way for a long, unmeasured space of time. Finally she looked at Pam again and allowed a faint smile to drift across her mouth. "Of course you're right, my dear. But fear does funny things to people. Jock is a strong man. No man I've ever known was stronger. He can face whatever comes along."

"And so can you."

"I hope you're right." Miss Ellie withdrew her hand. "Tonight. I'll try and tell him tonight. It's what I've really wanted to do from the start."

17

That evening, in the conditioned coolness of Southfork, Jock led Miss Ellie into the den and closed the room off to the rest of the family.

"Miss Ellie," he announced formally, "I want to talk to you."

"And I want to talk to you, Jock."

An expression of palpable relief washed across his face. "Well, now, then you go right ahead. What's on your mind, Miss Ellie?"

"No, you first."

"That's all right. Whatever I've got to say can wait."

"Jock," she said in a soft, low voice that he knew was lined with steel, "whatever it is, spit it out."

Nodding, he turned away and began stirring a pitcher of martinis. She watched him for a long time.

"Keep mixing those drinks," she said finally, "and you're going to have whipped cream."

"Huh?" He threw a quick, uncertain glance over his shoulder. "Right. I reckon they're done." He filled two glasses, then carried one to his wife.

She sipped and told him it was perfect. "I'm listening, Jock."

He nodded his head once in reluctant commitment. "Miss Ellie, I guess when a man and a woman have been married as long as we have, they can sense that something's wrong. . . ."

She watched him over the rim of the glass. "You're right. I guess we are beyond keeping things from each other."

"I could see it on your face."

"Jock—I wanted to talk."

"No keeping anything from you. You're just too damned cunning. You must have picked it up without my ever knowing."

"Or the other way round."

"The thing is, I never knew how to tell you. A hundred times I've been out on the edge of it, but I lost my nerve."

Miss Ellie blinked. Clearly Jock knew nothing about her visit to Dr. Danvers. He was troubled by something else. "Are you sick, Jock?"

"Me? Sick? Hell, no, Miss Ellie. I've always had the constitution of a horse."

"Not always, Jock," she reminded him gently.

"Well, now that itty-bitty trouble with my heart didn't add up to a hill of beans."

She straightened up. "Well, if you're not sick, what is it, Jock? You've got me half scared to death."

"I've got something to tell you."

"Dammit, man, don't you think I know that by now? All this beatin' around the bush. Tell me what?"

"About Amanda—" he choked out.

"Amanda?"

"Here I wait forty years, and don't you know, it would all come out backwards."

"Jock, I don't understand a word you're saying. Who is this Amanda you're talking about?"

"Miss Ellie"—he sucked air into his lungs—"I am trying to tell you about my first wife."

She stared at him without comprehension. "Your first wife? . . ."

"Yes, dammit. Before I ever met you, I was married and divorced. Long before I met you. Her name was Amanda."

Miss Ellie felt her joints lock in place. Her throat thickened. Resentment gave way to anger and anger to unbridled rage. Tears welled up behind her eyes, and she put her glass aside for fear she might drop it. Or hurl it into Jock's face.

"What," she bit off thinly, "are you talking about?"

"It's almost as if it never happened. Part of a dream. Or a movie I once saw. But back when I was out on that dove hunt with the boys, when those bushwhackers put a bullet into me, I wasn't sure I was going to make it. That's when I started thinking about Amanda. I realized I had an obligation to her—"

"Obligation!" Miss Ellie almost shouted.

The thing is she is not a well woman, Miss Ellie. Amanda had a complete mental breakdown shortly after we got married. Her doctor finally suggested to me that I get a divorce. He said there was no hope for her recovery, that she'd always be sick, always be an invalid, not a whole person. She had to be hospitalized, and I've been paying her sanitarium bills ever since. Well, when I was shot, I worked it out in my head that if anything happened to me there

19

ought to be some kind of trust fund to continue the payments for Amanda. I had to talk to you first, Miss Ellie."

The rage gathered in her then, like a twister coming over the near horizon, picking up force, without control. She came erect, and for a long beat Jock thought she was going to strike him. "You divorced a woman because she was sick!" she cried. "Turned your back on her when she most needed you!"

"Miss Ellie, the doctor said—"

"I don't care what the doctor said."

"I thought it would be best."

"And you kept this from me all the time, all these years."

"I wanted to tell you. Believe me. But I was afraid I'd lose you. Lose you to Digger. He was after you, and I was none too sure of myself back then."

Her words were edged with scorn. "What else haven't you told me? A marriage based on honesty, trust, that's what I thought we had. Now I discover you've been living a lie all these years."

"Miss Ellie, that was a long time ago."

"What does time matter? You walked out on her then. Deserted a sick woman. Tell me, Jock, if I get sick, are you going to desert me, too? Walk out and leave me alone?" She pulled away and stalked from the room.

Jock, alone and stunned, experienced a thrust of fear greater than any he had ever before known.

___ 4 ___

*I*n the living room J.R., Sue Ellen, Bobby, Pam, and Lucy had not failed to hear the angry voices from the den. If they could not hear the words, there was no doubt about the accusing tone used by Miss Ellie. And now they saw her come storming around the corner and head determinedly upstairs.

"What was that all about?" Bobby asked, expecting no good answer.

"Beats me," J.R. said, certain he knew the subject of the argument, concerned, too, lest he had gone too far in attempting to manipulate his father in his own self-interest.

Lucy spoke up in awe and fright. "I never heard Grandma sound so angry. What do you think they were saying?"

"I don't know," Bobby said. "J.R., you got any ideas on the subject?"

J.R. shrugged innocently. "What you heard is what I heard."

The reply satisfied nobody. "Maybe," Bobby said, "I'd better talk to Daddy."

"I'd stay out of it, if I were you," J.R. suggested mildly.

Bobby acknowledged the remark. "But I'm not you." He headed toward the den.

"Pam," Lucy said, clearly worried, "what do you think?"

"I'm sure it will all work out, whatever's wrong."

I surely do hope so. It just bothers the life out of me when Grandma and Grandpa get to scrappin'. It's like everything I can still trust and hold onto is coming apart."

Pam looped an arm around the younger woman's shoulders, trying to express more confidence than she truly felt.

In the den Jock finished one drink and poured himself another, then tossed back a long pull. He lit a cigarette, dragged heavily, and began to cough.

"Those cigarettes can be pretty destructive to a man who had a heart attack, Daddy," Bobby said.

Jock answered without turning. "Some things are more destructive to a man's well-being than a little tobacco." He killed off the martini and went after another.

"You mean to go off on one of those old-fashioned drunks the old-timers talk about, Daddy? Never knew martinis were the drink of the oil fields."

"Dammit, boy, don't lecture me."

"Sorry if it came out that way. Anything I can do to help?"

"No," Jock growled. "Not a damned thing." He took another long puff on the cigarette, then ground it out in an ashtray. "Dammit, Bobby, I been married to that woman for a hellish long time, and there are times when I can't understand a damn thing she means or wants." He rocked his full white mane from side to side. "Never did know what women wanted."

Bobby grinned. "When you find out, Daddy, let the rest of us in on the secret."

Jock grunted softly and turned away. But the serrated edge of his resentment had softened, and he began thinking of ways to bridge the gulf between himself and Miss Ellie.

Bobby remained with his father for nearly thirty minutes, their conversation proceeding in fits and starts, going nowhere, until finally he withdrew. Later that night as he and Pam prepared for bed, they discussed what had transpired.

"Miss Ellie still alone in her bedroom?" Pam asked.

"Apparently. And Daddy seems to have just about bedded down in the den. He's in there smoking and drinking like he's trying for another heart attack."

Pam stepped out of her panties and donned a flowing nightgown of transparent gauze. From his place in a deep chair across the room, Bobby remarked to himself once again on how stunning his wife was; the most beautiful woman he had ever known. He stood up.

"Shouldn't you say something to Jock?" she asked, beginning to brush her shining hair. "Remind him that he's doing himself harm?"

"I did. But talking to Daddy when he's on one of his rampages is like trying to coax a mad bull to be calm and reasonable." He stood behind Pam at her dressing table, hands resting lightly on her shoulders. The warmth of her delicate skin flowed into his veins. He kissed the back of her neck. She shivered.

"Bobby," she said softly, putting the brush aside, "I think I may be responsible in some way for what took place. Miss Ellie and I had lunch today. She told me some personal things, and I told her she shouldn't keep them from Jock."

Bobby drew her erect, and she came around to face him, arms sliding around his waist. His body was firm, strong, without an extra ounce of flesh. No man had ever excited her as much as this handsome husband of hers, no man had ever loved her more. Or loved her better, she added silently.

"What things?" he asked. "What can be so terrible that Momma would lose her temper that way? One thing about Miss Ellie, she's almost always in control, almost always on top of things. She's the strongest, most secure person I've ever encountered."

Pam bit back the impulse to tell Bobby what she knew. "I don't know—but I can see how on edge she is. Almost anything could have set her off."

"Why?"

Pam hesitated, then decided she could no longer keep Miss Ellie's secret to herself. "She found a lump in her breast."

Bobby stepped back as if struck, all color draining out of his face. His eyes skittered as if out of control. "Oh, Lord—a tumor?"

"Dr. Danvers' preliminary examination doesn't indicate a tumor. He seems to think it's nothing serious—benign. But your mother is convinced that it is a tumor, and serious."

Bobby turned away. "What about getting a second opinion?"

"Apparently they've done all the tests they can at this point. It's just a matter of waiting it out and Miss Ellie getting frequent checkups."

Bobby lowered himself to the edge of their bed, his face buried in his hands. Pam crossed to him, pressing his cheek up against the soft rise of her belly. He embraced her, and they held onto each other without speaking for a very long time. Then Bobby pulled away.

"I don't believe it," he said. "I know my mother, and it must be something more."

"What are you getting at?"

"Something else must have happened that we don't know about to set her off that way. Maybe a combination of things. Dammit, I wish I could do something—"

"But, Bobby, she seemed so concerned this afternoon about the way Jock was going to take the news."

"I don't understand that. He loves her, she knows that he does."

"Bobby," she said softly, "sometimes women believe that in order to hold their men they have to be perfect. Always perfect."

Bobby let that roll around his mind. "Maybe it's time for them to understand that a man can love a woman so much that nothing matters except that she's alive and with him."

She moved toward him, aware in every tingling nerve-ending that he was speaking to her now; she reveled in it. Awash in love and affection, in need, she went to his arms, and they kissed.

"There is nothing that could ever happen that would stop me from loving you," he said.

"Oh, Bobby, you make me so happy. I love you so much and want to give you everything you want."

He drew her down on the bed, hands stroking her gently. "You do," he said into her hair. "Everything I ever wanted."

5

Sue Ellen applied makeup with the exacting concern of a woman intent on appearing disinterested in her own good looks. Her face was a succession of contradictions: the open beauty of a Mardi Gras queen shadowed by a deep watchfulness, a quick, flaring suspicion; the vulnerability and physical helplessness of a sparrow combined with the lush sensuality of a tropical garden issuing thick, heady scents. Satisfied with her handiwork, she examined herself once more in the glass, her expression flat and her large eyes surprisingly dull. She stood up and put on the short, nubby knit jacket that completed the pink suit she had chosen to wear. A single gold chain, exquisitely wrought and obviously expensive, completed her attire.

Behind her J.R. was going through the complicated ritual of selecting a tie to complement his bland handsomeness. Each one he chose seemed to have something wrong with it, and he discarded one after another with rising exasperation, a man who knew what he wanted and intended to have it.

"What do you make of last night, J.R.?" Sue Ellen spoke in a voice without color or expression, the query put politely but without real concern for her husband's opinion. Polite verbal links in a marriage otherwise drifting onto the shoals of self-interest and mutual dislike.

"Last night?" He went on to another tie. "Damn things all look tired and worn out."

"That was quite an explosion from Miss Ellie, truly out of character, wouldn't you say?"

25

"I wouldn't say. Look at that grease spot! Now, you would think somebody around here would look after a man's ties."

"Meaning me, I suppose," she said under her breath. Then aloud: "I do not believe I have ever heard Miss Ellie raise her voice to Jock like that before."

"Here's one with a tear in it, just ruined. It'll blow over, these things always do."

Sue Ellen measured her husband from across the room with the still-eyed expertise of a judge at a livestock show: shoulders good, chest deep, neck thick, stance acceptable. But little else, she reminded herself: emotional content zero, human awareness zero, sympathy zero. It was evident that J.R. Ewing managed to exist in a world crowded with other human beings with neither concern nor care for any of them, himself excepted.

As if to confirm her thoughts, he swore at his collection of hanging ties—patterns, solids, stripes, knits—giving voice to his disappointment in them all.

She smiled without mirth, her immense blue eyes flat and tinged with pain. "You know what it was all about, don't you?"

"What makes you think that?"

"Believe it or not, J.R., as your wife I do have an abiding curiosity about you. I have made you my life's work, so to speak: 'What Makes J.R. Ewing Function?'"

"And have you uncovered anything to your satisfaction, my dear?"

"Hardly to any satisfaction. Information is being collected, hard conclusions have yet to be defined. You are a singular case, J.R."

"I take that as a compliment." He flicked another tie away in distaste. "You haven't answered my question, however. What makes you think I know what Momma and Daddy were fussin' about?"

"Simple, for a J.R. watcher. I could see how you avoided responding directly to Bobby's questions last night."

His mouth curled in what a stranger might have described as a smile; it was humorless, biting, edged with maliciousness. "My, my, sugar. Haven't you turned into the regular little analyst since you began seeing that headshrinker of yours. What's his name again? Oh, yes, Dr. Ellby."

She ignored the remark. "It's serious, isn't it? Between Jock and Miss Ellie, I mean?"

He held her glance for a brief interlude, then went back to his ties as if to a warm and comforting bed on a stormy night.

"I didn't really expect you'd give me an answer," she said quietly. "That would be too generous of you, too much the act of a normal husband toward his wife." She shrugged. "It is a fascinating prospect, however. What if Jock and Miss Ellie were in deep personal trouble? What if they actually went their separate ways? What if they went so far as to get a divorce?" She bared her perfect white teeth. "Am I getting to you, J.R.? Think of it, that precious Ewing empire of yours all fragmented and torn apart in a property dispute. Your power rendered to more reasonable proportions. You might even have to choose between Southfork and Ewing Oil or all the other family interests. You might just end up being an ordinary tycoon, just another minor Texas millionaire without a wiggly finger in everybody else's pie. That would just about do you in, my dear, being ordinary."

"What do you think of this one?" He held up a striped tie for her inspection.

"Very nice."

He slipped it on, then carefully made a proper knot. "You know, Sue Ellen, you do have a tendency to jump too far too fast. One small argument between folks married for over forty years does not mean a divorce and a property battle. The Ewings are still hanging tight, as they say. The Ewings are a family. And remember this: you are here only because it pleases my daddy and my momma."

Without a word Sue Ellen started for the door. His voice stopped her.

"By the way, after your therapy session, if your brain is not picked too clean to remember, stop in at the store and order me a couple of dozen ties."

From Southfork Sue Ellen drove swiftly and directly over to Braddock. There she entered Mitzi's Coffee Shop and took up watch at an empty table. She was working on her second coffee and fourth cigarette when a cowboy entered, moving deliberately toward the counter. She recognized him immediately—Dusty Farlow, all pared down handsomeness, somehow sensitive and rugged at the same time. A range worker vaguely out of place, as if he'd been set down by some cosmic error. He was smiling as he took his place at the counter, and even at this distance Sue Ellen responded, anxious to smile back.

"Another coffee, Mrs. Ewing?"

The voice brought Sue Ellen back, and she looked up into the waitress's face. "Yes, please."

The waitress poured and went away.

At the counter Dusty had heard the exchange, and he swung around on his stool. He eyed her with obvious pleasure and pushed himself erect, heading her way.

"Sue Ellen," he said, grinning hugely, sweeping off his worn Stetson in a graceful motion.

"Hello," she said shyly.

"Care for some company? If I'm not intruding. Unless you're waiting for somebody . . ."

"Please sit down."

The waitress appeared with a menu. He waved it aside. "I'm not very hungry this morning. Maybe some coffee and a double order of toast, plus about half-a-dozen eggs scrambled easy, bacon, home fries, and whatever else you got hanging round." The waitress left. "Sure am surprised to see you in this place," he offered.

"I'm not surprised to see you."

"You're not?"

"I knew you came here pretty often."

"You did!" A pleased expression creased his eyes. "Well, now that is very nice to hear."

Sue Ellen averted her glance. Her eyes were shining now, a hint of excitement, of anticipatory interest. But she was afraid, too, as if she were about to enter into a strange, alien world charged with imminent dangers and death.

"We had such a very nice conversation at the rodeo," she said. "I thought about you, about talking to you again. But now I feel very foolish."

"Don't. I wanted to get in touch with you, but I didn't want to cause you any difficulty by phoning the ranch."

"I understand. But you could have. It's not as if you're a ranch hand. Your family owns the Southern Cross Ranch.

28

That puts you on a par with the Ewings, maybe beyond them."

He shifted closer. "I hadn't planned on visiting with any of the Ewings. Except you, Sue Ellen. It was you only I wanted to see."

"Dusty—I don't want you to get the wrong idea about me, about us—"

The waitress arrived with his breakfast and placed it before him. "Some more coffee, Mrs. Ewing?"

"No, thank you, I have to go."

The waitress scurried away.

"At least keep me company while I finish my breakfast," Dusty said.

She eyed the litter of plates in front of him. "I don't know, I have an appointment in Dallas. You have enough food there to feed an army."

He laughed. "A few more minutes." He reached out and held her hand.

She hesitated. "I don't think I should." She sank back in her seat.

"You haven't asked me why I went to work over at the Funt Ranch instead of moving on, the way I usually do."

"I never thought about it," she said, elaborately casual. She was lying, and they both knew it.

"Want some of these eggs?" he asked, smiling. She shook her head. "I never eat this many eggs," he confessed.

She furrowed her brow. "Then why did you order them?"

"Would you believe, the sight of you makes me hungry—hungrier than I've ever been."

The implication of his words was not lost on her, but she refused to acknowledge them in any way. Under the table, however, one finely shaped leg began to tremble.

6

The storefront was an old taxpayer in a part of downtown Dallas already marked for better things. Here inexpensive shops and furniture stores sold complete suites of matched bedroom furniture for less than a thousand dollars. Here no hand-tooled boots and belts were seen, no six-hundred-dollar suits, no hundred-dollar Stetsons. This was a part of Dallas the business traveler never visited, a portion of the city that was of interest only to the real estate developers, the destroyers of the old and the builders of the new, the men who made their fortunes in cheap property and cheaper construction. It was here that Alan Beam had chosen to locate the headquarters.

Two workmen strung up the star-spangled banner. In red, white, and blue, it read: DRAFT CLIFF BARNES FOR CONGRESS. Too many words, awkwardly linked, Alan conceded to himself. But it put out the message and would flatter Barnes; both purposes took precedence over a smooth read. He took up a strategic position at the outside edge of the sidewalk and commanded the workmen until the banner was suitably centered and securely fastened in place. He felt a great deal of satisfaction; he was on his way.

A pretty girl named Celia came out of the store. She was one of the volunteers Alan had enlisted in what he had taken to characterizing as "The Sacred Cause." Celia carried a handful of Draft Cliff Barnes for Congress handbills. She displayed one to Alan.

"Does that meet with your approval, Mr. Beam?"

He examined the handbill, then gave her his most winning smile. "It measures up, sweetheart." He touched her cheek in reassurance, in surprising intimacy, in promise of pleasures and wonders to come. "Call me Alan, darling. We're all partners in this sacred endeavor."

Pleased and titillated, awed by her good fortune in joining the Cliff Barnes bandwagon in its preliminary stages, her head filled with fantasies of glamorous days and thick, sensual nights in the nation's capital, Celia went on her way, murmuring Alan's name aloud.

He put her out of his mind at once, seeking out a telephone. There were so many details to arrange. A young, ambitious man on the move couldn't afford to pause for even a moment. Not this early in the day, anyway.

J.R. sat alone at the huge conference table in his office. Scattered in front of him were offshore geology reports, ledgers, and economic feasibility studies, all pertaining to the drilling of oil wells in Southeast Asia. He studied one report with more than casual interest. Engrossed in the information, he didn't notice when Kristin entered carrying a lunch tray.

"Bet you're really starving, J.R." She spoke with the studied cheerfulness of an airline stewardess, trying to put herself forward in the best possible light.

He waved an indolent hand. "Put it on the desk, sugar." He kept on reading.

"But, J.R., you really should take a break, get some good nourishing food into your system."

He pushed the report aside, examined her as if for the first time. "Kristin, there are two very important functions you play in my life. One is doing a good job being my second secretary. The other takes place in that fine bed in your bedroom at the condo. I've got a mother and a wife; they take pretty good care of my health."

As she began to sputter an answer, the phone rang. Without thinking, she reached for it.

His hand came down on hers, hard and immutable. "Not the private line, Kristin. For a smart girl, there are some things it takes you a very long time to learn. A private phone means it *is* private, for my ears only."

31

"J.R.—" She fought for self-control. "You are absolutely the biggest—"

His grin was harsh and smug. "I know. Many people, men and women both, have characterized me that way. Now get back outside to your desk. Surely you have some work to do."

He watched the sway of her round bottom as she left. It was, he remarked to himself, worth keeping her around for that perfect fanny. He picked up the telephone.

"J.R. Ewing."

Alan Beam spoke without identifying himself. "Just wanted to tell you that we're open for business, J.R."

"I expected nothing less."

"Barnes for Congress. Can you believe it! Old Cliff is beginning to swallow the bait."

"Make sure he gets the hook all the way down."

"That's easy. I've rounded up a bunch of eager-beaver volunteers. They're all champing at the bit, ready to go. And the handbills are all printed and being distributed. We're under way."

"About those volunteers. Don't let them get too eager."

"I've got them under a tight rein."

"I wouldn't want so much enthusiasm that this thing gets out of hand. Make sure you don't elect Cliff Barnes to Congress or anything else."

"Trust me, J.R."

"I didn't get where I am trusting people, Alan. You might remember that."

"Just baiting the hook is all, J.R. The entire campaign would become a charade without funds, and you're the only source for that."

"Sounds good. It's time you made contact with the great man himself. Dangle the bait in front of his nose. Make him know what a great champion of his you are."

"I'm meeting him tomorrow."

"That's just dandy, Alan. You have brightened my day considerably. Keep in touch." He hung up without another word. Seconds later Kristin was back.

"You have an overseas call on line one."

J.R. reached for the other phone. He noted that Kristin remained in the office, closing the door behind her, and he decided to let her stay. She was, after all, a visual treat and

32

offered so much in the way of office entertainment. Perhaps later. . . . He spoke into the phone.

"Hank, is that you? You brought me in a gusher yet? What! Hell's bells, man, if that bloodsucker can't cut it, fire him and put somebody else on. Well, all right. I'll fly another driller out of Houston in the morning. Okay, I understand you, just make sure you understand me. Stay in touch." Dropping the phone back in its cradle, he leaned back in his chair.

"Trouble?" Kristin moved toward him, slow, languid, provocative.

"It's going very slowly in the Orient, slower than I like."

Kristin moved without haste behind his chair, hands going onto his shoulders. Methodically rubbing, she pressed herself against him.

"You are a winner, J.R.," she whispered against his hair. "You always have been and always will be. Even if you lose a battle or two, no way J.R. Ewing's about to lose the war."

"Nice to hear it, even if it does come from a party with a vested interest."

"I mean it. Just being near you fills some of my needs."

"Just being near me?"

"Working for you."

He took her hand, guided her around to the front of his chair. He touched her hip, then her belly, his hand rotating deliberately, moving lower.

She gasped and said his name.

"Doesn't take much, does it, Kristin."

"Don't be mean to me, J.R."

"Mean! Why, honey, I'm treating you the best way I know how, the way that pleases you most."

"I would do anything for you, J.R."

"Anything?"

"Just say the word."

"You know the word," he almost snarled. "You know all the damned words nobody says in polite society."

"Be kind, J.R."

"Get down on your knees."

"J.R. . . ."

"Do it now."

She obeyed.

"Now," he said, "earn your salary."

"J.R., treat me gently."

"I pay you well, Kristin, more than anyone of your limited office skills is worth. This is how you truly pay your way. Yes, that way, that soft and wet way you have. Just keep going, sugar, until you get everything you want. Do your best and your worst. . . ."

And she did.

That night Miss Ellie sat alone on the patio staring into the speckled Texas night. But all the beauty was lost on her, for that interval she existed within herself, sad, grim, increasingly angry. Bobby came out of the house behind her.

"Momma, how come you're out here all by your lonesome?"

She averted her face. "Just doing some thinking, is all."

"You all right?"

"Tolerable."

"Just tolerable?"

"It'll do."

"We missed you at dinner."

"I wasn't up to facing the lot of you."

"Would it help if we talked, if you told me about whatever's bothering you, what's wrong between you and Daddy?"

She spoke flatly. "No, I don't think it would help, son."

He persisted. "Pam told me about your visits to Dr. Danvers. Is that what the argument was about?"

"No."

"You told Pam you were going to tell Daddy."

In the darkness he was unable to see the almost tearful expression on his mother's face. "I try not to pry into your private life with Pam. Please show me the same consideration."

It was clear to Bobby that she had said her last word on the subject, and he kissed her cheek and went back inside. Miss Ellie began to weep silently.

The next morning Miss Ellie had just come out of her shower and finished drying herself off when the phone rang. She donned a robe and went into her empty bedroom.

"Hello," she began.

"That you, Ellie?"

34

"Yes, Harlan?"

"Yes, Ellie. The results of the pap cancer test came in. I don't like the results. I think you'd better get in here to my office as quickly as you can."

PART 2

Past Imperfect

$\mathcal{I}$t was spring, the weather clear and pleasant, the sun bright but not yet radiating the stultifying heat of summer. It was a time to make men and animals alike vigorous and anxious to get on with their day's work.

On Southfork there was activity everywhere. Corrals had been set up to accommodate the livestock, pens for the bucking horses and bulls, and stands for the crowds who would surely come as they did every year for the Ewing Rodeo. Posters had been tacked to telephone poles on every road into Dallas and Fort Worth, on over to Austin and west to Amarillo, as far south as Laredo and out to the gulf and Galveston. Competitors were expected from every corner of Texas, and as far away as Oklahoma and New Mexico.

There were mean steers that no man had ever ridden and unbroken range horses, equally dangerous to riders and themselves. Open ground had been marked for trailers and trucks, for the hundreds of tents that would begin springing up later that day, through the night, and into the next day. Workmen were sawing and hammering. Caterers were laying out trestle tables for the hundreds and hundreds of pounds of food that would be devoured all through the rodeo. Bars were set up for drinks, and freezers were rolled into place to chill the gallons of beer certain to be consumed. In the midst of it all, striding this way and that, shouting orders, giving instructions, making changes, was Jock Ewing in worn jeans and scuffed Red Wing boots, a straw Stetson stained and shredded, pushed low over his eyes. He was a man clearly enjoying his work, the years tossed aside, feeling young again. Miss Ellie, looking troubled but struggling to conceal it, came up behind him and said his name. He turned her way, eyes bright, cheeks glowing.

"Well, Miss Ellie, makes my blood run free and easy to see all this. Ain't nothin' like a rodeo to turn a Texas man to his youth. I got me a mind to enter the calf-ropin', show these young bucks how it's done."

"Stop that foolish talk, Jock Ewing," she barked, "and act your age. I have no intention of nursing a silly old man with a collection of broken bones in his body."

He frowned. "Something troublin' you, Miss Ellie?"

"McManus just phoned. One of his trucks broke down. The next load of lumber won't be here until one-thirty, maybe two o'clock. What's that going to do to the building schedule?"

Jock scanned the work area. "That ought to be just about right, the way things are going. No sweat." His brow crinkled with concern, and his eyes clouded over as he gazed into her still lovely face. Clearly his wife was no longer the beautiful young woman he had married, but she was still lovely, desirable, and he loved her very much.

"You all right?" he asked.

"Of course I am," she snapped, dismissing his concern. "I was just about to ask you the same thing. Wouldn't want an old tree to take too much punishment."

He laughed, a deep rich sound. "This old tree has roots that run solid and strong. I am enjoying myself for a change."

"Good," she said, as a workman came striding up to them.

He tipped his hat. "Excuse me, ma'am. That row of tables, Mr. Ewing—we're not exactly sure of where you want 'em placed."

Ellie stepped back. "I'll leave you men. I've got work of my own to do."

Jock watched her go for a moment before attending the workman. "Same as last year, Charley. Right over there. Come on, I'll show you."

In her bedroom Sue Ellen sat at her dressing table wearing a green Chinese silk robe that clung to her finely formed body like a second skin. She ran a brush through her hair a dozen times, trying not to hear the sounds of men sawing and hammering, shouting to each other. She put the brush down and pressed her fingers against her closed eyes, hoping to ease the tension she felt. A faint pounding in her temples, the tightness in her shoulders—all this hectic activity was more than she was able to handle, emotionally or psychologically. An almost overwhelming urge to weep took hold of her.

J.R., fully clothed, appeared behind her suddenly, hands coming down on her shoulders. "A lot of tension in your body, sugar."

"I'm all right," she said automatically. She retrieved the hairbrush.

His hand went under the silk robe, fingers kneading her shoulders. "Head hurt, darlin'?"

Her eyes rolled open. She wished he wouldn't touch her, wished he would go away. "It's all this noise."

He pressed his lips to the top of her head, his hands riding over her bare skin, cupping her full, heavy breasts. She shuddered.

"No need for me to rush off to the office. No need for you to be all this tight and tense. I have got a sure-fire remedy for your condition."

She shrugged and shifted away, and he was left standing with his arms at his side. She began brushing her hair again. "I'll be all right, thank you."

Anger and resentment rose in J.R. like a scarlet tide. "You really can't stand to have me touch you, can you, Sue Ellen?" She said nothing. "I'm your husband, if you remember. All very legal and proper." He waited; she kept brushing. "I've been very patient, Sue Ellen. Very understanding. But my patience is running out."

Her eyes met his in the mirror. "Your continuing desire for me, J.R., certainly is flattering. But entirely unexpected. What brought it on? You haven't been quite this interested in the past."

"You are my wife."

"So you finally noticed. You should have remembered the nature of our relationship a couple of years ago. It might have made a difference then."

"I have been making a real effort, Sue Ellen. You have to admit that. For your sake. For the sake of your child."

"*My* child—"

"Exactly. I have a right to expect something from you in return."

A faint smile curled her voluptuous mouth. "You'll forgive

41

me if I find it a little difficult to accept you in the role of faithful husband and loving father."

"I might become both, if you gave me the chance."

She stood up abruptly, forcing him backwards, and moved away from him. "You had an infinite number of chances a long time ago. You wasted every one of them. Now—well, now, J.R., I just want you to leave me alone."

"You are a bitch."

"Perhaps so. But I wasn't always. Whatever I've become, you played a major role in my transformation."

He spun away to where his attaché case stood, snatched it up, and went to the door, yanking it open. "Listen," he snarled. "Your little bastard is crying."

A flicker of emotion crossed Sue Ellen's face; she forced it aside. "The nurse will deal with *our* son."

He started to respond, thought better of it, and left. J.R. Ewing was not a man to waste much time on lost causes. When a man wanted to drink, he could always locate an available fountain.

But it was Pam, Bobby's wife, who got to Baby John first and lifted him out of his crib. She hugged him close and cooed soothingly. Gradually his crying ceased.

Pam stood there rocking back and forth, filled with affection for Baby John, suffused with a kind of warmth and love that she knew could be summoned up only for a baby. She didn't hear Bobby enter the nursery until he spoke.

"Hey, what happened? I was talking to you, and when I turned around, you were gone."

She faced him, a set expression on her face. "I heard the baby cry."

"Where's his nurse?"

"Mrs. Reeves has gone to warm up a bottle for him."

"He has a nurse," Bobby said softly. "He has a mother, a grandmother, a number of uncles and aunts, a grandfather. Why must it always be you who gets to him first?"

"What do expect me to do, Bobby, just let him alone in his crib, wet and crying?"

"Sweetheart, try and understand. He is not your child, not our child. Anyway, it's you I'm worried about."

Baby John was cooing contentedly now, and she put him back in his crib. "You needn't worry about me, I'm fine."

He embraced her. "Are you?"

She eased free of his arms, feeling guilty and anxious. But she said nothing.

Bobby went on. "It's not the end of the world, not having a baby. We're young still. Our turn will come, you'll see."

"And if it doesn't?" she asked grimly.

"Well, we have each other. That's what really matters. And when we're ready, when you're ready, we can always adopt a child."

"Your daddy would truly appreciate that, an adopted heir, wouldn't he?"

"This has nothing to do with anyone else. It's between us. Just you and me."

She went to him, and he held her. "I'm so afraid—"

"Of what?"

"That you'll begin to feel as cheated as I do. And hate me for it."

"Hate you! That could never happen. Never."

She placed her cheek against his chest, trying very hard to believe him. But she didn't, couldn't, and knew she never would.

Miss Ellie was seated at Jock's desk in the den, talking on the phone. Her face was lined, and puffs of skin supported her eyes. Sounds of the construction in back of the house filtered through to her, and she made a supreme effort to shut them out.

"We'll need another fifty loaves of bread," she said into the phone. "And a few hundred more tortillas—I want Raimondo to prepare tostados. Sausage and chicken, along with the cold beer and beans."

Bobby, still disturbed from his conversation with Pam, entered the den and seated himself on the corner of the desk, listening to his mother. Finally she hung up.

She leaned back and examined him soberly. "Where are you off to, dressed in jeans and an old shirt? I thought you were going into Dallas today."

"Nope. Change in plans. There are some discrepancies in last month's feed bill invoices. The accountants and I are meeting with MacGregor at the warehouse in Braddock to go over them. Momma, you look tired to me."

43

"No more so than usual," she said matter-of-factly. "What's Pam doing today?"

"She wants to go in and see Digger. That last attack of his scared her."

"A girl's got a right to worry about her father."

"She's worried and wants to make sure he's taking it easy."

"You think it's serious, do you?"

"Not so far as we can tell. But Digger's been pretty rough on his body all these years, Momma. Sooner or later flesh and bones give out, I hear."

"So do I," she said wryly. Then seriously: "You get older, Bobby, your body betrays you, no matter how well you've taken care of it. Things go wrong."

He heard a worried note in her voice. "Hey, Momma, are you sure you're all right?"

A rueful smile turned the corners of her mouth. "Just tired. Your father thrives on this kind of activity. But I'm getting worn down by it, I guess. Now let's change the subject. How is Pam really feeling? Do you think she's ready to go back to work next week?"

"I think it'll be the best thing in the world for her to do. Take her mind off herself."

Miss Ellie sighed. "Losing a child even before it's born. That's a traumatic experience for a woman, especially one like Pam who wanted a baby so very much. And she's lost two. That's bound to play tricks with her emotions and her mind. You be patient with that girl, son, treat her tenderly."

"I'm doing my best, Momma."

Sue Ellen materialized, and they greeted each other. "Is it just my imagination, Miss Ellie, or is there more noise than ever this year?"

"I get that feeling every rodeo we have. Workmen must be getting louder and louder."

Bobby laughed. "Guess I'll be on my way. Don't want to be late."

"You going into town, Bobby?" Sue Ellen asked.

"Just into Braddock."

Sue Ellen hesitated, wondering if what she was about to do was a good idea. But the sounds of the hammering and sawing, the shouts, reverberated inside her skull; she had to get away.

"My car's being fixed," she explained. "Would you mind giving me a ride? I could do a little shopping while you take care of your business. My head's beginning to ache from this incessant racket."

"Love to have your company," Bobby said.

She smiled. "I'll fetch my purse."

Five minutes later they were rolling onto Braddock Road in Ewing 4, Bobby's car. They made the drive to Braddock in silence, each lost in thought, grateful to be ignored. They rolled into the main street, past the shops and a newly constructed mini-mall. Everywhere there were flyers announcing the Ewing Rodeo. Spotting a parking space, Bobby pulled into it. They climbed out and walked a few yards along until Sue Ellen turned to face him.

"Do you have a lot to do?"

"I should be finished in a couple of hours at most. You?"

"Nothing special. I just wanted to get out of the house for a while. It's a pity my therapy sessions are only four mornings a week instead of five. It gives me something to do."

"I hope it does more than that."

She shrugged. "Who knows?"

"Your doctor, I hope."

"Don't be too sure. See you about noon. Hector's Place okay?"

"Fine."

They set off in opposite directions.

They met in the coffee shop at the Doubletree Inn off the North Central Expressway, simply two anonymous businessmen in intimate conversation. Facts and figures, dollars and cents, wheeling and dealing. A way of life in Dallas, respectable and accepted, admired—a proper way for a man to act.

J.R. drank black coffee. Alan Bean had a toasted English muffin dripping in butter and overlaid with strawberry preserves. Distastefully, J.R. watched him chew.

"Look," J.R. said gruffly. "There's only one thing I truly do want and that's to kick Cliff Barnes out of the Office of Land Management, right on his lily-white butt."

"I'm working toward it, J.R. Closing in every single day. Making progress."

"Don't sweet-talk me, Alan. I want action, not words."

"It's moving fast, J.R. If I didn't know better, I'd swear the whole movement was genuine. Six people here, a dozen there, Barnes for Congress groups springing up all over the district. What we need now is someone to head up the project. A man with organizational ability, someone to channel all that energy, so to speak, make sure it doesn't dissipate."

"Don't want it to be too good."

"Of course not. I don't intend to let this thing peak and burn out before Barnes falls for it, quits OLM and declares for public office."

"You're right about that."

"What we need is someone we can trust to get close to Barnes, keep him headed in the right direction, and not let some kind of an accident take place. We don't want Cliff getting elected."

"I wouldn't care for that at all. Got any ideas of who might fit the bill?"

Alan grinned arrogantly. "I'm full of ideas." He pulled a sheet of paper from his pocket, on it a typewritten list of names. "Here are some prospects. In order of desirability. I have been making a few inquiries. Discreetly, of course. These people all want what you want—Cliff Barnes on the street, on his heels, out of their hair and yours. But none of them's been especially vocal about it, so they would all look good to Barnes."

J.R. studied the list.

"There's one name missing," he said, "the best prospect of all."

Alan frowned; he hated being caught in an error. "Who's that, J.R.?"

J.R. grinned. "You, Alan."

"Me!" Alan was genuinely surprised.

"Nobody could do the job better, I'd say."

"But Barnes has to know that I work for you."

"For the *law firm* I sometimes employ."

"Still—he'll never let me near him."

"Wanna bet?"

"You've got a plan?"

46

"I've got a plan, all right, and it's a beaut. Sure to make us all happy—me, you, and mostly Cliff Barnes. Now you listen to what I say and follow instructions precisely. . . ."

Pam Ewing sat on the couch in her brother Cliff's apartment, legs crossed, growing impatient.

"Hurry up, Daddy, will you? Our reservation's for twelve-fifteen."

From the bedroom where he was dressing came Digger's voice, strangulated and brusque, the voice of a man used to living and working out of doors, making himself heard. "You and your brother—don't know what's got into you. Fancy restaurants, fancy duds, reservations before you can get a piece of meat to eat. Dammit, daughter, corner hamburger stand's good enough for me."

"Well, not good enough for me, Daddy." Her eye came to rest of a Ewing Rodeo flyer half concealed by a newspaper on the coffee table and her good humor evaporated. By the time Digger arrived on the scene wearing a suit and tie but still looking disreputable and rough-hewn, a man out of place and time in polite society, she was angry.

"Okay," he growled. "I'm ready."

Pam picked up the flyer. "What are you doing with this?"

Digger avoided her eyes. "They're all over the place. Can't get away from 'em even if you try."

"You brought one home to keep you company?"

"Don't get sarcastic with your father. I don't recollect bringing it home. Musta' been caught up in the paper. Yeah, that's it, caught up in the newspaper."

"Daddy—"

"Daughter—"

"We don't want any trouble."

"Now, just what are you getting at?"

"I read you like an open book, Daddy."

"I don't know what you're talking about."

"If you are planning to attend that rodeo, to try and see Baby John, you can put it out of your mind right this minute."

"I'm a grown man. Don't give me orders, daughter."

"Disabuse yourself of any such notion, Daddy."

47

"I don't need you telling me where I can go and where I can't. That child is my grandson."

"You know Cliff's the father, and I do. Bobby does, but not many more. You are not going to make trouble for any of us. We all have a full measure of it without you stirring the pot."

"I won't make trouble," Digger said belligerently. "But I don't back up from it, either."

"Promise you won't come. I know you. You'll say something you'll be sorry for, we'll all be sorry for. Give me your word."

"If I do, will you stop pestering me, girl?"

"I promise."

"All right, all right, anything to get you off my back."

Pam checked him out, certain he was lying and equally certain there was nothing she could do about it.

"Now can we go to lunch?" Digger went on. "I'm hungry."

Hector's Place was a replica of an old-fashioned Western café: rough-hewn planks inside and out, weathered and uneven, round tables without cloths, and sawdust on the floor. A long bar ran alongside one wall of the room, complete with mustachioed barmen wearing sleeve garters and red bow ties. Waitresses in short skirts with bouffant hairdos and nice legs scurried about carrying trays of drinks and food. The food was good, solid American-style cooking—steaks, chops, stews. The vegetables were fresh and homemade. The desserts were standard: apple pie, ice cream, rice pudding. The drinks were large and potent. At Hector's the varied clientele—men in business suits, cowhands, women in blue jeans and others in daytime dresses from Joske's or Neiman's—mixed easily.

At noon Sue Ellen showed up, laden down with the packaged fruits of her morning's shopping tour. She shouldered her way inside and promptly dropped one of her packages. Stooping to retrieve it, she let a second one fall. Convinced the entire pile was destined to go, she closed her eyes in despair and resignation.

"Excuse me, ma'am," came a steady baritone. "Let me give you a hand."

Her eyes snapped open. A cowboy crouched in front of

48

her, the dropped packages in his grasp. He rose, and she did likewise. He was slightly taller than she, with a warm smile and a manner she found immediately ingratiating. He was cute rather than handsome, with a comfortable way of holding himself, a man at home in his own skin.

"Thank you," she said. "I'll be all right now."

He ignored the invitation to return the two packages and instead relieved her of two more of her purchases. "This way," he said confidently. "There's an empty table."

He moved off, and she followed, admiring the compact set of his body, his easy swagger. At the table he stacked the packages in an empty chair, then saw Sue Ellen seated. "Looks to me as if you've been on a buying spree."

"I guess you could say that."

He took the packages she was still holding and put them with the others. "There, that ought to do it."

"Thank you for helping."

"My pleasure, ma'am." He was about to leave when Hector, the owner, came up alongside him. He was a big man with thick arms and shoulders and a menacing expression.

"I'm sorry, Mrs. Ewing," he said.

"What?" She was startled by his sudden presence.

"This man's bothering you. That doesn't go here, cowboy. On your way."

She saw the cowboy stiffen in place, was aware of his bony hands doubling up into hard fists. "No," she said quickly. "It's all right. He was helping me, Hector."

"Are you sure?"

"Listen, man," the cowboy started to say.

"It's all right, Hector," Sue Ellen said again. "He's helping me. He's with me."

Hector looked dubious but backed away from questioning her word. He apologized for the misunderstanding and departed as quietly as he had come.

"I think you'd better sit down for a couple of minutes," Sue Ellen said.

"Thank you, Mrs. Ewing. My name's Farlow, Dusty Farlow."

"Sorry about what happened. Braddock's a small town, and people tend to be a little overprotective of their own."

She felt as if Hector's intervention had somehow forced her into some kind of intimacy with Dusty Farlow, as if they had experienced some threatening danger together.

"No sweat," he said, smiling. "I'm the same way myself." He pulled out a flyer for the rodeo. "Are you this Mrs. Ewing?"

"One of them. There are a number of Ewings and a number of Ewing women."

"Well, ain't that a coincidence! I came all the way in from Odessa 'specially for the rodeo."

"What's your specialty, Mr. Farlow?"

"Dusty's the name. A little bit of this and that. Just like most cowhands, riding and roping, the usual. I expect you'll be around the rodeo grounds, then?"

"I expect I will since I live out at Southfork, summer and winter, day and night."

"Well, that'll be nice."

As Dusty was speaking, Bobby came striding up to the table. His eyes went from Sue Ellen to Dusty Farlow and back again, nothing showing on his face. "Hello."

"Oh, Bobby," she said, embarrassed and wondering why she should be. "My brother-in-law, Bobby Ewing, Mr. Farlow. Mr. Farlow helped with my purchases when a major disaster was about to befall me, Bobby."

The two men shook hands.

"Nice to meet you, Farlow."

"Nice to meet you, Ewing. Well, I'll be getting on. . . ."

"Thanks again, Mr. Farlow."

He touched his hat and walked away. Sue Ellen's glance trailed briefly after him before coming back to Bobby. "What a nice young man," she said cheerfully.

Bobby concealed his surprise. He couldn't recall when last he had seen Sue Ellen so bright and animated or so interested in anyone. It gave him something to think about over lunch.

Rodeo day. Southfork was awash in people and animals, a kind of charged carnival atmosphere. Corrals held broncos, bulls, steers, and calves. A four-piece band filled the air with country and western music, all toe-tapping airs. Clowns began entertaining the early-comers, the same clowns who would later keep deadly bulls away from fallen cowboys.

At the tables food was served in lavish amounts: chile and beans, barbecued and fried chicken, great juicy slabs of roast beef, roast leg of lamb, pork, Mexican sausage, potato salad, cole slaw, and beer in bottles, in cans, on draft.

Laughter and shouts of recognition, from friendly competitors who had not seen each other since the last Ewing Rodeo, could be heard everywhere. Cars kept pulling into the parking area, guests pouring out onto the grounds. There was excitement everywhere, a sense of anticipation, and soon the loudspeaker began to call spectators and competitors alike to the ring. The rodeo was about to begin.

Kristin, attending her first rodeo, was caught up in the surge of it. Her belly churned, and her mind spun trying to take it all in. With a happy smile on her beautiful face, she stood watching, ready for anything, anxious for anything. She was so lost in the moment that she never heard J.R. come up behind her.

"Enjoying yourself, sugar?" he asked.

She spun around, startled. "Oh, it's you."

"You expecting someone else?"

She ignored his reaction. "I've never seen anything like it. I had no idea it would be so—big. A family rodeo, you said. For a few friends, you said. A little get-together, you said."

J.R. gave her a pleased grin. "Got to admit it, when Daddy entertains, he does go all out."

"That's putting it mildly."

"Daddy has never been known for understatement."

"A family trait, I gather."

"That's what being a Ewing means in Texas, honey. Doing big things in a big way, maybe bigger than other folks even imagine."

"And that," she said, eyes sweeping the activity coolly, "is exactly what I like about them."

"Them? I didn't know you were that fond of all the Ewings."

She dropped a hand onto his chest, letting it slide seductively down to his waist, her fingers hooking behind the big silver Longhorn buckle he wore. "You. Just you, J.R."

51

"Remember it."

"After that last matinee in your office, how could I forget, honey?"

Her eyes went past him to the crowd around the swimming pool. She spied Sue Ellen standing motionless, watching them. There was a brief, aloof glance, and then Sue Ellen was gone, moving without haste through the crowd, seemingly not concerned by the show of intimacy between her husband and sister. Kristin's hand dropped away, her manner turned threatening.

"Damn!"

"What is it, sugar?"

"Sue Ellen, she's beginning to get to me."

"Is she now? What's she done?"

"Nothing. And that's the trouble. She just keeps walking around as if nothing bothers her."

"Maybe nothing does."

"The inscrutable bitch. Acting at being superior as hell to the rest of us."

"Maybe just to you, sugar."

"J.R., why don't you go—" She broke off and looked away.

Laughing thinly, he brought her back around. "Your sister really gets under your skin, doesn't she?"

"Yes, she does. My whole life I've had to put up with her airs and phony graces. Who the hell does she think she is, anyway? We both came out of the same place. I'm sick to death of it."

"Shall I tell you the difference between you, sugar? Sue Ellen's got something you only got a lien on."

"Meaning what?"

"Meaning me, sweetheart. A marriage certificate to a genuine pick-of-the-litter Ewing with a cowhide skin and sweet crude running in his veins. Remember, she is my legal and till-death-do-us-part wife."

"How could I ever forget? Don't I know just how much you value her? Don't you tell me every time we're in bed, every time I do for you in ways she won't? Don't you tell me every time you bump me and hump me? What is it you say? Oh, yes. 'Can't for the life of me see how two buns out of the same oven can be so different, one hot and rarin' to go all the time, the other cold and mean as a hungry shark.' Oh, I will never forget the loving relationship that exists between my darling sister and you."

The smile congealed on his mouth, his eyes still and burnished to a high, cold gloss. "You are my toy, sugar, a bauble to fondle and enjoy looking at. A pretty thing to divert me and pleasure me. However I choose to spend my spare time, in whatever sandbox, you are merely my playmate.

"But Sue Ellen is my wife. My first and lasting loyalty is to my wife and my child, my family. You're smart, Kristin, on top of being good-looking, so I know you are not going to forget what I've just said, are you, sugar?"

"I guess not."

"You aren't sure?" The threat in his voice was plain and heavy, a note she'd never heard before.

"I'm sure. I'll never forget what you said."

He squeezed her arm, hard. "You better not, hear."

The message was delivered, accepted, and profoundly understood.

The cowboys gathered in small groups around the corrals and the pens. They polished their best saddles, donned spurs and protective leather chaps, smoked, and talked.

"I've drawn a horse named Killer first time out. Anybody know the beast?"

"Ain't been in a rodeo yet didn't have a pony called Killer. Far as I'm concerned, everyone of 'em's a killer, a mankiller."

That drew a round of laughter.

"I know *this* Killer. Rode him over to the rodeo down in Laredo a month ago."

"What's your take on him?"

"He's none too big. Just an average rein. Shouldn't have any trouble with the nasty critter."

"Say," one of the cowboys said, "ain't you Dusty Farlow?"

Dusty nodded, whittling on a chunk of wood, bringing a primitive head into relief.

"I seen you in the steer wrestling some time back. You was mighty good."

"Well, I thank you kindly."

"Haven't I seen you someplace off the circuit?" another cowhand drawled. "Maybe down around San Angelo?"

Dusty kept on whittling. He had no desire to be identified with his family's ranch. "Maybe so. I do try to keep moving."

The cowhand laughed. "I know the feeling."

Dusty glanced up. Across the field a handsome woman was moving slowly. It was Sue Ellen Ewing. Even at this distance he was struck by her uncommon good looks, the proud way she held herself. A truly special lady, he told himself. He was sliding down off his perch atop the corral's top rail as if to go toward her when the cowhand addressed him again.

"How many events you in, Farlow?"

"What?" His head came around. "All, I reckon. Same as the rest of you trail bums." They were all laughing agreeably as he looked again for Sue Ellen. But she had disappeared into the crowd.

Then the announcer's voice blared out over the public address system: "Ladies and gentlemen, the next event is cowboy bareback bronc riding. There will be no saddles used. The cowboy is required to use a standard leather handhold, to have his spurs in the horse's shoulder as he passes the judges, then to spur the horse continuously through the eight seconds of the ride. The cowboy will be judged on how well he rides, how well he spurs, and how well the horse bucks. . . ."

"Dammit to hell," one of the cowboys muttered. "I surely do resent having to be responsible for the horses, too."

Jock was standing on the patio surrounded by a group of friends and some new acquaintances, basking in satisfaction over a job well done. The rodeo was on, the party in full voice, off to a good start.

One young woman said, "I've been looking forward to your rodeo for weeks, Jock. Last year was my first time, and I never had so much fun."

"I hope this time is just as good for you."

"Oh, it will be, I'm sure. But when are you going to start letting girls compete?"

"Compete with the men?" Jock was startled by the idea.

The girl nodded agreeably, her confidence overwhelming

in its easy brightness. "I can outride and outrope most of the hands you've got on this place."

"Is that a fact?"

"That's what my daddy tells me."

"He ought to know. Old Gene McKinney has been a top hand around San Antonio for as long as I can remember. I'm going to have to give it some thought, young lady."

"You can start by putting in some all-women's events next year."

"Well, maybe I'll do just that. Now you folks better amble over to the stands and get yourself some good seats before all of them are gone."

Miss Ellie looped her arm through his and led him off to one side. "Looks to me as if we're going to have a record crowd today.. They're still coming in."

Jock scanned the grounds. "Sure does seem like it. Weather holds this good, no one'll stay away. Hope you ordered enough food, Miss Ellie."

"As long as we've been married, Jock Ewing, you ever know me yet to run short of food?"

Laughing contentedly, he put his arm around her, and they strolled along.

In the arena was a cowboy astride a bucking bronc. He was riding bareback, left hand gripping a rope, right hand fanning air. His feet were high, raking at the horse's shoulders. Riding close alongside, a pickup man moved in as the ride went over the eight-second mark, the cowboy sliding to safety. The judges, in striped shirts, calculated their scores.

Bobby and Pam stood along the fence enjoying the competition. "Nice ride," Bobby said.

"I suppose so," she said, slightly distracted.

The announcer spoke over the loudspeakers. "That last cowboy ran up a score of sixty-six points, ladies and gentlemen. And now, in chute number two, Billy Boy Conrad on Minnie's Choice. Ride 'im cowboy!"

"I'm surprised," Bobby said. "I thought he was worth more points than that."

When Pam failed to answer, he turned toward her. "Something bothering you, honey?"

"No, I'm fine."

He ran his index finger across her furrowed brow. "Watch out now, else those creases are gonna become permanent."

"What?" A faint smile fanned across her crimson lips. "Oh. Am I getting to be a real drag for you, Bobby?"

He planted a kiss on her mouth. "I wouldn't put it that way myself. But it wouldn't upset me one little bit to see a smile on that beautiful face of yours, now and again."

"Bobby, I'm sorry. It's just that I'm afraid Digger's going to show up."

Now it was Bobby's turn to frown. "It's just like that brother of yours to tell Digger about the whole mess, just to make it worse."

"Cliff didn't mean to. It just slipped out."

Bobby was about to argue the point, let his resentment toward Cliff Barnes spill over, when he realized it would be foolish and counter-productive. Cliff and Pam were brother and sister, and genuinely fond of each other; old Digger was their father, for better or worse. "Look," he said, trying to be conciliatory, "you may have got this all wrong. Your daddy may not be intending to show up here at all. There's no love lost between Jock and Digger."

"That won't stop Daddy. He'll come, I know he will."

Bobby produced what he hoped was an encouraging expression. "Well, if he does, we'll do our best to make him welcome. This is a party and open to everybody. Now, come on, let's not spoil a great day by worrying. Okay?"

She hesitated, then smiled. "Okay."

"There! That's the smile I was talking about. Real nice, lady. Real nice."

He kissed her again as if that solved everything. But the fears each felt still existed.

A hundred feet away, a holding pen contained half-a-dozen lean and mean broncos. Standing on the rail were a line of curious cowboys, including Ray Krebbs, foreman of Southfork.

"That's first-class stock you're lookin' at boys," he said. "Brought in special from Fort Worth for your ridin' pleasure."

One of the cowboys guffawed. "Ray, you ever ridden one of them critters?"

"Never laid eyes on 'em till last night."

"Those are wild things, born to kill some poor cowboy."

"Well," Ray said, climbing down off the rail, "they are a purty sorry lot. Then you boys ain't no bargains, either. See you around."

He'd gone no more than a dozen yards when Lucy came up alongside, taking his arm, falling into step. He felt her firm young breast pressed against his elbow and sought to disengage himself without calling attention to the contact. She refused to release him.

"Oh, no, you don't. Ray Krebbs, you aren't getting away from me until you answer a few good questions I've got to put to you."

He smiled uneasily. "What's on your mind, Lucy?" He walked faster. "I got lots to do today."

"Not till you talk straight to me."

He stopped and faced her. "What's got you all riled up, Lucy?"

"You have, Ray Krebbs. Would you mind telling me what is going on? You have been looking right through me for nearly a week now. Just as if we were strangers, or I wasn't there. Where is your head at, Ray?"

"There's nothing going on." The lie was heavy on his lips. "I've been busy, is all. Just a busy working stiff, without much time for foolishness."

She inched closer to him, and without thinking he retreated a step or two. She grinned up into his face triumphantly, letting him know who was in control. "I always thought we were friends," she said. "*Friends.* I have always counted on you, and you could count on me. These days I can't even get you to say howdy, half the time." She eyed him narrowly. "Something I did or said, Ray? You have to tell me—"

"You didn't do anything."

"Then what's wrong?"

"It's nothing to do with you." He felt himself weakening, unable to keep it to himself any longer. "It's Donna."

Her brow rose. "Who is Donna?"

"Someone I was spending time with a little while ago."

"Pretty?"

"Purtiest thing you ever saw. And put together like a—oh, hell, Lucy, you know what I mean."

"Sure I do. Well, go on, what happened?"

"Turned out the lady had a husband."

"That does tend to make matters a bit sticky."

"Of course, she left him, finally. Told me she was going to get a divorce. I kind of hoped—"

"That serious, was it?"

"Just that serious. Then last week I pick up the newspaper, and there's an article saying she went on back to him."

She touched his arm sympathetically. "Oh, Ray, I am sorry. I've had my disappointments, too."

He shrugged. There was scant comfort to be derived from other people. This was something he was going to have to live with, work through by himself. For himself.

Lucy spoke again. "Didn't she phone you or write or anything, to explain?"

"Oh, yeah, she's been writing."

"And?"

"I haven't been reading the letters."

"You haven't—But, Ray, how can you do that?"

"I've kept them all. Maybe I'll read them someday. But not now. I'm just not geared up for that kind of punishment, Lucy. Now I really do have some work to do."

She let him go, wishing there was some way to reach him, to soften the pain he felt, to help.

"The score on that last rider, Dusty Farlow, is eighty-nine points. Congratulations, Dusty. And now coming out of the number three chute, Bobby Ewing trying to hang on on the back of Salome. Go get 'im, Bobby!"

Pam hurried away from the arena toward the house. Half-way there, Miss Ellie intercepted her. "Where you off to, Pam? Wasn't that Bobby I just heard announced? Aren't you goin' to stay and watch?"

Pam shook her head. "I can't watch Bobby ride. It makes me nervous. What if he got hurt?"

"He's a big boy, my big boy. He knows what he's up to,

what the risks are. And so do we all. Living can sometimes be a very dangerous business, Pam."

Pam chewed her lip. "I thought I'd check on Baby John."

Miss Ellie spoke with quiet understanding. "Pam, Bobby will be fine. And so will the baby. You can do yourself a favor and stop worrying. Just concentrate on getting well yourself."

"Yes, Miss Ellie, I'll try." She turned away before her mother-in-law could see the tears in her eyes. She knew she would never be well enough again, well enough to give Bobby what he wanted more than anything else, a child of his own.

". . . Bobby Ewing, a score of ninety big points! Now ladies and gentlemen the next rider is Jake Greenlaw coming out of chute number one on Dannemora."

Jock and J.R. stood side by side watching Bobby ride. Both were smiling.

"That's my boy," Jock said.

The words wiped the smile off J.R.'s face. "So am I, Daddy."

"I know that, son. It's just that when it comes to riding and roping, Bobby's top hand around here." Jock turned away from the arena, walking slowly along. He spotted Miss Ellie in conversation with a friend of hers and paused. "Your momma been looking all right to you lately, J.R.?"

"Just fine, Daddy. Why?"

"I don't know. Sometimes I get to imagining things, is all. I've been wanting to tell her about Amanda, you know, but somehow I can never muster the spine for it. You take care of that business concerning Amanda for me yet?" he said to J.R., anxious to change the subject.

"You can stop fretting, Daddy, I told you. The lawyers are setting up a trust fund for Amanda, just the way you want it. You just lean back and relax, ride easy. Leave it all to me."

"Yes, I reckon I will."

But J.R. couldn't believe that. Jock had never been the sort to leave vital matters in other hands. And that worried J.R. If Jock ever discovered that because of J.R.'s devious maneuvers, his subterranean manipulations, there were no assets available to turn over to Amanda, the balloon was certainly going to burst. Loud and clear ...

Digger arrived at Southfork at the same time that Bobby took his first ride. One look at the milling crowds sent Digger off in search of the nearest bar. It wasn't hard to locate.

"Bourbon and branch water, please."

The barman obliged, and Digger stepped away, glass in hand, shuffling slowly down toward the arena. It was Miss Ellie who spotted him first. She hurried over at once.

"Hello, Digger."

"Hello, Ellie."

"I must say this is a surprise. I wasn't expecting you."

"Couldn't stay away. Am I welcome here?"

She glanced at the glass in his hand. "As long as you stay sober and don't make trouble, you're welcome here."

"A tall order," he said glumly. He handed her the glass. "That ought to help some."

"I'm sure it will." She poured the contents on the ground. "You make yourself at home, Digger."

"No," he said softly, moving off, "I could never feel at home here. That's asking too much of a man."

J.R. watched Alan Beam for a moment or two. Among all the jeans and boots and straw Stetsons, the lawyer looked awkward in his Brooks Brothers suit and button-down collar. But Alan was the man J.R. had been waiting for. He swung around, and there was Kristin trailing behind. He pointed Alan out to her.

"I'm counting on you."

She flashed her most seductive smile and replied in a voice dripped with innuendo, "Have I ever disappointed you, J.R.?"

"Only your coffee, my dear. It leaves a great deal to be desired."

"That's a small fault—"

"Especially in one with so many virtues. Go on, do your best."

"You can depend on it."

Kristin waited until he walked away, then swung around and came face to face with Lucy. "Oh," she said, "hello."

Lucy summoned up her most awful smile. "Making progress with J.R., I see."

Kristin matched her, contrived sweetness for contrived sweetness. "I certainly hope so."

"Are you really trying to get J.R. away from Sue Ellen?"

"Is that what you believe?"

"I believe you must be the most amoral woman I've ever met."

"I hold you dearly, too, Lucy."

"Sue Ellen is your sister."

"I don't need you to point it out. Whatever my ambitions are, they certainly run higher than a ranch foreman."

"You mean Ray. But he's just my friend—"

"Of course he is," she answered, sweeping away, on her way to fulfill her primary obligations.

Someone jostled Sue Ellen's arm, causing her to spill her drink down the front of her dress. Annoyed, she used her hand to brush away the excess liquid.

A hand reached out, holding a clean handkerchief. She looked up to see Dusty Farlow. She smiled her thanks and mopped herself dry.

"You're a regular Galahad, always around when needed."

"I'd like to be, in your case."

She felt her cheeks grow warm. "I saw you ride. You were very good."

"Thank you. It's not hard being good at something you like to do."

"I wouldn't know."

"Isn't there anything you particularly enjoy doing?"

She returned his handkerchief. "I'm starving. I haven't had anything to eat all day. If you'll excuse me—"

"Mind if I join you? I'm sort of hungry myself."

She turned a dazzling smile in his direction. "I do believe

I've found something at last that I'd enjoy doing, sharing a meal with you. Shall we go?"

"My pleasure, Mrs. Ewing."

"The next event, ladies and gentlemen, will be calf roping. In this event, the cowboy must not reach the barrier before the calf. He must rope and throw the calf, then tie two hind legs over one foreleg. The tie must hold until passed by the judges. . . ."

On the far end of the competitors' area, away from all the action and noise, Dusty and Sue Ellen located a quiet place to eat off paper plates and talk.

"You really like rodeo work, Dusty? All the traveling . . ."

"It's a nice kind of life, if you can cut it. I've got no complaints."

"Haven't you ever wanted to settle down, be in one place forever?"

"Forever's a mighty long time." He laughed. "I guess I have at that. Sometimes. When the feeling comes over me, I sign on somewhere as a ranch foreman, or some such, and start acting like a normal human being. But sooner or later the restlessness returns, and I start wondering what it's like in some different part of the country, on some other ranch. Or there's a new rodeo to try, and so I pack my bedroll and move on. I guess that doesn't make much sense to a lady like you?"

"A little, maybe. I can see that what might seem interesting or important or nice one year might appear kind of dull and old another."

Dusty laughed, and his eyes crinkled up. "I don't know about that. Seems to me, I like the same things over and over again, just in different places. Food, horses, cows—"

She spoke without thinking. "And women?"

He answered easily. "Oh, sure, women, too. Especially women."

She felt her body grow tense. She enjoyed talking to this attractive young cowboy, enjoyed laughing with him; but this time she had gone further than intended. She didn't want him to misunderstand. "I'm sorry," she said. "I should not have asked you that."

"No harm. Coming from you, I will answer personal questions. Funny about that, I'm not sure why it is exactly. Maybe it's just crazy, but I feel very comfortable with you. Does that make any sense to you?"

She felt exactly the same way but refused to say so. She attended her food assiduously.

He went on. "I don't think I'd mind anything you said to me."

She made up her mind to choose her words with extreme care. After all, she reminded herself, she was a very much married woman. . . .

J.R. saw Sue Ellen talking to the lean cowboy. He paused for a moment to watch. There was something in the way each held himself, an air of intimacy that surrounded them, that bothered him. Even more was the interested, animated expression on Sue Ellen's face. An expression he couldn't recall having seen for a very long time. This, he warned himself, might bear watching.

Later, Bobby and Pam watched Dusty during another of his rides. Again he scored high, drawing loud applause from the crowd. Jock came up behind them, draping a heavy arm around each.

"Better be careful, Bobby. That cowboy does a real good ride. Who is he?"

"Name's Dusty Farlow," Bobby answered. "Comes from Odessa, I think. Sue Ellen introduced me to him over in Braddock yesterday. Seems like a real nice fella."

"Appears to be a good hand, that's for certain. Knows what he's about."

As befitted Ray Krebbs's status as Southfork's foreman, he lived in a cabin of his own, some distance from the bunkhouse. It was a simple affair made up of a small sitting area, kitchen and eating space, plus an adequate bedroom.

Certain that no one was likely to notice her, Lucy entered the unlocked cabin without apprehension. She surveyed the interior, trying to figure out where Ray would most likely conceal the letters from Donna Culver. She opened some drawers at random, sorted through piles of various items on a table top, came finally to the dresser in the bedroom. In the third drawer down, paydirt.

The letters were in a loose stack, together with a crumpled newspaper clipping, which Ray must have thrown away, only to retrieve it later from a wastepaper basket. She glanced briefly at the clipping before bringing her attention to the letters. She opened one letter and began to read. Her initial reaction was surprise, followed by a deeper interest, and finally satisfaction. The satisfaction of knowing she was right in coming to this place, right in intruding on Ray Krebbs's private life. It was only fair that Donna Culver's message was made known to Ray, fair to Donna and to Ray himself. She examined a second letter and was engrossed in its contents when the opening door to the cabin sent a rectangle of sunlight across the small room. Startled, Lucy looked up to see Ray standing there. The expression on his face was easy to read; he was unhappy to find her here, unhappy and angry.

"Dammit, Lucy! What are you doing? This is my home, and those are my letters."

"Ray! You don't understand."

"You don't belong here."

"I wanted to find out what was going on, help you, if I could."

"When I need help, I'll ask for it. You'd better go now."

She held out the letter. "I think you'd better read this."

He snatched it out of her hand, putting his back to her. His shoulders were held stiff and square, his legs planted firmly apart. A man with a deep fear and a deeper resentment.

Lucy spoke quietly. "Somehow, I never understood that the Donna you meant was Sam Culver's wife."

"Buttin' in where you've got no business," he muttered.

"Somebody had to do something. You're so stiff-necked, so damned proud and stubborn. You'd have spent the rest of your life moping around instead of doing something as simple and sensible as reading the lady's letter. Oh, sure, that way you just might find out what was actually going on and be forced to stop feeling sorry for yourself."

"I knew what was going on, all right."

"But not why. Sure, Donna went back to Sam. But not

because she wanted to. She *had* to. Poor Sam is sick and dying, did you know that? Donna felt a deep obligation to the man and wanted to help him, give him her support, be with him when the end came. Oh, you sure knew a lot, all right. But nothing that really matters."

Ray turned awkwardly, staring at Lucy in disbelief. His anger faded quickly to be replaced by wonder and concern. He began to read the letter. Once he looked up at Lucy, and she thought she saw tears in his pale eyes, but she couldn't be sure. Then he went back to the letter. After a suitable interval, Lucy departed, not making a sound as she went. Ray never knew she was gone.

Bobby was up for the calf roping. The signal was given, and he came charging out of the chute aboard a pony, rope flying. A flip of the wrist, and it went sailing in a graceful circle toward the fleeing calf. Bobby jerked back, and the loop settled over the beast. He reined in his mount, rope taut, and came flipping to the ground in one smooth movement. He wrestled the struggling calf to the ground and bound him in swift, sure strokes, then signaled the judges that he'd completed the tie.

At the fence, watching with professional interest, was Dusty Farlow with Sue Ellen beside him.

"He's good," Dusty said with admiration if not envy. "I can see where the competition lies. Are all the Ewings that slick?"

"My husband's even slicker, but not at roping calves."

"I'll have to keep that in mind. If I'm not careful, Bobby is just liable to turn me into an also-ran."

As one, they turned and strolled away. "Even if Bobby should win, he'd refuse the prize money. It'd go to whoever ends up second. Ewings don't need the prizes, they just enjoy winning."

Dusty spoke softly. "They're not the only ones."

She glanced over at him. His face was hard, set, a look of determination she had seen before on Texas men, a look that could mean trouble. Yet on Dusty it was limned with softness, as if he intended no harm to anyone.

He said, "I'm not saying that five thousand dollars wouldn't come in handy. It surely would. But there's more to

65

a competition than taking the prize. It's knowing you're the best. It's doing your best and winning if you can, short of killing yourself, that is."

She frowned, and he sensed the change in mood at once. "Lookee here, now, don't take everything I say too literally."

"You sounded like a couple of people who've been in my life."

"Men?"

She nodded.

"Well, whomsoever, I am not them. Believe me, I'm not Attila the Hun or some such. Winning is a normal human desire, isn't it? Don't you like to win?"

She stared sightlessly into the distance, not sure she even knew what the word meant anymore. But once she had. Once winning had been the most important fact of her life. . . .

She had always been the prettiest girl in the small West Texas town where she'd been brought up. In high school she had starred in the senior class play and pranced in front of the marching band at all the football games. In her first year at the university, someone had submitted her picture to the committee that ran the Miss Texas Beauty Pageant, designed to select a candidate for Miss America. Sue Ellen received a letter inviting her to participate.

Talent, grace, and beauty, the letter had stated. And for the first time in her life, Sue Ellen had grown afraid. This was no small-town competition where the other girls were chubby or plain looking or suffered from acne. These would be the best-looking young women in all of Texas, spectacular in face and figure. And they would be trained in dance or song or drama. They would be clever and witty and sophisticated, and she was sure she would be quickly eliminated. It would be best, she decided, if she did not compete at all, did not submit herself to possible embarrassment and shame and the inevitability of defeat. She put the invitation and the accompanying acceptance form in the back of her top bureau drawer.

That weekend she went home to visit her family. It was an uninspired interlude, as most visits were. There was talk of football games and wealth and politics, subjects that bored Sue Ellen. She found her mind drifting to the invitation back in her bureau drawer in the dormitory. It was her baby sister,

Kristin, already cool and driving and single-minded, who first perceived her preoccupation and commented on it.

"Something bothering you, Sue Ellen?"

She shook her head. "Not a thing, Kristin."

"You sure are awful quiet," her mother said, making it sound like an accusation of wrongdoing.

"Guess I'm anxious to get on back to school and my studies."

No one accepted that. Whatever else she was, Sue Ellen was not a student. She had never displayed any overriding interest in schoolwork.

"Something wrong?" her mother asked again. She was a pretty, thin-faced woman with bright, quick eyes, eyes that missed very little. She viewed life skeptically, as an ever-changing condition designed to frustrate her personal ambitions. She saw the future in terms of her two daughters. They would make good marriages to successful men and take care of their mother in her waning years. But those years lay far in the future, for she was a woman still interested in having a good time, still appreciative of a handsome man—if he had a substantial income, that is.

"Must be," Kristin said, with an overly sweet, almost malicious grin. "Sue Ellen's head is a thousand miles away. Bet you've gone and fallen in love with some poor plowboy up at school."

"Have not!" Sue Ellen said, too quickly.

"Is that what it is, Sue Ellen? You gone and got yourself involved with some worthless boy?"

"No, Momma."

"Then what is it? You in some kind of trouble?"

Sue Ellen clenched her lips together. "It's nothing."

"You tell your momma, hear."

So she did, and watched her mother's face tighten with resolve, an expression Sue Ellen had seen many times in the past. When Sue Ellen finished her recitation, her mother sat back and fixed her with an unblinking stare. The birdlike features were hard, glazed, the voice remote and without sentiment.

"Listen to me, girl, and listen good. What you and your sister have, all I've been able to give you, no thanks to your sorry father, is your good looks. Thank the Lord for that blessing. And in this world a girl has to take advantage of what she's got. You are smart as any of them, Sue Ellen, you can sing, and you can dance, you were just fine in that play you did in high school, and you're better to look at than any of them. So you enter that contest. I tell you, you get yourself chosen as Miss Texas and go on to Atlantic City. You become Miss America. Imagine it, my daughter. You can do it, Sue Ellen. The men you'll meet! They'll be flocking your way like bees around honey. I'll help you—sort them out, check out their backgrounds, get you matched with the best of them. Hear me out, girl. Make yourself a good marriage and you'll have a good life, everything you ever wanted. It's no different than one of those football games—there's winners and there's losers, and winning is everything. . . ."

Winning *was* everything. And she had in fact entered the contest, scored high in the talent competition, in the evening gown competition, and in the bathing suit competition. Shamed and shaking, she had forced herself to go out on that stage in a bathing suit that revealed more of her body than she wanted to reveal. The suit was so thin and so tight every curve and crease could be seen from the back of the auditorium. There had been rebel yells of appreciation and admiring whistles and, afterward, an abundance of men to make veiled offers to help her career if—if—

And Momma, right there to protect her. To make sure she was treated like a winner—she was indeed Miss Texas, looking every inch a queen. A true winner.

And inevitably, J.R. Ewing was the ultimate prize. A man who possessed everything a girl could ever desire, a man who promised everything forever and forever. Oh, yes, winning had been so important, until she was forced to live day after day and year after year with the debilitating results of that awful victory—used, abused, some essential part of herself lost forever.

"Oh, yes," she muttered in answer to Dusty Farlow, "winning is better than anything. . . ."

J.R. had choreographed every move. Dedicated to form and structure, to organization, he had plotted every detail, run it through with the principals. Now he stood not far from the main house with Kristin, exchanging pleasantries with whoever happened by. A few yards away, Alan Beam. Slightly tense, watchful, drawn up with the edginess of an athlete about to run an important race. A shadow flitted across J.R.'s face, and Kristin, alert to his ever-changing moods, spoke quickly.

"What's wrong?" She followed his gaze. Beyond the press of people, Dusty Farlow was walking with Sue Ellen, their heads together, lost in conversation.

"Why should you care?" Kristin said, without thinking.

J.R. snapped out his answer. "She's my wife. How many times must I tell you? I do care."

"You're jealous!" she said incredulously. "I don't understand you. Here you are, playing around with your wife's sister, and God knows how many other women, and you get jealous when Sue Ellen even talks to another man."

He bared his teeth in what appeared to be a smile; Kristin knew better. "You're right, you don't understand. Jealousy has nothing to do with it. *Family* is what it's all about. Family, and my authority. Family, and concern for what belongs to me."

"My God, J.R., you don't *own* Sue Ellen."

He blinked once. "My, my, you are naive." He made a small gesture that caught Alan Beam's attention, nodded, and looked away. "Enough of this social chit-chat, Kristin. It's time to go to work."

She straightened up, her breasts straining under the tight western shirt she wore. She wet her lips. "I'm ready."

"You should have become an actress, Kristin. Make-believe is your natural milieu."

Alan came up behind her, his arm circling her waist. "Shall we slip off somewhere together, Kristin?"

"Not too far," J.R. cautioned. "I want you where I can see you. Where everyone can see you. And, Alan, don't get too caught up in your work, don't enjoy yourself too much." He paused. "Well, well, look who's arrived in time for the big show."

Miss Ellie and Digger came out from behind the house, walking unhurriedly and talking, the way old friends with much to say talk. "This is going to be better than I anticipated. Imagine it, Cliff Barnes will hear the story first-hand from his very own daddy's lips. Couldn't be better. Okay—you two get started, curtain's going up. . . ."

Miss Ellie and Digger, oblivious to J.R.'s scheming, no matter how it might involve them, kept walking. She was saying, "So you had to come back, you missed Dallas too much."

He laughed raucously. Miss Ellie had always made him feel good, had always provided a pleasure in life no one else could offer. "Getting away from Dallas did me a lot of good, I don't mind telling you. Those months in California, they gave me time and space to get my head straight. Put some money in my pocket, honest money, the kind that comes to a man for doing hard work. I got to tell you, Ellie, it was good to work hard and earn my own way, get paid for it. I've been on the wagon ever since."

"What about that bourbon and branch you were carting around earlier?"

He grimaced behind his grizzled gray beard. "A temporary lapse. Anyway, you came along just in time to save me from myself."

They went on silently for a few strides. "Digger, I want to ask you something—"

"Anything."

"Have you finally stopped blaming Jock for every evil that's befallen you? Is that why you're here?"

He turned away and answered evasively. "I've never held you responsible, Ellie. You know that. You did what you had to, and I've respected you for it."

"So did Jock, Digger. I wish you'd remember that part of what happened." She paused, hoping he would respond; he made no answer. "It concerns me, Digger, all this bad feeling dragging on. What happened between you and Jock was bad enough—all that's in the deep past. But now your boy and mine, Cliff and J.R.—they are out for blood, Digger, both of them. In the old days they might have shot it out. I don't like it. I don't know where it's going to end, and it frightens me."

Digger pumped up his lungs, his jaw set. He shared the identical fear but was unable to confess it aloud, was unable to release the feelings of betrayal that he had nur-

70

tured for so many years. He said nothing and kept walking.

"Digger," Miss Ellie said. "Why are you really here?"

He made his reply in the most sincere voice he could produce. "Why do you think? To see that new grandson of yours and wish you well. Hell, woman, I ain't as bad a fella as that husband of yours has made me out."

Ellie felt the tension drain out of her. She believed Digger. She wanted to believe him.

"And the next event, ladies and gentlemen, is cowboy saddle bronc riding. For this event the cowboy must have his spurs in the horse as he passes the judges, he must spur throughout the ride, he must not touch the horse or saddle or himself with his free hand . . . ."

Kristin took up a position away from the crowd, in the open and visible to anyone who cared to look. It was a provocative stance, one booted heel hooked into the lower rail of a corral, breasts and belly thrust forward, lips parted in invitation.

Alan Beam moved in closer, hovering over her. "Shall we get the show on the road?"

"Show a little passion, Alan. Fake it, if you have to."

"I was about to suggest something similar to you. Give me a smile, a little encouragement."

"You're not supposed to like it, simply to perform. Think you can do that, Alan, put on a good performance?"

"As good as you've ever had, lady."

"My, my, I do believe you are boasting."

"Any time you'd like a sample—"

"Oh, wouldn't J.R. love to hear that."

He paled. "You play rough."

"I've had a good teacher. But don't worry, Alan, I won't give your secret desires away. Hold on to them, sugar, in this world you can never tell what odd couplings will come about, given enough time. All right—consider yourself encouraged, though not a whole bunch."

"That's your style, isn't it, Kristin, always getting what you want without giving away very much? Very little of value, that is."

"Don't be nasty, Alan, or I'll have you cut to size."

"I bet you would."

"Depend on it. Enough palaver. If you're ready, my dear, I am very much in the mood. I doubt that you'll enjoy this as much as I will."

She drew back her arm and slapped him as hard as she could. His head rocked back, and his cheek began to sting, tears coming to his eyes.

"Don't you ever talk to me that way!" she said in a loud, shrill voice.

Everywhere within earshot conversation ceased, eyes shifting their way. Lucy, a soft drink in hand, stared in wonder, trying to hear every word.

J.R., in conversation with a stockbroker from Dallas, turned to see what was happening.

Digger and Miss Ellie froze in place, watching.

To all of them, it seemed that Alan was trying to soothe Kristin, quiet her down. But with little success. Her voice rose again.

"How dare you suggest such a thing! I am a nice girl, a good woman. You have no right—"

J.R. rushed over, a shining knight to the rescue in antelope boots and a white Stetson.

"What is it? What's going on?"

Kristin choked back her tears. "He insulted me."

"Look, J.R.," Alan said, "she's a good-looking woman, and I'm only human."

"That does it, Beam. You've gone too far this time. Forgotten your place. Kristin is my sister-in-law, she's *family*. You get your butt off Southfork and do it now."

"Just a minute. I can explain."

"Up north, where you come from, things may be different. But this is Texas, boy, and we treat our women with respect and honor. You don't have much time left."

"You don't understand."

"I understand, all right. You're a filthy-minded no-good sonofabitch, and if you're not out of here in two minutes, I'm going to climb up one side of your head and down the other. Now git!" J.R.'s big right hand flashed out and landed on Alan's cheek, a resounding slap. The lawyer staggered under the force of the blow and almost went down.

He backed off. "I'll get you for this, J.R. I swear it. Nobody, nobody treats Alan Beam this way."

A contemptuous smile snaked its way across J.R.'s mouth. "I ever see you around this ranch again and it'll be your ass, boy. Come near a Ewing one more time, and you'll wish you'd never left home, hear!"

"You haven't heard the last of me," Beam cried as he headed toward the parking area. "You'll pay for what you've done today. All of you."

Not far away, Dusty and Sue Ellen had seen it all, heard every word. "Who are those people?" Dusty asked. "Anyone you know?"

"You could say that. The big man is my husband, and the lady whose honor he's salvaged is my little sister."

Dusty took a beat to reply. "I guess your husband is what is known as a Texas gentleman."

Sue Ellen didn't attempt to disguise her amusement. "No one's ever called him that before. As for my sister's honor, I doubt that it was in need of much protection. It never has been in the past."

Dusty arranged a pleasant expression on his face. "Seems like your husband is about to join us."

"Maybe he's concerned about my honor."

"I don't intend to cause you any distress, Sue Ellen."

"If anyone does, it won't be you. And don't be concerned about J.R., he has only a limited inventory of chivalric impulses, and I'd say he's exhausted his reserve for today."

"Oh," Dusty said easily, "I'm not concerned."

J.R. came striding up to them, a scowl on his face. Sue Ellen beat him to the punch. "Mr. Farlow here has been commenting on how well you handled that situation, darlin', on how much the Texas gentleman you are. J.R. Ewing, I'd like to introduce Dusty Farlow."

Dusty extended his hand; J.R. ignored it.

"He's right," J.R. snapped out. "We Texans are very protective, you might even say possessive, of our women, Mr. Farlow. We take a real interest in just who they spend time with, and why."

Dusty answered in an exaggerated drawl. "I reckon I know

73

that, being Texas born and bred myself, Ewing. Never did take kindly to having my toes trod upon; expect you're exactly the same." Then, to Sue Ellen: "Excuse me, ma'am, it's about time for me to ride. If you're still free, I might just see you again, after the next event." He tipped his hat and walked away.

"Not much for facing up to things, is he?" J.R. said.

Sue Ellen laughed up at him. "That's not somebody you can bluff or frighten, J.R. There is nothing that cowboy wants or needs that you can deprive him of."

"If that means you, sugar," he said in a serrated voice, "don't be too sure of yourself. You're as much my property, bought and paid for, as the car I drive, and you better not forget it."

"Riding Crossroads, Bobby Ewing, scoring one hundred eighty-eight points. Next up on Stargazer, Juan Negrete."

Alan Beam climbed into his car and started the engine. He was about to back out when he heard someone calling.

"Hey, wait a minute!"

He saw the pretty blond girl running toward him. No more than twenty, she was full bosomed with a strong and shapely figure. She came up to the side of the car, hand outstretched.

"Hi, I'm Lucy Ewing."

He reminded himself of the job he had undertaken. He kept his face closed, his manner sullen. "I've had my fill of Ewings for the day."

"I don't blame you. This can be a very difficult family at times, especially J.R. What a bastard he is."

"You'll get no argument from me." He took her hand and held it longer than was necessary. "I'm Alan Beam."

"I admired what you did."

"Oh?" he said cautiously.

"Not everyone around Dallas has the guts to stand up to J.R. He's a bully, always pushing people around, and he's got the power and the deviousness to do it."

"So I discovered. He'll find out I don't scare so easily."

"So I noticed," she said, smiling. Very gently she withdrew her hand. "I just wanted to say hello, let you know all Ewings aren't bad."

"I'm glad you did."

"See you around sometime, then."

"Not if J.R. has anything to say about it."

She took a beat. "He doesn't."

He watched her walk away, her pert little backside swaying delightfully. Alan was flabbergasted; what a stroke of good luck!

In the arena Dusty was riding a horse named Danger Sign, and dangerous he was. Dusty was jolted out of the saddle like a shot, hitting the ground hard. He scrambled for safety. Only when he was outside the corral did Sue Ellen, watching closely, allow herself to breathe again.

Kristin, standing a yard behind her, spoke insinuatingly. "Better watch out, sister. You are beginning to make a public spectacle of yourself. People are beginning to talk."

Sue Ellen came slowly around. "I do believe you've supplied a full measure of dramatics for the day, dear Kristin. No one's going to take much interest in my behavior after that performance of yours. No one will pay any attention to what I do or say."

"J.R.—"

"Oh, yes, there is always J.R. I've got to give you credit, Kristin, it took me eight years to figure J.R. out. You've managed to do it in a few short months."

Kristin pulled back as if struck. "I don't know what you're getting at."

"I think you do."

"He's your husband, Sue Ellen, not mine."

"I thought you'd forgotten that."

"I don't know—"

"You know, in every sense of that word, Kristin. But I will spell it out for you. I was referring to my dear husband's peculiarity of wanting only what someone else wants or has. If no one wants me, J.R. certainly doesn't. But if a man, any man—Dusty Farlow, for example—displays any desire, then J.R. discovers his own passions running close to the surface. Isn't that why you'd rather Dusty didn't pay any attention to me? That way J.R.'s ardor for his legal bedmate will cool, leaving so much more for you."

"Surely you can't believe—"

"I believe, Kristin. I do indeed believe the very worst of you and of J.R."

"I'm your sister."

"That never stopped you before. It will never stop you in the future. Now if you'll excuse me, I promised to meet Dusty after his ride."

Bobby's last ride was done, and he was satisfied, if not exultant, over his performance. He and Pam were walking up toward the main house, hand in hand, when they spotted Digger with Miss Ellie.

"I told you," Pam said, despair in her voice. "I knew he'd show up."

"Well, there's only one thing to do, get him out of here, and fast."

"That may not be so easy."

They hurried forward.

"Digger!" Pam cried.

The old wildcatter swung around, face drawn up defensively. He had heard his daughter use that tone before. It neither pleased nor frightened him; it was just one more difficulty in a life filled with problems.

"Daughter," he said mildly.

Miss Ellie's anxiety surfaced immediately. "It's all right, Pam. I've already told Digger he's welcome."

"You shouldn't have come, Daddy, and you know it."

"Man gets married, has children, raises a family best way he knows how, and what happens—he's cursed with an uppity daughter. Ain't nothing worse than a child trying to run her daddy's life. Back off, girl."

"You mean to make trouble, Daddy," Pam said.

Miss Ellie broke in. "Nonsense, Pam. Digger and I go back a long time. We're old and dear friends. Digger's come to see my grandchild, and I'm glad of it. It's time this ridiculous family feud came to an end."

Bobby squeezed Pam's hand, intending to silence her; she understood the message. In front of Miss Ellie they were unable to go on, unable to stop Digger. They would have to find another way.

"Pam," Miss Ellie said commandingly, "you and Bobby go

on up to the house. I'm going to find Jock, tell him Digger's here. Get this thing straightened out once and for all."

". . . points, which puts Dusty Farlow into a commanding lead and with only four riders remaining . . ."

Sue Ellen said, "Looks as if you might win after all, Dusty. What will you do with the prize?"

"Nothing in particular."

"Don't you care about the money?"

"Not really. Not much."

"You don't mind being poor?"

"I like it a whole lot better'n being rich."

"Rich?"

"My folks own the Southern Cross Ranch."

"The Southern Cross in San Angelo? But that's one of the biggest—it's worth—"

"Yeah. Worth a hell of a lot."

"I don't understand. Doesn't the Wayne family own the Southern Cross?"

"Uh-huh. My momma's name was Farlow."

"I see. But you spend your life drifting, a rodeo bum. Why?"

He shrugged. "I was turning into someone I didn't like very much. Does that make sense to you?"

"I think so."

"You seem to have some doubts."

"I don't think we should talk any more."

"Why?"

"People are starting to take notice."

"That didn't bother you a minute ago."

"It does now."

"Why? Why did you like me better when you believed I was a down-and-out cowhand? Because you didn't have to take me seriously then? Because I wasn't any kind of a threat to your position, to your marriage? Because being poor meant I had to be no-account, easy for you to dismiss from your mind, from your life?"

"I have to go."

"Rich or poor, I'm the same man, Sue Ellen. Someone you

have to deal with. A man you happen to like. You've sure as hell made that clear. It's true, isn't it? Admit it."

She took one long look into his pale eyes before walking away. "I admit," she said quietly, and left him standing alone.

Pam was unable to get Digger off her mind, unable to put an end to her concern over what her father might do. With Bobby's help she sought him out and isolated him in the den. She tried to talk some sense into the stubborn old man. He listened for a while, head rocking from side to side in disbelief.

"Will you calm down?" he said finally.

"Daddy," she went on, as if not hearing, "when Miss Ellie brings Jock in here, I want you to just announce how tired you are, how much you want to go back to Cliff's apartment to be alone and rest—"

"No sir," Digger protested. "Ain't gonna do it. Not until I see my grandson."

"Oh, for crying out loud, Digger," Bobby said. "You keep saying *your* grandson. Jock and Miss Ellie, they are going to see it a lot differently."

"Well, now, maybe it's time they learned the truth. Cliff and Sue Ellen are responsible for Baby John and not J.R., no matter what the legal papers say."

"Daddy, please," Pam implored. "You don't understand what you're doing."

"I know what I'm doing, all right."

Bobby broke in. "Digger, if you so much as say a single word about Baby John's parentage—"

"Don't threaten me, boy. Bigger folks'n you have tried it and come out weepin' and wailin'. I ain't too old to hand out a few good licks still, if I have to. So you—"

"Oh, Daddy," Pam said. "Stop it. Talk sense. We are trying to keep everybody in orbit. You go shooting your mouth off and no telling what's liable to happen."

Digger set his jaw. "I am waitin' to see my grandson."

"No," Pam said. "Jock's grandson, Miss Ellie's grandson. Not yours."

"All right," Digger conceded. "If you two would stop

78

treatin' me like I only got half my wits, it might help. I'm tellin' you loud and clear I want to see that boy. That's all. Then I'll go. Peaceful as you let me."

Bobby exhaled slowly. "Peaceful is the word, Digger. Let's not forget it."

Before anyone could say another word, Jock and Miss Ellie entered the room, Miss Ellie hopeful and smiling, Jock tense with the knowledge that he was about to undergo an unpleasant ordeal.

"I found him," Miss Ellie said.

Jock nodded once. "Hello, Digger."

"Jock."

The two men regarded each other warily, with the stiff-legged uneasiness of a pair of pit bulls. It was Jock who made the first move, wishing to forget the past, if only Digger would allow it. "Ellie tells me you've come out to congratulate us on our grandson—that right, Digger?"

Digger pulled his eyes away from Pam, looking right through Bobby. "I want to see the boy, right enough. There can be no doubt about it."

"See, Jock," Miss Ellie said.

A pleased smile split the bleak mask that Jock's face had become. "Well, all right. Come along, then. I'll show him to you. Believe me, Digger, that boy is something worth seeing, I tell you. Shoulders like a halfback, great strong legs and the look of brains. Wait'll you see 'im."

Jock led Digger out of the den, the others trailing apprehensively behind. In the nursery they all crowded around the crib.

"Look at that boy!" Jock crowed proudly. He lifted the infant out and held him high for all to see. "Was I tellin' you the truth, Digger? Ever seen a better-lookin' young'un?"

Digger answered in a strangely subdued manner. "Be all right if I hold him?"

"Daddy," Pam said in warning.

"No reason why not," Miss Ellie said.

Jock turned the baby over to Digger, pride etched in every crease and seam of his leathery face. Digger looked down at the child he cradled in his arms.

"He's awful quiet," he muttered.

79

"Hell, man, you ought to hear him yell. Damnedest voice you ever heard. A real big set of lungs, a Ewing through and through."

Digger stiffened in place. It was getting to be too much for him. His mouth opened and shut again.

"Don't you agree, Digger?" Bobby said, as if seeking to force acquiescence out of the old man. "He sure does look like a Ewing."

Digger looked around. Ranged in a circle, all Ewings; even his daughter, Pam. He longed to confront them all with the truth, to use this child to regain his pride, to revenge himself for past indignities and defeats.

"I don't know about that," he said.

"Well," Miss Ellie said pleasantly, "he certainly has got a good deal of Sue Ellen in him. Anybody can see that. But he's J.R.'s son, all right. Looks just the way J.R. did when he was a baby. Beautiful. You know, Digger, we almost lost him. Twice, in fact. Before he was born, even; and the kidnapping. What terrifying days they were, waiting, hoping, thinking we might never have him here with us, after all our years of wanting him. We expected to love him, but I don't think any of us knew until then just how much we would. How much he would mean to us."

Seeing Ellie's beaming face, seeing the years drop away as she spoke of her joy at loving Baby John, Digger discovered that he could do or say nothing to hurt her. He had caused her grief in the past, he could not do so now. He delivered the baby back to Jock.

"That's a fine grandson you've got, Jock. Handsome and strong. Thanks for letting me see him." He hurried out of the room without another word.

"Why, I do believe there were tears in Digger's eyes just then," Miss Ellie said. "My, how that man has changed."

But Pam, looking after her father, knew better.

Smiling, Dusty came up to Sue Ellen. She eyed him soberly.

"It's almost over," he told her.

"Almost . . ."

"I meant the rodeo."

80

"I'm sorry, I didn't."

"Please, Sue Ellen, don't do this. It isn't often that something like this happens. The way I feel—"

"You hardly know me."

"And you hardly know me. It doesn't matter. We both feel it. You won't deny that."

"No," she said almost inaudibly.

He reached for her hand. She took a backward step. "Let's not throw it away, Sue Ellen. It may never happen to either of us again."

"I'm married."

"Ordinarily that would stop me. I'm not looking for a passing fling with a married lady. But this time—I think we deserve each other, Sue Ellen. I can see how unhappy you are, and I am a lonely man who wants someone to love and someone to love him. You must know that I mean what I say."

"I do," she murmured.

Neither of them saw J.R. come out of the house and start down the hill toward them.

"I don't know," Sue Ellen said to Dusty. "It's all so new, so difficult. You have to give me time."

"All the time you need or want."

J.R.'s voice cut through the mood of the moment like an angry blade. "Time to do what? Exactly what are you two planning behind my back?"

"Oh! J.R.!"

"That's right, sugar. Your ever-lovin' husband. I think it's time you rode out of here, cowboy. You're not welcome at Southfork anymore."

Dusty held his ground. "Word is you're a hard character, Ewing, but not so hard as you like to believe. Anything were to happen to Sue Ellen, I'd not look kindly on it. You get my message, I'm sure."

"On your way, Farlow, before I have you thrown off the ranch."

Dusty's grin was mirthless. "Care to try that by yourself, Ewing?"

"Oh, please, Dusty," Sue Ellen said. "Please don't make any trouble."

"Whatever you say, Sue Ellen. It's been a pleasure talking to you, getting to know you. Ewing, I'll always be around." He left swiftly.

J.R. took Sue Ellen's wrist and led her roughly back to the house, upstairs.

"Let go of me," she demanded once.

"Make a scene now, darlin', and I'll finish it. And you won't appreciate my methods."

"Where do you think you're taking me, J.R.?"

He stopped in front of the door to their rooms. "Why, right here, sugar, our bedroom. Where else?" He opened the door and shoved her inside, trailing close behind. She whirled around to face him.

"Whatever you've got in mind, give it up, J.R. Nothing you do is going to work."

"I want to see your smile, sugar. The same smile you turned on that two-bit cowhand. Come on, sugar, let's have it now."

"Go to hell."

In a single, swift motion he took hold of the front of her blouse and yanked her toward him. She fought but was unable to break free. "Let—me—go!"

He shoved her backward onto the bed. For a moment she didn't realize what was happening, then she recognized his intentions.

"No, J.R.! Damn you to hell—no!"

"Is it so hard to do? After all, I am your husband whom you love dearly and are sworn to love, honor, and obey. Surely that rates me certain privileges. At least the same privileges as that cowboy has."

"You can fry in hell—"

His laughter was empty and cold. Holding her in place, he tore at her shirt front. It popped open. "My, aren't you getting daring? No bra, honey? What will people say?" He squeezed her breasts, and she gasped in pain. "How did Mr. Farlow enjoy them? Did he appreciate what a prize you are? Best-looking girl in south Texas. How much did he see, Sue Ellen? How much did he get to touch? How much did he use you? Here, Sue Ellen? Here? Here?"

She wrenched out of his grasp, rolling to the floor, coming up to her feet at once, backing away. He went after her.

"Just pretend I'm him. Just pretend, and see if that won't work up your feelings, your desires. Pretend, and enjoy what I'm about to do to you."

He lunged forward, and as he did she brought her knee up into his groin. He bent double, groaning. She slapped him as hard as she could across the face.

"J.R., you are disgusting."

He went to his knees, moaning and clutching himself in pain.

"You need a woman, J.R.? Go out and find Kristin. She'll be happy to oblige all your fancies, I'm sure."

He forced himself to stand. "You're right. She will, and she'll be a lot better at it than you ever were. I've wasted enough time on you." He stormed out of the bedroom.

She remained behind, weeping softly.

"Ladies and gentlemen, the winner of the overall prize, as best all-around cowboy of the Fifteenth Annual Ewing Rodeo, the star of this year's show—Dusty Farlow!"

PART 3

Miss Ellie

"*A*m I boring you, doctor?"

Dr. Ellby, Sue Ellen's psychiatrist, sat comfortably in his black leather and rosewood Eames lounge chair, feet resting lightly on the ottoman, making an occasional note with a ballpoint pen on a yellow legal pad. From her place on the therapist's couch, Sue Ellen could not see him. But she could hear the low rasp of his breathing, always regular, a sibilant counterpoint to her emotional anguish. She had been talking to him for uncounted minutes without interruption, only to abruptly go silent; and the silence closed in about her like an oppressive hood, cutting her off from all forms of life. Including Dr. Ellby.

"Well," she said insistently. "Am I boring you?"

"Do you bore people generally, Sue Ellen?" His voice was cultured, clear, the unaccented tones of a radio announcer. Nothing to identify his beginnings, nothing to mark him and set him aside as different or special, ordinary or unique. Just *there*, she thought; and that eternal rasp.

"I've had no complaints."

"Yet you believe you're boring me?"

"Just asking."

"Why do you think you're boring me?"

"Ask a question, get a question. I suppose that is professional technique. It's what I hate most about you, doctor. No, I guess that's not entirely accurate. I don't hate you. How could I, when you remain a cipher to me. There must be a reason to get angry, it doesn't simply occur in a vacuum."

"To some degree you're right."

"But not entirely," she said, voice dripping with sarcasm.

"Not entirely," he agreed flatly. "You can experience an emotion without always knowing why, or having to justify it."

"I suppose you're right. Still, I'm convinced some of your other patients must be much more interesting to you than I am."

"Why would you believe that?"

"My husband said that of all the psychiatrists in Dallas you were the one most likely to get me into bed."

There was no alteration in the tempo or intensity of his breathing. "Is that what you think?"

"I don't know what to think."

"Do you believe it would be proper psychiatric practice for a doctor to sleep with his patients?"

"I imagine it would complicate matters somewhat."

"In what way?"

She swung up into a sitting position. "Ah, there you are! You look vaguely familiar. Have you been the one breathing behind me all this time?"

"Are you feeling a great deal of hostility toward me, Sue Ellen?"

"More than I can express."

"Won't you tell me why?"

"Yes. It's because you have no accent."

He showed some surprise, to her surprise. "No accent?"

"Yes. Any shrink worth his salt would have a Viennese accent, a salt-and-pepper beard, and wear gold-rimmed glasses. Ideally, you should be short and pudgy. Instead, you are tall and good-looking and talk like Walter Cronkite. It ruins a perfectly fine freudian fantasy."

He made a note. "About your hostility—is it because I haven't tried to seduce you?"

A burst of laughter broke out of her. "I don't want to be seduced. Not by you or anyone else."

"Not even your husband?"

"Most especially not by my husband. I'd like a drink of water."

He gestured. "Won't you help yourself."

She went over to his desk, aware that he was studying

88

every move she made, and poured water from a carafe into a glass. She sipped it and put down the glass.

"If you were a Viennese gentleman, you would have brought me the water instead of making me go after it."

"Do you really want to discuss my social graces? Wouldn't you like to tell me what is really on your mind?"

"My mind is a blank." She went back to the couch and sat down, crossing her legs, avoiding eye contact with Dr. Ellby. "Completely blank."

"Do you think that's possible?"

She allowed her eyes to flutter shut, and a vision of Dusty Farlow faded into view. He was smiling, arms extended, inviting her to come to him. She opened her eyes, not looking at Ellby.

"I met a man—"

A long silence followed.

"About the man you met?"

"He's just a common cowboy."

"Does that trouble you, his social and economic inferiority?"

"He's not inferior in any way."

"Would you mind explaining?"

"His family owns a very large ranch. Actually, he's quite wealthy in his own right. But he lives like an ordinary ranch hand, a rodeo bum—"

"How do you feel about that?"

"No big deal, actually. I don't know why I'm even discussing him with you. What do you want to know about him?"

"What would you like to tell me?"

"Damn your questions!" She uncrossed and crossed her legs. Thinking of Dusty, a weakness came into her middle, traveled downward between her thighs. She wet her lips. "I hardly know the man. There isn't much to tell. I talked to him over coffee and at the Ewing Rodeo. Actually, we talked a great deal at the rodeo. Actually, I went to a coffee shop over in Braddock every day hoping to run into him. I don't know why?"

"Don't you know why?"

"I guess I wanted to see him. I was afraid to see him. Does that make sense? He wants to see me." She broke off and began pacing the room.

89

"How do you feel about that?"

"What? Oh, well, I guess I like it. I'm flattered. I am a married woman, after all."

"Does it make you feel wicked?"

"It makes me feel—oh, dammit, can't you understand? He wants to go to bed with me. He wants to make love to me. He wants to be intimate in every way with me."

"And how does that make you feel?"

She shook her head, sat back down, then stood up again and lowered herself carefully to the edge of the couch, adjusting her skirt neatly over her knees. "I am cold. All frozen up inside. I have no desire for sex."

"In which case you have no problem, do you?"

"He's reminded me that I'm a woman, a human being with human desires."

"Then you feel something for this man?"

"I didn't think I'd ever feel anything again."

"Do you intend to see him again?"

"Do you think I should see him?"

"What do you think?"

"I don't know. I'm confused. I'm frightened. I think about him constantly. I fantasize—do you know what that does to me, a woman like me? I lie in bed at night next to J.R., listening to him snore and imagining it's another man next to me—Dusty—imagining his hands on my body, stroking me, caressing me, making me want him. Oh, damn you, Ellby, tell me what to do!"

"Apparently you are not as sexually disinterested as you indicated. This man, this Dusty, he seems to be healing the wounds you incurred. This is the first time you've mentioned him, or any man, the first time you expressed any sexual interest at all. How do you feel about an extra-marital affair? Does it offend you?"

"It doesn't seem to bother J.R."

"You are not J.R. Have you forgotten your affair with Cliff Barnes, what happened to you when you decided to fight fire with fire?"

"I think that Cliff was exactly that, an attempt to strike back at my husband, to gain some measure of revenge. But Dusty, he's different."

"Different? How is he different?"

"I truly care for him."

"Are you sure?"

"I'm not sure of anything any more. What am I going to do?"

"Always be Sue Ellen, I imagine. The only person you can be."

A harsh sound broke out of her. "And who is she? What is she?"

"That," he said standing, signaling the end of the hour, "is what we are here to find out, isn't it?"

Cliff Barnes welcomed Alan Beam into his private office, got him seated, and assessed the youthful-looking lawyer: handsome in a lean, dark-skinned way, with bright, intelligent eyes that met his own almost too steadily, a practiced act designed to impress and conceal, if not deceive. At the same time Cliff was impressed with the younger man's eagerness and apparent sincerity; his interests appeared to be Cliff's interests. Appeared, he stressed to himself silently.

"I have a very comfortable position with Smithfield and Bennett," Alan was saying, by way of qualifying himself and his reason for coming here. "I would not be making waves if I didn't think it would all work out both to your benefit and mine. I truly believe you can run for public office and win."

Cliff leaned back in his chair, his chin resting on his laced fingers, watching Alan. "I heard about your little difficulty with J.R., out at Southfork."

"He made me look bad when there was no reason to. When I was in no position to defend myself. I can't forget that. Who told you about it?"

Cliff shrugged. "The best of sources, from my point of view. My father was there, saw and heard it all, and Digger has more reason to hate the Ewings than many of us."

"Okay, so you know what took place. You know that I'm finished with J.R. Ewing."

"And you mean to get even by riding my back?"

Alan took a deep breath. "In part, yes. But it's not that simple. Sure I want to hurt J.R., hurt him bad. I figure you are the one who can paint the target on the right spot. I know about your work with the OLM, how you've hurt Ewing enterprises already. But all you've done is give the

bull an itch. He knows how to scratch. I think you can
deliver a telling wound. I think you can draw blood."

"How's that?"

"Vengeance isn't sufficient. You've got to profit yourself at
the same time."

"You said you were still solid over at Smithfield and
Bennett."

"That's sixty thousand now, maybe even a hundred thousand in a couple of years. I am a very good lawyer, Cliff, very
good at what I do. At whatever I do. I can be good for you,
too."

"Keep talking."

"I like money well enough, don't get me wrong. But I'm
also young enough and ambitious enough to want to make a
very clear mark on society."

"And just how do you intend to do that?"

"By hitching my wagon to a star, a star that's heading
right into the highest part of the sky."

"Which means me?"

"Yes, sir."

"Just one thing you seem to forget—I am not running for
public office. I like the work I'm doing now."

"Of course you do. And that's part of why I've come to
you. There are too many guys running around making noises
about how much they want to help people, and they get
nothing accomplished. You're different."

"How so?"

"You're dedicated, true. But you're also competent. You
say you'll do something, you do it. But—"

"But?"

"But you're locked into a job that limits you. Sure you can
annoy the Ewings now and then, but working out of OLM
you'll never stop them. They're too rich, too powerful, with
too many good connections that will slow you down, hobble
your case, eventually put you out of business."

"Which brings us right around to elective office."

"Yes. You stand for the things the voters in your district
want. People honor you with their confidence, they trust you.
They will vote for you. It's a natural situation, Cliff. Run for
Congress. Endorse the Draft Barnes movement."

"No."

"Why not?"

"You said it. I'm competent. If I run, I want to win. If I go for it, I have to be convinced that I can win. I don't believe in lost causes. I don't believe in learning how to lose. Losing hurts, and I do it without grace."

Alan grinned. "I don't intend for either of us to lose. Here, feast your eyes on this list of individuals and organizations that I've already lined up to back you. And that in a very short time with limited staff and limited funds. I tell you, we can win."

Cliff ran his eyes down the list. "There are some good names here."

"Now do you believe me?"

"I'm flattered."

"Then you'll run?"

"I'll say this—I'm impressed. You've been a busy boy."

"This is only the beginning. Will you endorse the movement?"

"Not yet."

Alan floundered, seeking an argument that would work. "I can put you in Congress."

"It will take more than a few names on a list. It takes volunteers, organization, money."

"I can put it together."

"When you do, I'll know you can do it."

"Then you won't stop me?"

"No," Cliff said slowly, "I won't stop you."

A broad grin sliced across Alan's face. "That's all the encouragement I need. I believe in you, Cliff Barnes, and I'm going to make you a winner. I'm going to put you into one of the main corridors of power."

"And yourself right alongside?"

"All the way, Cliff. All the way to the top."

——— 8 ———

*I*n a private room in the Dallas Memorial Hospital, Pam watched her mother-in-law transfer a few things from an overnight bag on the bed to the closet.

"Pam, you didn't have to come up here. I don't want you to be late for work."

"I spoke to Liz. I'm taking the day off."

"That's not necessary. All they're going to do is run a few tests. And remove the cyst. Nothing to it."

"Miss Ellie, I know you think there's going to be more to it than that. And even if there isn't, you're going to be in the hospital overnight. Don't you think you ought to let Jock know?"

"Frankly, I don't."

"I could call for you."

"Please don't do that, Pam."

"Not if you don't want me to. But how do you expect to spend a night away from Southfork without Jock knowing you're in the hospital? The man will be worried sick. Shouldn't you be the one to call him?"

"Pam, I am pleased that you're concerned about my well-being and Jock's. And I love you dearly. But as far as what I tell or don't tell my husband—well, dear, that is none of your business."

Pam smiled wanly. "I'm sorry. It's just that I feel specially close to you so I guess it is my business, after all."

Miss Ellie's eyes flashed angrily. "Pam, you stay out of this."

Pam shook her head. "I just can't believe you'd think that Jock wouldn't stand by you at a time like this."

"What you believe right now is irrelevant, of no consequence. What I do or don't do is my decision to make."

Before Pam could reply, a nurse entered. "As soon as you're ready, Mrs. Ewing, we'd like to begin the testing procedures."

"I'll only be a moment. My daughter-in-law is just leaving." She fixed Pam with a steady gaze, and the younger woman, after a brief hesitation, walked out of the room. In the corridor she came to a pay phone and dialed. A few rings and she heard: "Ewing Oil."

"Bobby Ewing, please."

Then the secretary's familiar voice came on. "Ewing Oil, executive offices."

"Connie, it's Pam. Is Bobby in?"

"Just a moment, Mrs. Ewing."

Miss Ellie, wearing a hospital gown and robe, was perched on the edge of the bed when Dr. Danvers appeared with another physician.

"Ellie, this is Dr. Mitch Andrus. He'll be doing the actual surgical procedure. Dr. Andrus is an experienced and excellent physician."

"I'm sure he is," Ellie replied. She felt very tense, almost to the edge of her self-control. Her eyes skittered from one man to the other and back again.

"Mrs. Ewing," Dr. Andrus said, "let me try to explain everything."

"Please."

"Shouldn't we wait for Jock?" Dr. Danvers asked.

"That's not necessary," she replied quickly. "Go ahead, doctor."

Danvers seemed surprised. "You're sure?"

"Quite sure. Please tell me what it is you have to do."

Andrus answered with professional detachment. "The area with the cyst will be removed, and we'll have a frozen section done to test for cancer. When the report comes through, we'll know how to proceed."

"Meaning," Miss Ellie said in a small, tight voice, "that

there is a chance that I may need major surgery. A mastectomy."

Danvers replied. "Ellie, even if we discover a tumor, it may not be malignant."

"It will all be done very quickly," Andrus said. "We'll send the tumor down to the lab while you're on the table. The results will come back rather rapidly."

"Ellie," Danvers said, "there is one thing we have to discuss, however. If we do find a malignancy, you have a choice other than mastectomy. Lumpectomy—where just the tumor is removed. That would be followed by special radiation treatment. It's an area in which we're gaining more and more experience and—"

"No," Miss Ellie said. "I don't think so. If you have to, if it's medically indicated, do the mastectomy."

Andrus nodded. "I know this is difficult for you, Mrs. Ewing, but I believe a patient should know everything, every possibility."

"Go on, please."

"I do what is known as a modified radical. I leave the muscles, which will give you better use of your arm later on, but I do remove all of the lymph nodes."

"All right," she said in a small voice.

Danvers spoke. "Ellie, in about six months, depending on how things proceed, I will arrange for you to see a plastic surgeon for reconstruction."

"Make me as good as new, Harlan?"

"Not exactly. But they do excellent work these days. It's an important psychological boost."

"Anything else I should know?"

"Only one thing," Danvers said. "If we have to do a mastectomy, do you want us to wake you first so we can talk and give you a chance to think about it again?"

She almost laughed at the naiveté of the question. "No. I haven't thought about anything else for weeks now."

Danvers offered her some papers. "I'm going to need your signature, Ellie."

She nodded, saying nothing. She wrote her name at the bottom of the various official forms. She handed them back to Danvers, who held her hand for a long moment. He smiled encouragingly and led Dr. Andrus outside.

After a minute or two, Miss Ellie walked over to the closet and opened it. A full-length mirror hung on the back of the door. She opened her robe, unbuttoned the gown, and studied her body. It hardly seemed possible that her still firm, almost youthful breasts could be corrupted by disease. She was no longer a young woman, yet she still took pride in the way her body had held up, the skin taut, the flesh solid. She remembered how many times Jock had gazed lovingly at her nakedness, had expressed the joy he took in her body, in its strength and suppleness, in the pleasure he found in it. She never heard the nurse come into the room.

"Oh, Mrs. Ewing, I'm sorry—"

Miss Ellie reluctantly turned away. "I was wondering if I will ever again look the same. Is that silly?"

"Not silly at all. Is there anything I can do for you?"

"I just wanted to remember—"

The nurse struggled to keep her professional composure. "I have to get you ready."

Ellie lay alone in the room, waiting. Trying not to be too afraid, trying not to think. At the same time she warned herself not to close herself off from life, no matter how cruel and mindless that life might become. As long as she lived, she wanted to remain aware and sensitive, know what she was experiencing and feeling. She wanted always to be the most, the best Ellie Ewing it was possible to be.

Jock came into the room. "Miss Ellie," he said, concern and alarm in his voice.

"I didn't want you to know."

"You should have said something. I'm your husband. I have a right to know."

"It may be only a minor operation. I'm sure that was all explained to you."

"Yes, but Bobby said you're worried they'll find cancer."

"They might."

"Why keep it from me?"

"I was afraid to tell you."

The nurse entered with an orderly. "Sorry, Mr. Ewing. We have to take Mrs. Ewing up to surgery now."

Jock reached for Miss Ellie's hand. "Afraid? Of what?"

97

She retrieved her hand. "If they find cancer, Jock—if it's bad—will you leave me the same way you left Amanda?"

Jock stood in place, unable to move or speak or think. He watched them roll his wife away and wondered what the future held for them.

___ 9 ___

$\mathcal{P}$am, Bobby, J.R., and Jock were in the waiting room. Impatient. Skittish. Unable to sustain a conversation. Wishing they were somewhere else. Wishing none of this had happened, had to happen. Bobby checked his watch; less than five minutes had passed since the last time he had looked. Pam stood up and sat right back down again. J.R. stared at some middle point in space. Jock swore under his breath.

"I'm going to get Daddy some coffee," J.R. said at last. He started for the coffee machine at the far end of the corridor.

"Don't want any coffee," Jock growled.

"Help settle your nerves."

"Don't want any, dammit. Don't anybody around here understand the mother tongue?"

"Isn't it time they came down and told us something?" Pam asked. "What time is it?" She looked at her watch.

"Maybe one of us should call the ranch," Bobby said. "Lucy will be home from school by now."

"She'll be worried," Pam said.

"Where's Sue Ellen?" Jock asked gruffly. "Dammit, J.R., why isn't that wife of yours here? She's family, too, isn't she?"

"She had an appointment with her therapist today."

"Past time for her to be finished, isn't it?"

"I suppose it is."

Bobby interrupted. "I'll call the ranch, as soon as we know something."

"Maybe," Pam said absently, "it would be better if I went home and talked to Lucy. To Sue Ellen."

"Maybe."

Sue Ellen galloped her horse until the animal broke into a sweat and began to snort, great muscles twitching under his skin. She turned him into a tree-shaded glen and dismounted, allowing him to cool down. She put her back against a large tree and closed her eyes. She held herself very still, trying not to think, not to anticipate. Nothing was going to occur that she could not deal with capably. Nothing. Nothing.

Moments later she heard another horse coming into the glen. She kept herself in place, unwilling to show any reaction, any sense of excitement or pleasure. She heard the horse stop and whinny, heard *him* spring lightly to the ground.

"Is this where I catch the bus to Lubbock?" he asked lightly.

She opened her eyes. "You shouldn't have phoned me, Dusty."

"I had no choice."

"It's better if we never see each other again."

"I can't believe that. Anyway, you're here. I'm here." He sat down beside her, careful to make no bodily contact. "This is nice."

"This is crazy."

"Maybe so. Don't you have a crazy side? Did you ever think of climbing Reunion Tower in downtown Dallas? Or scaling the Eiffel Tower? I sure as hell did."

"I never did. Not once. I guess I'm much more cautious than you are, straighter."

"Well, that's all right. I'll teach you to think about such things. Help you cut the ties that bind you so firmly to the ground, teach you to fly free, fly as high as you want to."

"Dusty. I'm not ready to fly. I'm just learning to walk again."

"I know you've been hurt."

"More than once."

"Remember I met your husband."

"If it was only him—I think I could have handled that. If

100

you get hurt enough times, you become gun-shy, flinch easily. I'm afraid—of so many things."

"If you want to tell me, I'm ready to listen. But don't think you have to. I accept you the way I see you, that's all that matters to me, and it's all good."

"I don't know if I'm ready to trust another man. Not yet."

"Leave J.R."

"I tried once. He dragged me back."

"This time you'll have help. He won't find dragging so easy this time."

"You don't know my husband. He finds a way to break any man who stands in his way. A man who took his wife away—my God, there's no telling what J.R. would do."

Dusty took her hand in his. "Physically, he would find me a long ton to haul. Believe me, he couldn't break me that way. And otherwise—well, don't forget, there's a lot of money behind me, if I want it, a lot of power. And my family knows how to use it."

"Slow down, honey. What makes you think I'd leave J.R. for you? You're skipping ahead mighty fast, too fast for me."

"I didn't say leave him for me. If you want to leave him, for any reason, I'll help you."

"Why?"

"Do you really have to ask? Because I care."

She looked away. "You don't know me very well. I'm a snob, and I can be a bitch if I don't get my way. You know why I married J.R.? I wanted to be part of all that Ewing power and position and wealth. I wanted the social standing the Ewing name could give me."

He shifted closer to her. "Do you expect me to believe you're all that bad?"

"Yes—"

He kissed her. At first she held herself stiffly, then slowly her lips gave way, softening, parting, accepting his tongue, her arm going around his neck. Abruptly she broke away. Her face was flushed, and she was breathing rapidly.

"Please, don't do that again. Not now, not now."

"I'll wait as long as you want, until you're ready."

101

She came up to her feet and went toward her horse. He helped her mount.

"Will I see you again soon, Sue Ellen?"

"I may never be ready," she said, before riding away.

10

$\mathcal{L}$ucy sat on the patio alone. Some books were spread out on the table in front of her, but she had given up all pretense of studying. Something was clearly wrong. Nobody else was anywhere on Southfork: not Bobby or Pam, not J.R., not Jock or Miss Ellie. And none of the servants seemed to know where the others had gone. Lucy felt deserted, alone in a once familiar and reassuringly populated world. She felt like a character lost on some alien landscape or desolate moon, devoid of life. Of course, she told herself, such ideas were absurd, silly, self-indulgent. Everywhere around her there was life: humans, cows, chickens. Although in this terrible heat, the chickens were not faring too well. Neither for that matter were the cattle. Death was everywhere; death of heat stroke, of dehydration. Water holes were dried up, and the prairie was cracking under the strain. It occurred to her that she was hot, thirsty, weary, and should retreat to the air-conditioned sanctity of the ranch house. She made no move to go.

She was thinking about Alan Beam when Pam drove up and climbed out of her car. Pam looked fresh and pretty in a loose-fitting print skirt and a pink blouse, her perfect round arms exposed to the air. She was a beautiful woman, one of the most beautiful Lucy had ever seen. Lucy had no hopes of ever being as beautiful as Pam; she, Lucy, was pretty, cute, pert and feisty, all those things. But beautiful? No way.

"Hi, Pam," she said with forced cheerfulness.

Pam was crying. "Is Sue Ellen here?"

"Nobody's here."

"Let's go inside. This heat is unbearable. I've got something to tell you."

"Yes." Lucy couldn't make herself move. "I've been thinking about doing that myself."

Taking her by the hand, Pam led Lucy into the den. Lucy shivered. The cool air chilled her.

Pam wiped her eyes. "Sit down."

"I'm too cold to sit."

"It's about Miss Ellie."

Lucy stiffened in place, her bright blue eyes glazed, unseeing, impenetrable. "Is that why you're crying?"

Pam nodded. "I was going to phone, but I couldn't. I wanted to see your face."

"Is she dead?"

"Oh, no, no."

"Nothing like that. It's just—"

"You are crying," the girl said logically.

"She's having surgery."

"Surgery?" Lucy had never even had a hangnail removed. Surgery. A foreign word out of a language she had never comprehended. Good health was a constant of her young life. Doctors were an occasional inconvenience for physicals or shots; never anything more. She had never suffered pain to her flesh, had never broken a bone, chipped a tooth, suffered more than a seventy-two-hour virus. Surgery entailed anesthetics and blood transfusions, scalpels; suffering, ugliness, and death. She didn't understand and said so.

Pam began again. "Miss Ellie has been concerned about a lump in her breast. Dr. Danvers and a couple of other physicians who were called in are sure it's a cyst—"

"A cyst?"

"Nothing to worry about."

"But they are operating?"

"To remove the cyst, just as a medical precaution. Better safe than sorry."

Lucy found it all too alarming to digest. "Why," she asked with considerable heat, "was Grandma so angry at Granddaddy? I never saw her so upset. Was it because Grandma needed—to go to the doctor?"

"I don't know. None of us do. Neither of them is talking."

"Then there's nothing to worry about?"

Pam began to weep again. "I don't know. I left the hospital before the procedure was over. I wanted to tell you myself. I wanted to be with you when you found out."

"I'm sure Grandma will be fine, absolutely all right. Perfect."

"I hope so. But we all have to be prepared."

"Prepared?" Lucy paled. "I don't know what you're talking about. I don't want to hear any more." She clapped her hands over her ears. "I won't be!" she shouted "I won't be! I won't be *prepared!*"

"Prepared? Prepared for what?" It was Sue Ellen who spoke, striding into the den in her riding clothes, face lined with dust. "Is this a Boy Scout convention? Be Prepared, isn't that the Boy Scout motto?" She tried to smile.

"Sit down," Pam ordered.

"Is something wrong?"

"It's Miss Ellie. She's in the hospital. They are operating on her now—"

"Oh!" Sue Ellen said, sinking down into a chair.

Jock, Bobby, and J.R. were alone in the hospital waiting room. The plastic coffee cups on the low tables were half drained, the ashtrays filled with burned-out cigarettes. Jock ran his fingers through his white mane.

"I can't understand that woman," he said for the fifth time in twenty minutes. "Checking into a hospital and not saying a word to me. Forty years of marriage, sharing everything, and she doesn't say a word."

Bobby looked up. His face was strained, drawn, tight at the corners of his finely etched mouth. "Daddy, why don't you tell us what's been going on between you and Momma?"

Jock stood up and looked away. "Nothing to tell. At least not now. Oh, hell, I just don't want to talk about it. J.R. can fill you in, if he wants to. I got to walk around, work off this tension." He strode out into the corridor.

Bobby turned angrily to J.R. "You knew all along!"

"Now hold your water, little brother. It was a confidence, nothing sneaky."

"Seeing how it's you that's involved, I find that hard to believe."

"Okay, here it is. Daddy was married and divorced before he met Momma."

"I don't believe it!"

"True enough, Bobby. And when he told Momma, she exploded. Imagine Daddy keeping a secret like that from all of us for all those years."

"This is going to take some getting used to."

"For me, too," J.R. drawled thoughtfully.

Out in the corridor, a nurse came up to Jock. "Mr. Ewing?"

"Yes, ma'am." He felt his heart begin to pound. Fear gathered in a thick, wet knot in his middle. His big hands clenched. "I'm Jock Ewing."

"Mrs. Ewing is back in her room now, and Dr. Danvers would like to see you."

"My boys are in the waiting room," Jock said. "Will you tell them, please?"

"Yes, sir."

He hurried off toward Miss Ellie's room. He entered cautiously. Miss Ellie, pale and small to the eye, was back in the bed, still asleep from the sedatives. Standing next to the bed was Dr. Danvers. He, too, seemed pale and under strain.

"How is it, doctor?" Jock asked.

"Hello, Jock."

"Harlan, how is she?"

Danvers raised his eyes to Jock's. "Ellie was right."

"Right?"

"I'm afraid so."

"Malignant?" Jock said with as much dignity as he could summon up.

"Yes, Jock. Her breast was full of cysts—and there was a small cancer nearby. It never registered on the mammogram."

"What are you telling me?"

"We had to perform a mastectomy. Jock, when Ellie comes out of it, we're going to have to tell her—"

"Tell her?" Jock said without comprehension.

"That we had to take her breast."

Jock staggered as if hit, and Danvers put out a hand to steady him. Tears filled Jock's eyes as he gazed down at his sleeping wife. How would she be able to live with this, he asked himself.

How would he?

PART 4

Last Imperfect

*O*nly three months earlier, it was quiet in the maternity ward of Dallas Memorial Hospital. A few new fathers studied their crinkled, recently born offspring through the glass of the nursery window. A new mother, a half-smile on her face, came shuffling along the corridor, holding on to her once-again flat stomach as if it might spill forward. Two attendants wheeled a woman into delivery. A nurse marched along with brisk competence, as if on her way to perform some medical necessity; in fact, she was bound for the cafeteria and a quick coffee with her intern lover.

Nearby, J.R. was in conversation with Dr. David Rogers.

"I believe it'll be for only a few more days. Then we'll send the boy home to you, Mr. Ewing. Meanwhile, we'll do our best to make him as comfortable as possible."

"I'm sure you will, doctor. You know how anxious we all are, especially my wife and I."

"Understood, Mr. Ewing. Trust us. Now if you will excuse me, I'm on call."

J.R. turned away, and his eye fell on a newspaper lying on a chair in the lounge. Frowning, he picked it up and read the headline: PROMINENT DALLAS BUSINESSMEN FREED ON BAIL.

Heading the long story was a photograph of Jeb Ames and Willie Joe Garr, taken as they were leaving prison. Both men seemed grim, serious, as if on their way to an appointment, with something very private on their minds. J.R. read the entire story, turning gloomier with every paragraph; he was not happy to have them back in town—he had wished them a long and difficult term in prison. He tossed the paper aside; he would deal with Willie Joe and Jeb when the time came, as it inevitably would.

He turned back to the nursery and saw Sue Ellen standing

111

in front of the glass. In a floor-length robe of blue satin, her hair precisely coifed, her face carefully made up, she looked younger than her years and incredibly beautiful. Yet, through it all, there was a dull pallor of skin and spirit, as if some essential aspect of her being had been irrevocably damaged. J.R. came up behind her, placing one hand at the small of her back. She shuddered.

"Come on, darlin'. It's time to go home, back to Southfork. Go on, get dressed."

She continued to stare at Baby John—John Ross Ewing III. The child slept peacefully in the small hospital crib. He was undersized, but perfect, and seemed to be well.

"You hear me, Sue Ellen? We got to be goin'."

"So soon?" She spoke without expression as if there remained within her only a minimal amount of spirit and life force.

Taking her elbow, he guided her back toward her room. "No need for you to be frettin' about the baby. Doctor says he's doing just fine. In a few days he'll be coming home."

She shrugged his hand away. "Why should I worry? I'm not worried. About anything. I'm sure it will all work out in the end. Everything."

Neither of them noticed the man at the far end of the corridor watching them covertly. When they were gone, he walked leisurely to the nursery window to examine Baby John through the glass. As far as Cliff Barnes was concerned, he was looking at his own flesh and blood. His own son. And he meant to make sure the world knew it.

Braddock Pasture was a vast sea of green, flowing into the clear blue sky at the horizon. Half a dozen cowboys on horseback were gently but efficiently edging cows and their calves, some steers and bulls from the outlying ends of the pasture toward a trap containing a dozen or so of the already culled cattle.

On horseback, Jock was at the trap, examining the animals as they came in. He pointed to one calf. "That one! Something's wrong with him. Cut him out and let's take a looksee."

A cowboy rode up, loop in hand, working the calf away

from his mother. At the same time Bobby came riding up, reining in alongside Jock.

"I heard what you said. I found a cow dead with screwworm south of Braddock country this morning."

Jock scowled. "That ain't so good."

The cowboy had pitched his rope over the neck of the calf and with the help of a second cowhand flipped the animal over. Jock rode in for a closer look.

"That's it, all right," he said with disgust. "Screwworm. Hell's bells, we'll have an epidemic on our hands if we don't take care of it fast."

Ray Krebbs came riding up, driving three cows and their calves ahead of him.

"They okay?" Bobby asked.

"Looks to me like screwworm," Ray replied. "The small ones are infected."

"Damn," Jock muttered.

In the trap a cowboy was smearing the calf with ointment.

"Okay," Bobby said to Ray. "First thing in the morning, we start riding all the pastures, checking the herd. I want every animal examined."

"You got it, Bobby."

Jock said, "All that prickly brush up in Little Horn is bound to cause us some trouble."

"No help for it," Ray said. "It's got to be done." A movement along the road caught his eye. "Car coming."

They recognized it at once, J.R.'s Mercedes. Ewing 3, as it was known around the ranch.

A broad grin split Jock's face. He kicked his horse into motion and galloped off toward the road, Bobby right behind him. They waved their hats in the air, shouting greetings. From their positions the cowboys began to wave and shout.

In the car Sue Ellen gave no indication that she heard or saw anything. Beside her, J.R. frowned. "There's Daddy and Bobby." He slowed the Mercedes to a stop. "The boys are mighty glad to see you, Sue Ellen, to have you back. Let's get out and say hello, sugar."

"I don't think so."

"But they expect it."

"I'm too weary. I'd like to lie down."

For a moment he was unsure about what to do. Then he put the car back into gear and drove on.

At the side of the road, Jock and Bobby watched them go.

"Well, now," Jock said, "wasn't that a mite peculiar? I wonder if anything's wrong."

Bobby didn't answer; he was silently asking himself the same question.

The Ranch Lounge was tucked away in the corner of a downtown office building in Dallas, one of those sleek watering holes that could be put down in any large city in the continental United States without anyone noticing the difference. For the most part, the people would look and dress and talk the same; think alike and be comfortable in each other's presence. In the dim light men drank with other men's wives, sleek well-dressed women talked intimately, and young men and women made connections that might last for a lifetime or one night. Pam Ewing and her brother, Cliff Barnes, sat in a remote corner, hunched over a low candle that burned steadily in a hand-hammered Mexican holder. To a casual onlooker it would have been plain—neither of them was having a very good time.

Pam fingered her glass. "You don't understand what Sue Ellen is like right now. You haven't seen her every day, the way I have."

His voice was harsh, inflexible, his face set. "She's been ill. Like most of us, she'll recover." He signaled the waitress for another round of drinks.

"I've had enough," Pam said.

He paid no attention. "That baby is mine."

"You can't be sure of that."

"I'm sure, and so is Sue Ellen. So are you. And so is J.R., damn his eyes."

"You've got to give her time. Time and a chance to get her emotions together, get her head straight."

He snorted. "I love her."

"Then you'll understand, be warm, sympathetic."

"I want to see my son."

"I know how you feel, Cliff."

"I doubt that."

She went on as if he had said nothing. "I don't like what happened, but you're my brother. I can still sympathize with you."

"Then you'll help me."

She set her jaw. There was in her lovely face the same stubborn resolve her brother showed, with perhaps an added strength he seemed to lack. "You must try and remember, Cliff, there's not just you to consider. Or the baby, for that matter. Think about Sue Ellen, how she feels now. What she's going through. Emotionally, she is a mess. It's as if she's walking a tightrope. Any distraction, the slightest disturbance, and she's certain to fall."

"I don't think you understand, Pam. I can help her. She loves me, and I love her. I am determined—"

"Keep on the way you're going, and you'll help her right back to the bottle, if you're not careful."

"Months ago," he said bitterly, "she wanted to come to me. Be with me. I should have let her."

"Maybe you should have. Maybe a lot of this mess would have been avoided if you had let her. But you didn't."

"I only tried to do what was best for her."

"What was best for your career, you mean. Isn't that a fact, Cliff?"

Before he could answer, the waitress brought the drinks. She emptied the ashtray, then finally left.

"That's not fair, Pam," he said, keeping his temper under control. "You know J.R., the way he is—"

"J.R. plays a role in all our lives. But just this once, let's leave J.R. out of it. This time, finally, accept responsibility for your own actions, your own life."

He swallowed half of his drink and lit a cigarette. "Whatever I may have done, none of it matters now."

"What does matter to you, then?"

"That I love Sue Ellen. That I want her. That I want Baby John, to claim him as my own."

"I'm warning you, Cliff—"

He waved her words away. "Come on, Pam. You can't possibly believe she's better off with that monster she's married to than with me."

"That's exactly what I do believe."

He pursed his lips. "Makes a brother feel good to know how his sister truly feels about him."

"I love you very much, Cliff. But I understand you very well. You are selfish and self-serving. You will do no good for Sue Ellen or the baby. I'm convinced of that."

He tossed down the remainder of the drink, then fixed her with an unyielding stare. "Nothing you say is going to change anything. My mind's made up. I want them both, and I am going to have them, no matter what I have to do."

Pam felt deeply disturbed. She knew that in his warped desire for revenge against the Ewings he was capable of any act, no matter how irrational. Somehow, she was going to have to make him see the truth. But how?

On the patio at Southfork, Lucy was with two of her friends from school, Wanda, a lithe redhead, and Sherrill, a pretty, intense brunette. They were all very busy studying a catalog as well as a number of official-looking sheets of paper, periodically making notes on a yellow pad. Lucy chewed thoughtfully on a long brown pencil.

"If only I can move this history course," she mused. "That would leave me afternoons completely free for cheerleading practice."

"You're best on the squad now," Wanda said. "Get any better'n you'll show the rest of us up."

Sherrill sighed and stretched. "Why do we have to study history? Who cares what happened yesterday, anyway?"

"You sure don't," Wanda said sweetly.

If Sherrill heard, she gave no indication. "I don't understand half these requirements. All I care about is the differences between boys and girls, and I know all there is to know about that now."

"I bet you do," Wanda replied, smirking.

"Hush, you two," Lucy said. "Somebody'll hear."

"Oh, dear," Sherrill said. "That isn't exactly what I meant to say."

"There's another history course Tuesday and Thursday mornings," Lucy said. "I can take that, if I can get out of music."

"Better not," Wanda warned. "Old Lady Dodd teaches

that one. She's the strictest teacher in the whole school. She gives out more F's than anybody else."

"I thought you were planning to study this semester, Lucy," Sherrill said.

Lucy groaned and rested her chin in her hand. "All the studying in the world's not gonna turn me into a first-class brain." A car turned into the driveway, and Lucy sprang to her feet. "They're here!" She ran forward, down the patio steps, her friends close behind.

J.R. climbed out of Ewing 3 and hurried around to help Sue Ellen. "Hello, Lucy. Girls."

The girls answered as if one. "Hello, J.R."

"How's the baby, J.R.?"

"Doctor says he's doing fine. Be able to come home in a few days, more or less."

He helped Sue Ellen ease her way out of the car. She looked around as if seeing Southfork for the first time, unaware of her husband's nearness.

"Welcome home, Sue Ellen," Lucy said. "I'm glad you're back."

Sue Ellen accepted Lucy's kiss on the cheek with almost regal indifference.

"I am very glad to be back." She issued each word formally, polite but without conviction.

J.R., having removed Sue Ellen's luggage from the car, put an arm around her, directing her toward the house. "You must be tired, sugar. Let's get you settled in."

She nodded and with an almost imperceptible movement, dislodged his arm. She moved off toward the house with deliberate, stately grace. A woman in no hurry to get where she was going.

The three young women watched her go, then huddled together, Wanda speaking in subdued, secretive tones. "I thought you said she was fine."

Lucy replied cautiously. "She is."

"She is not," Wanda insisted. "You think I don't recognize 'fine' when I see it. That is a lady on the brink of something or other."

"Oh, shoot, Wanda, you don't know anything about it."

"You listen to me, Lucy Ewing. My momma had herself a

117

breakdown two or three years back, and I remember she held herself in that same stiff way, as if she was afraid she was going to come unglued or something."

"I tell you Sue Ellen is fine. Isn't she, Sherrill?"

"Oh, my. Well, I don't know. I think what I think is that I agree with you, Lucy, except where I agree with Wanda. Am I making any sense?"

"About as much as usual, honey, so don't worry about it."

Sue Ellen's bedroom was bright and cheerful, a pronounced contrast to her mood. She was cool and withdrawn, a woman so badly hurt that she had retreated to some dark and private place deep inside herself where—she hoped—no one, nothing, could ever harm or hurt her again. So much pain: a marriage that had steadily disintegrated into constant conflict, repeated insults and denigrations, verbal and physical abuse from a man she had respected, loved, and trusted. Until she had realized that she was merely another one of his many possessions, an object without feelings or a soul, without fears or hopes. Someone—no, something—to display, show off, a beautiful thing to be draped on J.R. Ewing's arm when required.

She had sought the love and assurance she needed elsewhere. Cliff Barnes. So full of supportive talk, so many sweet words, vows of eternal affection and concern. And out of that had come another betrayal and the sense again of being used badly. She made a silent vow to allow no one to ever injure her again. To keep those vulnerable parts of herself behind impenetrable walls, to be safe and secure within her own person.

Now she examined her surroundings as if not quite able to believe where she was. J.R. put the valise down and embraced her.

"I want you to know—I am very glad you're home."

She stepped back.

"I mean it," he said, spreading his arms in sincere surrender, an indication of how utterly harmless he truly was.

She turned her back toward him.

"I am going to try to make you happy to be here, Sue Ellen."

"I am happy." She spaced the words to extract from them all meaning, all impact. Three separate and empty utterances. A mechanical concurrence, take it as you like.

"Give me a chance," he said. "I'll make it all up to you."

"I think I'd like to rest now."

"Give me a chance. I can make it up, for everything. I'll wipe out the past."

"The past?"

"The boy. Haven't I accepted him fully? As my son. J.R. Ewing III. He's got my name, every legal right to be my heir, my rightful descendant in every way. He'll never know about—about anything that's happened. I've forgiven you, Sue Ellen. It will all be forgotten, never mentioned around Southfork."

"Yes," she said reflectively. "I believe I would enjoy a quiet time before dinner."

"You won't give an inch, will you?"

"An hour should do."

An angry retort died behind his lips. "Anything you say, sugar. It's good to have you home again."

She lay down across the bed and closed her eyes, hands delicately folded over her breast. As if in prayer. Or in death.

At almost exactly the same time that J.R. brought Sue Ellen back to Southfork, Jeb Ames and Willie Joe Garr appeared at his office in the Ewing Building in Dallas. They had the look of men with a mission that allowed them no rest: eyes hot and searching, faces set in an angry cast, their bodies under clothes that fit too loosely, pitched forward as if about to attack some unseen enemy.

The secretaries, Connie and Louella, were busy working when the two men arrived. It was Louella who greeted them with less grace than she was capable of displaying.

"Mr. Ames! Mr. Garr! What are you doing here? I mean—may I help you?"

Jeb Ames smiled mirthlessly, his rough face made rougher by eyes that were shining hard and impenetrable. "I know what you mean, sweetie, and that's okay. We dropped in to see J.R. Heard he had a baby and want to congratulate the man in person. Touch the flesh, so to speak."

"You heard?" Connie said, not thinking.

"Even where they had us. Walls do not a prison make, not when important goings-on are happening. Oh, we heard, all right."

"Only we are not in prison any longer," Willie Joe Garr said in a rasping voice full of mockery. "In case you have any doubts"—he held out his hand—"feel and make sure." He laughed coarsely when Connie pulled back instinctively.

"I'm sorry," Louella said. "J.R. isn't here right now."

Jeb Ames said, "With his wife and baby, I imagine. They still in the hospital?"

"The baby is," Connie answered nervously. "Sue Ellen went home today. That's where J.R. is—" She broke off, vague guilts coursing through her. She wondered if she'd ever learn to keep her mouth clamped shut.

"Lucky fella, that J.R. Wife gets into a serious auto accident when she's very, very pregnant, and wife and baby both survive. In good health, are they?"

"They're just fine," Louella said.

"Well," Jeb Ames said, "you tell him we were looking for him, hear?"

"Yes, sir."

"You tell him we'd sure like a few of his precious minutes to talk up old times, to remember this and that, to offer our best wishes. You tell him what I said."

"Oh, yes, sir, Mr. Garr. I certainly will."

The two men pivoted around and left as hurriedly as they'd come. Connie, wide-eyed, turned to Louella. "Those two scare me silly. How in the world did they get out of jail so fast?"

"Parole. When you're Ames and Garr and the charge is only manslaughter, I guess you don't stay in prison very long."

Connie shivered. "I'd feel a lot better for all of us if they were still behind bars."

"So would I."

Later that afternoon Miss Ellie wandered into the den at Southfork and discovered J.R. mixing himself a drink. He greeted her with a polite kiss, inquired about her health, and offered to make a drink for her.

She declined. "I think I'll wait for your daddy, thank you."

"He been out on the range all day?"

"All day. That man works too hard for somebody his age."

"Don't you worry about Daddy. He's strong as a bull in his prime."

"But he's not in his prime, not any more. And I do worry about him. He's my husband, and I love him very much." Then, reluctantly: "I thought Sue Ellen looked much too pale for my tastes."

"She'll be just fine."

"And slightly withdrawn."

"Normal postpartum blues. And the effect of the accident."

"Maybe. But I don't like it."

"Don't you start worrying about her. Doctor says there ain't a cotton-picking thing wrong with my wife. Healthy as a young colt."

"Physically, maybe."

"Now, Momma. It's just a matter of time. Woman needs to rest a little is all. Relax. Find out that all the troubles she's had are gone, over, long forgotten."

"Forgotten by her?"

"Everything's gonna turn out splendidly."

"Is it?"

"If I have anything to say about it. You'll see, Momma. You'll be proud of me yet."

She eyed him directly. "I hope so, son, I certainly hope so."

He took his drink and went outside, not caring to pursue the conversation. He was just making himself comfortable on the patio, swirling the ice in his glass with one finger, when Jock's car drew up in the parking area. Jock and Bobby climbed out, both dusty and sweat-stained, two men with a hard day's work behind them. Jock led the way up to the patio. He lifted the glass out of J.R.'s hand and drank thirstily. "Ah, I sure did need that. How's Sue Ellen? And the baby?"

J.R. accepted the return of his nearly empty glass. "Doctor says they couldn't be better. Both of them. You okay, Daddy? You look tired."

"One of those days. Found some calves with screwworm."

The ranch and its day-to-day operation held scant interest for J.R. "How far along?" he asked automatically.

"Ten, maybe twelve days." He reached for the glass again, emptying it in a single swallow. "We're working on it."

Bobby said, "Tomorrow we'll put on some extra hands, to work the pastures over."

"It gets out of hand, you'll have big trouble."

"Hell's bells, J.R., it ain't gonna get to that. We'll stop it first."

"I sure do hope so, Daddy. Ewing Enterprises has problems enough with the oil market, the way things are right now. Don't need short beef sales to add to them."

"You tend to the oil, J.R., Bobby 'n' me will handle the ranch. Ain't that right, Bobby?"

"No need for you to trouble yourself, J.R."

"Reckon you're right, little brother." He watched his father and brother go tramping into the house, past Lucy coming out.

"Oh," she said. "Didn't know you were here."

"Can I get you something cool to drink, sugar?"

"Don't bother. I can take care of myself."

J.R. examined his niece. "Don't know what you got against me, Lucy. I keep trying to be nice to you, but you just don't slack off at all, do you?"

"I can't make up my mind about you, J.R. Whether you've actually changed or not. Anyway, I was used to the old J.R. the kind it was so easy to hate. This new edition—well pardon me for saying so, but I don't find it easy to trust you." She broke off and indicated the driveway, a car speeding up braking to a dusty stop. "Pam's home. That'll make Grandma happy. We haven't all been home for dinner in a long time."

Sue Ellen, unable to sleep, lay on her bed with her eyes open. Staring fixedly, seeing nothing. Determined to maintain an empty brain, uncluttered by thought or feeling, to drift through a murky world untouched, unhurt, unscarred. She stood up and smoothed her skirt, touched her hair as if by reflex, and left the room. On the landing she paused. Pam was coming up the stairs. Their eyes met, and Pam's face broke into a smile.

"Oh, Sue Ellen, I'm so glad you're home. We've missed you so around here. How are you feeling?"

Sue Ellen's expression never changed. Without a word she spun around and went back into her room, closing the door behind her.

A sense of *déjà vu* came over Pam, a flood of anguish at Sue Ellen's obvious dislike. Once before she and Sue Ellen had been at swords' points and then as now she had been unsure as to why.

Nearly two years earlier Pam had walked into the den late one night to discover Sue Ellen pouring straight bourbon down her throat as if to quench an unquenchable thirst. Sue Ellen had been unsteady, eyes unfocused, and she had picked her way to a chair as if on a balance beam.

"Checking up on me, sister-in-law," Sue Ellen had begun.

"Don't you think you've had enough to drink?"

"Enough! Depends on the life you lead. For me enough never comes, if I'm still conscious."

"I'll help you upstairs."

"I don't want your help."

"What do you want, Sue Ellen?"

Sue Ellen's face had seemed to melt then, her voice cracking. "Would you believe—I love my husband. I truly do, which is why I married the no-good sonofabitch. Why doesn't anybody around here understand that? I tried every way I know to make him love *me*."

Pam had been deeply affected by Sue Ellen's anguish. "Don't make it worse—"

"You ever count your blessings? I have. And what do you think mine add up to? J.R. is what, always J.R. The country club, the committees, the invitations, the parties—they all come because I'm *Mrs.* J.R. Ewing, his satellite."

"No. You're an attractive woman. Intelligent. Warm and loving."

Sue Ellen cocked her head in defiance. "I had lunch today with a man. He thought I was attractive. But would I have been so attractive if I weren't Mrs. J.R. Ewing?"

Pam reached for Sue Ellen's glass. It was empty. "Let me help you upstairs."

"That plane has crashed, and they're gone. J.R. and your Bobby. Both of them are dead."

"No, they're coming back, both of them."

Sue Ellen's face wrenched up into a twisted mask. "Wait till you're just Pamela Barnes again. You were nothing, you'll be nothing without the Ewing name. Just another little gold-digging tramp—"

"Please, Sue Ellen . . ."

"Bobby pulled you up out of the gutter. How many men paid your bills before you found a Ewing to pick up the tab?"

"Paid—nobody ever paid my bills! I made my own way, at a job, same as I'm doing now. If I have to, I can take care of myself."

Sue Ellen began to weep. "If J.R.'s dead, what will I do? I lose everything. I haven't even got a child, and I want one so much."

Pam had begun to weep then, remembering the loss of her own child, experiencing vividly her own renewed maternal desires. And in that moment the two women came close together, sharing their mutual misery and fear. They had held each other, rocking gently, Pam murmuring, "I know, I know," until Sue Ellen had cried herself to sleep.

That had been a long time ago, and though neither of them had ever talked about that night, neither had ever forgotten it. And they had approached each other warily ever since, with suspicion, each expecting to be attacked again.

After this latest encounter, Pam made her way to her bedroom. Bobby, already showered and shaved, was in the last stages of dressing for the evening. They kissed and examined each other.

"You look tired," she said.

"I'm fine. Don't worry about me."

"But I do, ever since that plane crash—"

"You still think about that?"

"Every now and then something reminds me."

He kissed her again. "That was a long time ago. I'm here and well."

She smiled ruefully. "Did you have a bad day?"

"Some sick cattle. Nothing that can't be handled. What about you? You don't appear too cheerful to me."

"I just met Sue Ellen. She didn't even say hello. Just ducked back into her room. It's going to be difficult."

"Give her time. When she understands we're on her side, no matter what, she'll come around."

"I'm not so sure. I think she hates us. Every last one of us Ewings."

"Maybe I ought to have a talk with her."

"If you think it'll do any good."

"Can't do any harm. Be back in a couple of minutes."

He discovered Sue Ellen in the nursery, a cheerful room decorated expressly for Baby John and awaiting his return. Bright wallpaper and drawings done by Miss Ellie, red, white and blue furniture imported from France, and a litter of expensive toys. A music box was playing "The March of the Toy Soldiers" while brightly painted miniature figures danced in awkward steps.

"Sue Ellen—"

"Yes?" She spoke without turning.

"It's Bobby."

"Yes, Bobby? Hello, Bobby."

"How are you feeling?"

"The doctor says I'm fine."

"It's good to have you home."

"So everyone keeps assuring me. Isn't this a lovely room?" The music box wound down. "Momma spent weeks decorating—"

"Everyone is so nice."

"We all love you, Sue Ellen."

"And the baby."

"Yes, and the baby. But not *only* the baby. You must believe that."

"If you say so, Bobby."

"Sue Ellen, please. Don't shut us out. You need friends, family. Everyone does. Don't push me away." His concern distorted his evenly featured face. "Let me try to help, Sue Ellen."

A pleasant, distant expression was draped over her lovely face, the pale eyes still and looking at nothing in particular. She stood motionless, waiting.

"I'd never use what you told me that day about you and Cliff Barnes, about Cliff being the father of Baby John. I'd never do anything to hurt you or the baby. You have to believe that, Sue Ellen. You can trust me, I swear it."

She blinked her eyes around to meet his, and a point of light appeared as she stared at him coolly. "I don't know what you're talking about, Bobby."

Stunned at what he'd just heard, he retreated a step, unable to assimilate her denial, her rejection of reality, as he knew it. Then she smiled—polite, pleasant, devoid of the slightest hint of emotion.

"It's getting late. It must be time for dinner. We mustn't keep the others waiting." She walked out of the nursery, leaving a deeply disturbed Bobby behind.

Little Horn pasture was rugged and unrelenting, crowded with dense, prickly brush that concealed individual cows from sight and made finding and immobilizing them hard and difficult work. Bobby, Ray Krebs and a third cowboy located a cow and her calf, spent half an hour running them down before bringing them to a halt. While they were watching, the calf sank to the ground on its side. The mother moved between calf and cowboys, trying to shield her offspring.

At a distance Ray circled the animals slowly. "That calf is just about dead, Bobby."

"Damn," Bobby said. "Okay, you go on." He took a rifle from its saddle holster and dismounted He aimed and fired quickly. It was not a job to be relished, but it had to be done. "All right," he said to the cowboy, "bring the ointment and we'll finish up here."

Sue Ellen made no attempt to get out of bed that morning. J.R. dressed in silence, waiting for her to make a move, getting annoyed when she didn't.

"You're not getting up?" he said at last.

"Not at the moment."

"Don't you feel well?"

"I feel all right."

"Your color is better today. Matter of fact, you look terrific."

126

"I'm glad you think so."

"Momma's gonna start worrying about you."

"Your momma has had three sons. I'm sure she'll understand that my need to rest is perfectly natural."

He sat down on the edge of the bed and took her hand. "You remember that little Greek restaurant we used to go to?"

"I remember it."

"I was there a few days ago—" She showed no interest. "Just a business lunch." He felt compelled to explain.

"It doesn't matter."

"Anyway, it was still first-rate. What if you and I were to stop by there for lunch after we visit the baby today?"

"I'm not visiting the baby today."

"What?"

"The doctor said it was important that I get enough rest. I don't think running back and forth to Dallas is exactly what was meant by that."

"But the baby—"

"The baby is well taken care of."

"Darlin'—"

"J.R., you want to go into town and look into that nursery window at all those sleeping children, well, all right. I do not. Now if you don't mind, I'd rather not discuss this any more. I'd like to get some more sleep."

Her eyes rolled shut. He stood up.

"I'll see you tonight."

When she gave no response, he snatched up his briefcase and stormed out of the room.

In the dining room breakfast was being served buffet style: warmers of eggs, sausage, bacon, ham, hot cakes, and fried beans; biscuits and butter; fresh milk and coffee; and three kinds of fruit and orange juice. Lucy and Miss Ellie were at the table while Pam was serving herself.

"Bobby seems so worried about the cattle," Pam said. "Is it serious?"

Miss Ellie answered. "Not if it's caught in time. But it is a great deal of work for everybody involved. Checking the entire herd, cutting out those infected and treating them, destroying those who are too far gone."

J.R. entered and put his attaché case aside, offering greetings to everyone by name, kissing his mother. The familiar grin was plastered across his bland face as if painted in place. He poured himself a cup of coffee and drank it as quickly as he could. He was in no mood to linger for family chit-chat, not after his confrontation with Sue Ellen.

"What time do you figure to be at the hospital, J.R.?" Miss Ellie wanted to know.

"'Bout twelve-thirty or so, Momma."

"I thought I'd drive in with Sue Ellen this morning. What if I take you both to lunch?"

J.R. stared at the bottom of his cup, then put it aside with almost delicate finality. "Sue Ellen won't be going into Dallas today." His voice was harsh, biting, leaving no doubt in anyone's mind of his feelings.

Pam and Lucy exchanged a quick look but said nothing, each pretending to a concern she didn't feel. Miss Ellie put her eyes on J.R., probing and insistent, looking for more than he might say.

"Why is that?" she asked in a mild, controlled voice.

"Doctor told her to stay in bed for a few days. Woman after childbirth—they're always a bit worn down, ain't that a fact, Momma?"

"Is it, son?"

"So I hear." He gave an uncomfortable laugh. "Now, Momma, there's nothing to worry about. Sue Ellen just needs to take it easy for a while. Now, I've got to run, got a very important appointment first thing this morning. Better hurry. Have a nice day."

Snatching up his case, he was gone. Moments later they heard the smooth, powerful sound of the Mercedes motor as he drove away. None of the women spoke for a long while, until Pam broke the uneasy silence.

"It's not unusual for new mothers to need rest."

"No," Miss Ellie murmured absently. "No, it is not." There were unanswered questions in her manner.

Lucy said, "I'll be glad to ride you into town this afternoon, Grandma. As soon as I get back from school."

"What? Oh, yes, thank you, dear. That would be very nice."

They chatted on, but it was clear to each of them that they

held the same concerns and were desperate for answers that would not come.

Ewing 3 drew to a smooth stop in front of the Ewing Building. J.R., the ever-present attaché case dangling from one hand, leaped out and started toward the tall glass doors of the main entrance. Halfway there he paused, lost in thought, then turned and moved quickly through the morning rush of workers into the next block. There, a jewelry store, sedately placed, tastefully furnished, extremely expensive. He studied the window display, all glitter and gold, made up his mind, and went inside. You could get more with honey than with vinegar, couldn't you?

In Dallas, wheels within wheels whirred and spun webs of intrigue and eventual danger. Life around the Ewings progressed in directions none of them could foresee, as events and characters unknown to anyone at Southfork, unknown to each other, entered the game. Friends and enemies, allies and competitors, all focused on the Ewings in hope of gaining rewards of the flesh or the spirit. Of finding revenge.

For Cliff Barnes revenge was the reason for his being, the drive that brought him out of the deepest sleep, alert and plotting ahead, the life force that thrust him springing into his future without heed of danger. Cliff Barnes wanted many things out of his life; but first, to get even with the Ewing family.

In his private office in the Office of Land Management, he consulted with Harry Shaw, one of his aides. Shaw was one of those Texans, slender and taut, who always appeared at ease in western clothes; dress Levi's, a cowboy shirt and jacket, expensive lizard boots. Yet he was a city man, never having set foot on ranch or farm. Born and bred in Dallas of city people born of city people. The sort of Texan outsiders seldom considered, the kind who made the Lone Star State into one of the most prosperous in the Lower Forty-eight.

On the wall of the office was a map of Texas, every county clearly indicated, every oil well clearly marked. And in red, every piece of land, every arroyo and flatland, every well and refinery burned with the Ewing brand. All other oil properties took second place to the Ewing holdings, in Cliff Barnes's view. He tapped the map with a wooden pointer.

"Here, here, here—we've stopped them cold in those areas. But look at all those green flags—dammit, Harry, they've got plenty of drilling sites left and ready to go. And the word is they are leasing more every week."

Harry Shaw cleared his throat. "The Ewings are not exactly dumb, Cliff."

"I know that. But we've got to cut 'em off at the pass."

"Which pass, Cliff? There are only twenty-four hours in a day. If we spend all of them concentrating on the Ewing properties, it isn't going to look good. People will begin to ask questions. Raise doubts about the legitimacy of our purpose."

Cliff swore under his breath. There was no arguing the logic of Harry's words. As much as he wanted to apply pressure to Ewing Oil, as much as he wanted to damage the family, he had no intention of risking his own position. His power was limited—effective when shrewdly applied—but not absolute and hardly infinite.

"We must be able to move in on them somewhere else, then."

Shaw opened a folder he held in his lap and studied a report he had received a day or so earlier. "There are three choices open to us right now. I'm convinced that the Palo Seco field provides the best opportunity. We've had a lot of complaints from farmers up there, and a move by us at this time would be well received."

"Are the complaints substantial?" Cliff felt a certain amount of slippage in his resolve, as if some subterranean fear had suddenly inhibited him. "I don't want to go out on a limb and—"

"Maybe you're right. There are sufficient complaints, but none of them are solid. Without facts and figures, that sort of thing. We could hold back for a week or two."

"Did you check out that Environmental Impact Study on the new Lindero site?"

Shaw nodded briskly, closing the folder. "It looks good to me."

Frowning, Cliff sat back down behind his desk. "Something fishy there."

Shaw went on, a new urgency in his voice. "Don't turn down the study, Cliff. There's no sound reason to. If your battle with the Ewings begins to look too much like a personal vendetta, you'll be cutting your own throat. Hurting yourself more than you'll hurt them."

"I'm not convinced."

"Then listen to this. There are rumblings coming out of Austin that I don't like. The politicians up there are beginning to ask questions."

"The Ewings are behind that."

"Of course they are. Did you think they'd lay back and let you walk all over them? They're fighters, that bunch, and it would be a mistake to forget it."

"What are you suggesting?"

"Stay cool. Stay loose. Else you're gonna find some damned State Senatorial Investigating Committee breathing down our necks, *your* neck. They'll ask a hell of a lot of questions, and some of them may be impossible to answer without looking bad. Do us both a favor, Cliff—go slow."

Cliff drove his fist into the palm of his hand. "Damn! The Ewings think they can buy off the entire state government."

"They can sure exert a great deal of influence on it. It's the American Way," he ended, grinning.

"That works both ways."

"Exactly."

"All right, I'll slow down. But it doesn't mean I'm giving up the attack."

Shaw sat back in his chair, relieved. "The war goes on, to be fought on a field and at a time of our own choosing." He rose, smiling pleasantly, having accomplished his purpose. "See you later."

Cliff waved him out. Alone in the office, he hesitated only briefly before picking up the phone and dialing.

"Dallas Memorial," an operator answered.

"Maternity Ward, please."

"Maternity."

"Could you tell me how my—I mean, how the Ewing baby is doing?"

"He is doing splendidly, sir. Gaining weight and strength. Are you a member of the family?"

"Just a—friend. How much longer will he be in the hospital?"

"I'm afraid I can't answer that."

"I see. Thank you."

He replaced the receiver and sat without moving for a long time. There was so much to think about—his work, his life, his son. . . .

"Any calls?" J.R. demanded as he burst into the waiting room of Ewing Enterprises. His secretaries looked up from their work. They recognized J.R.'s dark mood and wasted no time on niceties.

"Mr. Smithfield is waiting in your office, sir," Louella said quickly. "With a Mr. Beam, an associate."

"Any calls, I said." J.R. grimaced.

Connie read off the call sheet. "Mr. Ames and Mr. Garr each phoned twice this morning. They stopped in yesterday afternoon, too. They insist they must see you soon."

"Let 'em wait," J.R. said, heading for his office. Inside sat Harv Smithfield, white-haired and handsome, erect and well constructed for a man in his seventies, still vigorous, still anxious to do a day's work, his mind sharp and probing. With him was Alan Beam, lean and ferretlike, a young man clearly ambitious and seeking moves to make that would advance his career.

Smithfield made the introductions. "Alan is a brilliant new addition to Smithfield and Bennett, J.R. New blood keeps the gears oiled and turning smoothly."

Alan delivered his most charming and innocent smile. J.R. grunted and went behind his desk, indicating that the others were to sit.

"You're not a Texas boy?" J.R. said.

"I'm from Chicago, sir. But I hope to make Dallas my home."

J.R. busied himself with some papers.

"Your daddy joining us?" Smithfield asked.

"Not today. There's some sick cattle out at the ranch, and he and Bobby have been out doctoring the herd day and night."

"Hope it's not serious."

"It'll work out. Now about business, Harv?"

"Well, I wanted you and Alan to meet. He's our resident expert in environmental law, and these days that seems to be occupying a great deal of our attention."

"That should help." J.R. turned to the younger man. "Harv's been Ewing Oil's lawyer for as long as there's been a Ewing Oil. He and my daddy go back a long time."

"I'm looking forward to working on Ewing's problems."

"What problems are those?" J.R. asked coolly.

"Now, J.R.," Smithfield said soothingly, "no need to give the boy a rough beginning. He's smart, he's good, and he's a hard worker. Take my word for it. If anyone can make hash of Cliff Barnes's tail, this lad can."

"We'll see."

Alan smiled. "I've been studying the problem, sir. It has some very interesting aspects."

"I call what Cliff Barnes is trying to do to my business something stronger than just interesting."

"Yes, sir," Alan replied quickly. "Stopping production on that well in Odessa, claiming contamination, well that was really a masterstroke."

J.R. showed his annoyance. "This isn't a tennis match, Beam. This is business, a hard and often ruthless business. I don't admire the techniques of my enemies."

Reaching into his briefcase, Alan brought out a bound report. "I've always found, sir, that business or pleasure, it pays to give the devil his due." He extended the report, and J.R. accepted it. "I've roughed out—to coin a phrase—a game plan."

The intercom began buzzing as J.R. scanned the report. He flipped a switch, still reading the report. "Yes? What is it?"

"Willie Joe Garr on line two."

"Tell him I'm busy. I'll be busy all day." He released the switch and glanced up at Alan Beam. "This is interesting—and good."

"Thank you, sir."

"Call me J.R. All my friends do."

Harv Smithfield leaned back in his chair, breathing easily. The sparring was over. If the marriage had not actually been consummated, at least the first date was going well. Better than he had hoped, in fact.

Willie Joe Garr slammed down the phone and began pacing the grubby motel room he and Jeb Ames were sharing. "The rotten mother, he won't even take our calls."

"We can't force him to talk to us."

"The hell we can't. I've got some ideas. . . ."

"Willie Joe, I've spent enough time in the slammer. Don't come up with anything that's gonna put me back inside."

"Jeb, I've always been the brains of this partnership, and nothing has happened to change that. I've got an idea—foolproof, guaranteed to put large amounts of money in our pockets and leave us free to get back up to the top. Just you listen to me."

"All right, I'll listen, but—"

If Willie Joe heard the doubt in his partner's voice, he gave no sign as he began talking. Low and fast.

Pam and Lucy stood side by side, peering through the nursery window at Baby John, as they had all begun calling the newborn infant. Around them the usual bustle of a maternity wards: nurses rushing to and fro, doctors strolling the corridors, parents, grandparents, friends, come to admire the new offspring. Next to Pam stood another woman. Her name was Priscilla Duncan, and she was smiling as she gazed at the babies.

"Aren't they adorable?" she said.

Pam agreed that they were.

"But so tiny."

"Yes, they are. But we can be sure everyone of them will grow bigger."

Priscilla Duncan smiled more broadly at Pam, as if they were old, dear friends.

A nurse joined Pam and Lucy. Pam turned to her. "Do you think it would be all right if I gave my nephew his next feeding?"

The nurse hesitated. "I don't know, Mrs. Ewing. Usually the mother is the one—"

"My sister-in-law isn't feeling too strong," Pam said in a coaxing manner. "She won't be coming into town today. You don't want to deprive the baby of a relative's presence."

The nurse hesitated, then relented. "It's not usual procedure, but if you'll follow me——"

Pam winked at Lucy and trailed the nurse into the nursery. Lucy stood at the glass, grinning approval as Baby John began sucking at the bottle. He was, Lucy decided, like all the rest of the Ewings, hungry for life.

The family gathered for drinks before dinner on the patio that afternoon. Bobby, J.R., and Jock were at the bar, pouring and drinking, reflecting on the day's activities. At the table Sue Ellen flipped idly through a magazine, not terribly interested. Occasionally one or another of the others would glance her way, obviously concerned.

"Well," Jock said to J.R., "if Harv Smithfield recommends this Beam fella, I'd put money on him."

"Oh, Alan's bright, all right, without a doubt. He's already researched the law backwards and forwards. Maybe he can come up with a way for us to stomp Barnes into the ground."

Jock growled. "Don't count on the law, boy. It ain't never done right by us and never will. Besides, Cliff Barnes is pretty shrewd himself, probably got a legal trick or two up his sleeve."

"Maybe. But somehow we have to stop him. Unless, of course, little brother here can think of a good reason why not."

Bobby spoke calmly, without haste. "You know, J.R., try as hard as I can, I can't come up with a single good reason. You've got my permission to go on."

"Well, thank you, little brother."

At that moment two cars pulled into the driveway. Pam and Lucy. Exchanging greetings, they joined the others on the patio.

"You been to the hospital?" Bobby wanted to know.

"Uh-huh," Lucy offered.

"Well," Jock said impatiently, "how's my grandson?"

Miss Ellie laughed aloud. "*His* grandson! You'd think Jock Ewing played a direct and creative role."

Jock glowered with mock menace at his wife. "No dirty talk from you, Miss Ellie. Well, let's have it—how is the boy?"

"Small," Lucy said, "but gorgeous."

Pam said, "The doctor says he's gained another full ounce since yesterday."

Lucy, at the bar, called over her shoulder. "Anybody want a drink?"

"The usual for me," Pam said.

"Sue Ellen?" Lucy said, and just as quickly realized what she had said. A hush fell over the group as they awaited Sue Ellen's answer.

"Just some club soda, please."

There was an almost audible sigh of relief that Sue Ellen had resisted temptation. Lucy poured the soda, and Sue Ellen took it and headed for the pool, moving languidly. J.R. waited a beat or two and went after her. He found her seated on a wooden bench staring into the still water. He sat beside her. For a long time neither of them said anything. Until J.R. could remain silent no longer.

"Darlin', you are goin' to have to take a little more interest in things."

"Interest? What things are those, J.R.?"

"Life in general, sugar."

"Life in general is of little concern to me right now, in case you haven't noticed."

"I have noticed. And so has everyone else, in the family and outside."

"Where would you suggest I begin this interest in things?"

"You could start with your child."

"I don't think he's suffering from any lack of attention."

"You are his mother," he started out angrily. Then, more quietly, almost petulantly and querulously, "You wanted a baby so much. Now.... Don't you care anything for him at all? Your own flesh and blood."

She answered in a flat voice that carried an implicit message: don't be a fool! "Of course, I do."

"It doesn't much look like it."

She poured the club soda into the pool in a slow, thin arc, then smiled at what she had done as if taking some secret delight in the accomplishment. "Appearances are very often deceiving, J.R."

"Meaning what?"

"Meaning nothing is as it appears to be. You sidling up to

me this way. Anyone watching might get the idea that you actually were concerned for my well-being."

"I am."

"I find that hard to accept."

"I'm your husband."

"And have been for some time. Why the sudden interest, the public displays of affection?"

"We can salvage our marriage, Sue Ellen. Others have done it, so can we."

She sat up straighter, her plump breasts pressing against her shirtwaist. She was, J.R. reminded himself, a remarkably attractive woman, a delight in the bedroom when she chose to be. Inventive, daring, tender and not so tender, according to mood, hers and his. A thick, warm desire oozed up into his gut, and he reached out to her. She stood up, giving no sign that she'd noticed. She stepped closer to the pool, and for a long, uncertain moment he thought she might dive in, fully clothed.

"Look," he said, standing behind her, "I know this is not an easy time for you. It's not easy to go through what you have and quit drinking cold turkey, the way you did. I admire you for it. I'm proud of you. You are a person of character and will power, of determination."

"I'm weak and vacillating. Without confidence or hope. I belong nowhere, J.R., a flit of a girl coming into middle age and confused and frightened. As for my drinking—well, I never considered that a problem. I kept telling you all that. But no one listened. Especially you, J.R. You never did listen to me about anything."

"I am listening to you now, sugar. To every word you say. I believe if we try, really try, we can work out all our other problems. I want to, Sue Ellen. I really want to."

She stared at him with blank eyes and an expressionless face. He grew jittery and felt the need to do something with his hands. He remembered his visit to the jeweler that morning and reached into his pocket, pulled out a ring box, and opened it.

"Here," he said. "This is for you. I bought it this morning. It's a maternity ring, complete with a handful of diamonds. Very expensive, very beautiful, don't you think?"

He extended it, but she made no move to accept it. At last

she raised her eyes to his. "You bought me one time, J.R. That's my limit. There's no buying me any more. I'm no longer for sale."

J.R. stood with outstretched hand, gazing into the space his wife had just occupied, aware that she was moving back up toward the house, leaving him behind. And alone.

"Everyone's so busy these days, we hardly ever get to see one another, except at the dinner table."

"Aren't those long hours for a man Jock's age, Miss Ellie?"

"Sue Ellen, some men take to babying. My Jock's never been one of them. I did a little too much of it, anyway, last year after his heart operation. I'm sure Bobby and Ray will make certain he doesn't overwork himself."

Sue Ellen turned her steel-blue eyes on Miss Ellie. "You're so smart, so strong, you're always in control."

"Not really. I've made my share of mistakes, Sue Ellen, and I expect I'll make some more. Many more before I'm through. Just not too many, I hope."

Sue Ellen allowed a wan smile to touch her lips, and just as swiftly fade away.

Miss Ellie continued reflectively. "Don't brood on the past, my dear. It never does much good. You have the whole future to look forward to; and, from where I sit, it looks fine. J.R. is my son, and I love him dearly. But I admit that I don't always like him or like what he does. He is a hard man, fiercely ambitious, and somewhat careless about whom he damages. He hasn't behaved this well since he was six years old. Maybe having a son is what he needed to settle down.

"And maybe it's just what you need, too, Sue Ellen. A child gives a man and a woman a different perspective. It brings continuity into their daily lives. To be totally responsible for another human being, to wonder if you're doing this right or that wrong—it makes you humble, makes you more tolerant of your own parents' failures and, of course, your own.

"Jock and I longed for another grandchild for a very long time, Sue Ellen, and, in giving us Baby John you have made us very happy. I can't wait until he comes home from the hospital. And Jock"—she laughed softly—"will undoubtedly spoil the baby rotten, just as he did our own children."

She broke off, frowning, measuring her daughter-in-law. "But there is something more Jock and I want, Sue Ellen. We want you to be happy, too."

Sue Ellen forced her voice into a light, airy register in an attempt to appear cheerful, if not ecstatic. "Oh, I am happy, Miss Ellie. Very happy. J.R. has never been kinder or more understanding. And the little boy—I don't think I've seen anything more beautiful in my life."

Lucy joined them, perky and sprightly, a gleam of anticipation in her eyes. "Want me to take you into the hospital, Grandma?"

"I don't know, dear." She addressed Sue Ellen. "Were you planning on going into Dallas today?"

Sue Ellen spoke without hesitation, her face straight, her eyes clear. "Of course," she lied. "In fact, I'll get myself together, and we can all go together." As she stood up, she staggered, her hand going to her brow. She sat back down, still holding her head.

Miss Ellie went to her. "What is it, dear? Are you all right? Would you like some water?"

"Just a touch of dizziness, Miss Ellie. I'll be all right in a minute, and we can leave."

"Leave!" said Miss Ellie. "You are not going anywhere. I want you to go right upstairs to your bed and lie down. New mothers are subject to spells of one sort or another. I should know."

"Shall I help you upstairs?" Lucy said, eyeing Sue Ellen sidelong.

"No, thank you, dear. I'm sure I can make it by myself."

They watched her go. Then Lucy and Miss Ellie went outside and got into Lucy's car. "You know, Grandma," Lucy said as they drove away, "I believe that Sue Ellen has no desire to see her baby."

"Nonsense!" Miss Ellie said sharply. "Of course she does. He's her son."

"I know. But parents don't always want to see their children. Or have anything to do with them. Mine didn't."

Miss Ellie stared straight ahead. "Lucy, that's just not true."

"I don't want to fight with you, Grandma, but I know better. Seems to me, my momma and daddy didn't want me when I was born and haven't wanted me since."

"I'm sure you're mistaken. Circumstances—"

"Then tell me this: why aren't they with me? Why have they left me alone for so long? Why don't I ever hear from them?"

Miss Ellie had no good answer to supply, and they drove the rest of the way into Dallas without exchanging another word.

At the hospital, standing at the nursery window, Lucy became aware of a woman standing nearby, a vaguely familiar face. At last she recognized her as someone who had been watching the babies the last time she had been here: Priscilla Duncan, although she didn't know the woman's name. She nodded politely and turned her attention to Baby John. Miss Ellie, meanwhile, was standing to one side in conversation with one of the physicians attending Baby John, Dr. Rogers.

"Then you think the baby will be fit to leave the hospital soon, doctor?"

"About as soon as his parents want to get him home, Mrs. Ewing."

Her excitement grew. "But that's wonderful! I hadn't though it would be so quickly."

"He's doing better than we all expected. There's no reason to keep him longer. Tell his mother she can come get him tomorrow."

Lucy turned away from the nursery to join Miss Ellie and the doctor just as Pam stepped out of the elevator and came their way. Lucy waved. "Pam!"

"I didn't expect to find you all still here," Pam said. "I'm so pleased."

"Grandma couldn't tear herself away. You know how some people are about grand*sons*."

"I'm finding out," Pam said in a bantering tone.

Miss Ellie put on a mock scowl. "You should have seen the fuss I made over you, Lucy, when you joined us. Girl or boy, a grandchild is a very special creature." She turned to Pam. "Baby John can come home tomorrow."

Pam clapped her hands. "That's marvelous!"

The doctor said, "He's right up to weight, and all his tests come out affirmative. There's nothing we can do for him here that his mother can't do better at home." The paging system squawked, and Dr. Rogers heard his name called. "You ladies will have to excuse me, that's me they're after."

"Goodbye, doctor," Miss Ellie said. "And thank you very much."

Lucy waited until he was gone. "Now can we go have some lunch? Grandma's taking me to Anselmo's, Pam. Want to come?"

"I'll take a raincheck, thanks."

"You don't know what you're missing. Best Italian food in Dallas."

"I know." She patted her waistline. "I'm not as young as you."

Lucy laughed with delight.

"Bye, dear," Miss Ellie said. "See you later."

Pam strolled over to the nursery window and took up her position, seeking out Baby John among the other babies. "Aren't they sweet?" she cooed aloud.

Next to her Priscilla Duncan nodded. "Just as sweet as can be," she murmured.

That morning J.R. met with Alan Beam in the Ewing office. Beam got right down to business, a trait J.R. found admirable in a young lawyer.

"The site is perfect, J.R. Drilling's been going on in the area for years with no adverse effects. The population's far enough removed not to care a damn what goes on."

J.R.'s voice grew softer, his manner more diffident, the way it often did when he was concerned, vitally interested, or enraged.

"That's one of those land vacancies, isn't it?"

Alan laughed. "You know what they say: 'A vacancy is a piece of land surrounded by oil wells.'"

J.R. failed to join in the merriment. "Most of the good ones have been snatched up."

"True enough. But there are still vacancy hunters sniffing around. In any case your daddy filed a claim with the state on this land maybe twenty years ago. Bought it at a bargain price."

"Not much chance of oil being found now."

"From what I hear, just the opposite is true."

J.R., always careful, had run his own tests on the vacancy. He knew the prospects for striking it rich better than Alan Beam did. Or anyone else for that matter. "Well, fact is, I've already set a crew to work in that vacancy. Drilling commenced more'n a week ago. So if Mr. Cliff Barnes wants to come down on us about that site, we've given him cause enough."

Alan inched forward to the edge of his chair. The prospect of a good fight stimulated him, unloosed the adrenalin in his system. "I can draft a foolproof Environmental Impact Study. If Barnes rejects this one—bingo! Abuse of power, especially in light of the other wells put down in that section."

"My daddy has the notion that the law is not the best way to deal with Barnes. He may be right."

The intercom went off. J.R. reached for the switch. "Yes, what is it?"

Louella's voice had a distinctly uneasy ring to it. "Mr. Ames and Mr. Garr are out here. They insist on seeing you."

J.R. considered briefly. "I'm in a meeting now. Maybe some other time." He sat back in his chair, gazing thoughtfully at Alan.

"Do you want me to forget about this?" Alan asked.

"No. No, I don't think so. Seems to me it's worth taking a shot at. Nothing much to lose."

The words were no sooner out of his mouth than the door burst open, and Jeb Ames entered, trailed by Willie Joe Garr. Unable to keep them out, Louella, behind them, spread her hands helplessly.

Ames placed his big hands flat on J.R.'s desk, his face pushed forward aggressively. "Why is it, J.R., me and Willie Joe here are beginning to get the idea you don't want to see us?"

J.R. waved Louella away. He waited until she had closed the door behind her before speaking. He manufactured his most ingratiating grin, but his blue eyes remained motionless, glazed, unfathomable. "Boys, you understand business. Nobody's done more of it than you have. Just been busy, fellas, that's all. Now you're here—what can I do for you?"

142

"We want to talk," Garr said roughly.

"Must be pretty urgent, you busting in here thisaway. Disturbing the peace, you might say." His laugh was brittle and short. "Don't seem to me that it's too smart for folks out on parole to go around creating a ruckus, isn't that what you'd say, Alan?"

"The law takes a dim view of parolees acting in an antisocial manner."

Garr glared at Beam. "Who the hell is he?"

"My lawyer," J.R. said happily. "An officer of the court, so to speak."

Ames broke in. "Our talk is urgent, J.R., in your best interests as well as our own. And most of all, it's private."

Alan stood up. "I'll come back another time, J.R."

"Thank you, Alan." He waited until the younger man was gone. "All right, now what can I do for you boys?"

Garr lowered himself into a chair. "Don't we even get offered a drink?"

"I'm kind of particular about who I drink with."

Ames shook his head. "Be reasonable, J.R., and we'll try to be."

"Not when you bust in here like a couple of wild-eyed maniacs. Not when I know how easily you two bastards can destroy a human life."

Ames made a face, as if remembering something distasteful. "We were trying to protect you as well as us by getting Julie out of town. If that girl had shot off her mouth to Cliff Barnes, you'd have been finished, too."

J.R. made no attempt to hold back the anger. "Did you have to kill her? Dammit, there are other ways to handle people like that. She wouldn't have talked to anyone. I'd've seen to it."

Garr shrugged. "It was an accident, you know that."

Ames sat down finally, observing J.R. across the desk as if for the first time. "The way I look at it, what happened was as much your fault as ours. And it's us who've done all the paying up to now. Time behind bars is always hard time, J.R. We took it and kept still. We took it all and never complained. You might not fare so well in the joint, you might not like it at all."

"Are you threatening me?"

"Just telling you how it was, is all."

Garr spoke in a gravelly voice. "It's your turn to pay, J.R., same as we did. Only your way won't hurt as much."

"Meaning what?"

"Meaning," Ames said, "we need cash. And quick."

"And lots of it, J.R."

J.R. began to laugh until all good humor washed out of him and his face firmed up, mouth stretched taut. "You think I'm about to hand over a bunch of money to you boys? What for? Old times' sake? Let's get one thing straight—you have got absolutely nothing on me."

"Don't be too sure—" Garr started to say.

Ames gestured for him to be quiet. "All our money is tied up in litigation, J.R. We are being sued by everybody for just about everything. No way we can put our hands on a penny of it until the suits are settled."

"Seems to me you boys sure did manage to get yourselves in a pickle barrel full of hornets."

"You owe us, J.R.," Garr said. "You owe us plenty."

J.R. came up to his feet. Tall and wide, he was a man occupying more psychic and physical space than most. A man of authority, power, and immeasurable wealth. He looked down on his two visitors. "Even if I had the money in my hands, which I do not, I wouldn't give you boys a nickel. Not a nickel."

They came out of their chairs, as if the movement had been rehearsed, each one stalking around one end of the desk with menace in their stances.

J.R. beckoned them on. "Come on, boys. That's exactly what I want, exactly what you need. Prove how dumb you really are. Lay a hand on me, and I'll have you back in jail by sundown. My lawyer witnessed you break in. My secretaries. Go ahead, try something."

That stopped them. "We need money," Ames said menacingly.

"Get out of here," J.R. replied.

Ames nodded and went to the door. "You win this time. But it's not over yet. We're gonna see to it you're real sorry about the way you're treating us, J.R."

"Real sorry," Garr echoed, following his partner.

"The only thing I'm ever gonna be sorry about," J.R. called after them, "is it wasn't you instead of Julie who fell off that roof."

Feeling smug and satisfied, J.R. sat back down. Victories no matter how small, always provided him with a profound feeling of accomplishment, the renewed sense of his own superiority. Ames and Garr were easy for him; he had always been able to handle them.

Bobby, wearing soiled jeans and a sweat-stained work shirt, returned to the big house at Southfork after a hard morning on the range. A shower and a change of clothes, before he headed into town, were in order. Starting up the stairs to his room, he met Sue Ellen descending.

"You're home early," she said pleasantly.

"I'm going into Dallas for a while."

She continued past him, the exchange completed, as far as she was concerned. He hesitated, turned, and said her name. She paused, not looking back up at him.

"Yes, Bobby?"

"I plan on stopping off at the hospital to see the baby. Why don't you come along?"

"Why, thank you for thinking of me. But that's not going to be possible. I'm not feeling up to it this afternoon. Another time, perhaps."

She continued on her way. He hurried after her, catching up at the bottom of the staircase. "Sue Ellen, you can't go on like this."

"Like what? I don't know what you mean."

"Avoiding me. Avoiding issues. Avoiding life itself."

"I'm very much alive," she said deliberately. "You don't seem to understand, Bobby. I'm not avoiding anything. I am simply following doctor's orders: resting, trying to get myself well again."

"Did your doctor advise you to ignore your baby and forget the past? I don't think so, Sue Ellen. You can't get well that way. Things don't disappear because you pretend they don't exist. You can't wipe out the past by denying it ever happened."

For a brief moment her pain surfaced and was apparent

145

on her face. A quick intake of breath, a slight shift, and a tranquil, unruffled expression returned. She gazed up at him quizzically.

"What is it you want from me, Bobby?"

"I want you to get well. I want to help you, if I can."

"Oh, you can."

"Tell me how."

"By leaving me alone. Please."

Less than two hours later, Bobby drove up to the hospital, parked his car, and headed for the main entrance. Ahead of him he saw a familiar figure. Bobby called out with a surge of annoyance.

"Cliff!"

Cliff Barnes responded, waiting for Bobby to catch up.

"What the hell are you doing here?" Bobby asked angrily.

"The Ewings don't own this hospital."

"Dammit, man, you are going to start some big trouble around here, and there is no way you are going to like the results."

Cliff's face darkened, his fingers folded up into fists. "You're my sister's husband, the only Ewing who faintly resembled a human being. But don't try to push me too hard, Bobby. You'll discover I don't back off from trouble."

"I warned you to keep away—from Sue Ellen and the baby."

"Take your warnings and stuff 'em."

Bobby took a single stride forward, head ducked aggressively low.

"You mean to start a brawl right here on the steps of the hospital? That's okay with me. Just think of the headlines in tomorrow's papers."

"Oh, you are a bastard, Cliff."

"Just butt out, Bobby. This is none of your business. This is between Sue Ellen and me."

"Maybe that's how it once was—but no more, Cliff. We're all involved now, the entire family. It would be a fundamental mistake on your part to believe that I am going to sit quietly by and let you cause more trouble."

"You can't stop me. That child in there is mine. Have you forgotten that?"

"You really don't care how many lives you have to destroy, as long as you get what you want."

"How many Ewing lives? You're right. I don't care."

"And what about Sue Ellen?"

"I love Sue Ellen. I want her. Her and our son."

Bobby shook his head grimly. "Cliff, listen closely. This is a warning. Sue Ellen can not handle any more pressure right now. She's not well enough, she's walking right along the outer edge of her tolerance. Try to force her to choose between J.R. and you, and you'll drive her straight back into that sanitarium."

"Get out of my way."

"J.R.'s in there now, Cliff. Visiting with *his* son. Before I'll let you go in, I'll wipe up the ground with you."

Cliff hesitated, then said, "I won't take you on, Bobby. Not this way. Not when I know I can't win. I don't make futile battles. But let me tell you this—I want them, both of them, Sue Ellen and the baby. And I intend to get them. Any way I can."

He stepped around Bobby and hurried down the hospital steps toward his parked car. He got into it and sped away without a backward glance. When he reached his office, he stormed over to his desk, calling for Harry Shaw.

"Something you want, Cliff?"

"Damn right there is. That Ewing Oil Impact Study on the Midland Field? It is rejected. A dead issue. I want the files on every piece of land they own or lease, every prospective drilling site. I want every vacancy deal explored, the legalities sifted through. If there are any discrepancies, let's instigate legal action. I want to hit those Ewings where it hurts."

"Cliff, take it easy."

"To hell with taking it easy. I'm going to make those damned Ewings sweat blood until they give back everything that rightfully belongs to me."

First light spread over Southfork like a steel-gray scrim, the sky clear and promising another crisp, cool day. Down at the corral, Bobby was checking his saddle and tack, which was up on the corral fence. He heard footsteps coming his way but did not respond.

"Morning." It was Pam.

"Morning." He kept at his work. "You're up pretty early."

"So are you. I want to talk to you."

"All right, talk."

"I'm sorry about last night."

"So am I."

"I wanted us to make love."

"Not half as much as I did."

"Then what happened?"

"We had one of our Barnes-Ewings wars again."

"That has to stop. I love you, Bobby, I want you. Whenever we fight, I feel just sick about it."

"Okay, let's make a pact. No more fights. Especially at bedtime." He took her in his arms, and they kissed, then clung to each other.

"Oh, Bobby," Pam said. "Tonight. I'll make it up to you tonight."

"And me to you."

"I can hardly wait." She slipped out of his arms. "Is everything going okay about the calves?"

"We should have it all under control by tonight. Look," he said abruptly. "This damned Barnes-Ewing feud thing is getting on my nerves. It keeps getting between us, you and me, making it harder for us to be honest with one another."

"Everything's so complicated. Cliff—J.R.—the baby. I never know what to do, what to say."

"It's that way for me, too. Yesterday I saw Cliff. He was at the hospital."

"Oh, that fool brother of mine!"

"I've warned him to keep away from both of them, Sue Ellen and the baby."

"He will, Bobby. He has to. He just doesn't understand yet how fragile Sue Ellen is right now. When he does, he won't want to make things worse for her."

"I'm not so sure. I tried to explain all that to him. It didn't make much of an impression. He's determined to cause trouble."

"He won't. We won't let him."

"Saying that's a lot easier than doing it. Maybe you'd

148

better talk to him, tell him if he makes a move, any move, I'll tear him apart. Tell him that J.R.—all of us—will make a scandal big enough to ruin him forever in these parts. No matter what he does, he can't defeat the Ewings."

"You believe that?"

"Tell him," Bobby answered grimly. "Tell him if the Ewing name has to be dragged through the mud, Cliff Barnes's tail is going with it. And it will be the bumpiest ride he's ever taken—you tell him that."

"I will," she said softly.

It was later that same morning that J.R., dressed for town, joined Jock at the breakfast table.

"You're off to an early start," Jock observed.

"I've got a breakfast meeting with some overseas oil people. They leaving the country today." J.R. poured himself a cup of coffee and seated himself.

"What's it about?"

"There's a new field opening up off the Asia Coast. Might be something in it for the cartel. I'm not sure yet."

Jock grunted, shoveling bacon and eggs into his mouth. The years had in no way dimmed his appetite. "Ames and Garr made any move to get back into the cartel?"

"Not yet. They're hog-tied with litigation and short of capital. Doesn't give 'em much room to operate."

"The jury might have called it manslaughter, but those two are murderers. They should have been put away forever. I don't want Ewing Oil to have anything to do with them."

"Neither do I, sir." J.R. finished his coffee and made ready to leave.

"You want me to take Sue Ellen into the hospital? I don't think she should be driving yet. Your momma tells me she had a dizzy spell yesterday."

"I'll be back to pick her up. By the time you're back in this house tonight, Daddy, you'll have your grandson to play with."

A pleased smile spread across Jock's leathery face. "Well, now won't that be nice." His face became serious. "Things any better between you and Sue Ellen, son?"

"I sure am trying, Daddy."

149

"I can see that you are, son. Keep up the good work."

Bobby entered the dining room, and greetings were exchanged. "Ready to go, Daddy? The truck's here."

Jock stood up. Bobby snatched a sweet roll from the buffet, eating as he went.

"How much of the herd we gonna lose?" J.R. wanted to know.

"Not too bad. A dozen calves in all, maybe. We caught it just in time."

"That's something, I guess," J.R. said.

Bobby was annoyed but said nothing; hard, dirty work was something J.R. failed to acknowledge. Work that saved all but a dozen calves. Hell, yes, that was something. Something damned good.

It was just short of eleven o'clock that same morning when J.R. returned to the ranch. He located Sue Ellen seated at the pool, a glass of iced tea in her hand. He kissed her hair and squeezed her shoulders and asked her how she was feeling.

"Well enough, I guess."

"I like that bathing suit. Seems to me your figure's better than ever."

She gave no indication that she had heard the compliment.

He made an effort to subdue his resentment. "Reckon it's time for you to change, anyway. I'm anxious to get into Dallas and pick up that boy of ours."

She glanced at him strangely, as if not comprehending, then pulled her eyes away. "I don't believe I'll be able to go with you, J.R."

"Not go with me! What in the hell do you mean by that?"

"I've had a bad headache all morning. I thought some sun and a cool drink might help. It hasn't." She stood up. "I think I'd better lie down now."

He watched her go, his insides churning, wanting to strike out, to give pain, to cause anguish. Instead, he stood locked in place, his limbs quivering, waiting for the rage to subside. Nearly five minutes went by before he went after Sue Ellen. He found her stretched out on her bed, wearing a multicolored caftan.

"You're getting dressed and coming with me to the hospital."

She blinked. "I told you, I can't."

"Won't, is more like it. You can fool everyone else around here with your fake headaches and phony dizzy spells, but not me. There's nothing wrong with you, and both of us know it."

"The doctor said it was vital that I stay calm."

"To hell with the doctor! All I care about right now is that you start acting like a wife and a mother."

"I'm doing my best."

"It's not good enough. You have my momma and my daddy, everybody in this family, scared silly about you. You haven't displayed a bit of maternal feeling. Haven't you any sense of decency, of what's proper and fit?"

"Don't talk to me about decency."

"We are not going to turn this into a discussion of my behavior. It is you we are concerned about right now." He advanced toward the bed. "Now are you going to get dressed, or am I going to have to do it for you?"

"Do you intend to drag me kicking and screaming out of here?"

"If I have to. Now what's it to be?"

"I do believe you mean it."

"Depend on it. Now get up."

For a long moment, she made no move. Then she sat up resignedly. "I'll get dressed," she said without emphasis.

"I figured you'd see the sense of my argument. You've got five minutes, and then we leave—one way or another."

They made it to the hospital without incident, hardly a word exchanged. As J.R. swung Ewing 3 into the parking lot, they spotted police cars around the main entrance, flashers slowly turning. Uniformed officers were everywhere, plus radio news cars and television news vans. Men carrying minicameras on their shoulders were filming everything in sight, and reporters with microphones were interviewing doctors and nurses and an occasional police detective.

J.R. helped Sue Ellen out of the car. "Wonder what's going on?"

A man with a microphone came rushing up. "Mr. Ewing, Mrs. Ewing, have you any comment to make at this time?"

"Comment?" J.R. exclaimed. "About what? We're here to pick up our son, take him home."

Other newspeople clustered about, firing questions. "Are there any leads, Mr. Ewing?"

"Has there been a contact yet?"

"Any ransom demands?"

"Hey, take it easy, people," J.R. cried, guiding Sue Ellen toward the hospital entrance. "Whatever it is, it has nothing to do with us."

"You mean you don't know?"

"They haven't been told."

"Oh, my God!"

"What is it?" J.R. asked. "What in hell are you people carrying on about?"

"Mr. Ewing, Mrs. Ewing—it's your son, John Ross III—"

"What about him?"

"He's been kidnapped!"

The hospital was aswarm with police, in uniform and in plain clothes. Men and women from the forensic squad were checking the nursery, the corridors, the stairwells, and elevators for potential clues. Everywhere questions were being asked, answers noted and subjected to the cynical and skeptical minds of experienced detectives.

"When was the last time you saw the baby?" was a query asked over and over.

"When I fed him," one nurse answered. "About nine-fifteen."

"And what time did you examine the child?" another detective inquired of the pediatric resident physician.

"About ten o'clock, I'd say. I completed a routine exam about ten."

Detective Lieutenant Simpson escorted J.R. and Sue Ellen into a small room set aside for them. He got them seated before straddling a chair himself. He was a dark, intense man with lively curious eyes and a lipless mouth. There was a no-nonsense set to his body, as if he were prepared to spring into action an instant before anybody else would do so. His glance went from Sue Ellen to J.R. and back again.

"Does anybody have any idea—?" J.R. began.

Simpson shook his head. "So far, no one seems to have seen or heard anything."

"You'd think that in a hospital—" Sue Ellen said.

"Exactly the opposite, Mrs. Ewing. There are always so many people around, wandering in and out. Doctors, nurses, patients, visitors. It seems people simply stop paying attention."

"But to just walk out with a baby—"

"Yes. Well, nothing like this has ever happened in this town before. We'll do our best to find your boy, Mr. Ewing. I have a few questions."

"Whatever you say, lieutenant," J.R. agreed. He sent an inquiring glance at Sue Ellen. She sat stiffly in her chair, hands folded properly in her lap. Whatever she might have felt, none of it showed on her face, which remained a stunned alabaster mask; beautiful, stony, giving off no messages.

"Is there anyone who you can think of who would have done such a thing?"

"No one," J.R. answered at once.

"About half the state of Texas hates my husband," Sue Ellen put in without a change of expression.

"I see," Simpson said. "Anyone in particular?"

"I can't imagine anyone I know doing such a terrible thing."

Simpson looked to Sue Ellen for verification; she averted her glance.

"Any help you folks can give us—?"

J.R.'s mind reached back in time. A flood of names and faces came rushing into view: business and personal enemies, men he had beaten in some deal or other, husbands whose wives he had seduced, women he had treated badly. He shook his head. "There is nothing," he said.

"Mrs. Ewing?"

"I can't help you."

"Well," Simpson said, standing, "I guess that's it for now. We'll follow normal procedure in a case like this. We'll do our best to find your son."

J.R., on his feet, felt his strength flowing back into his limbs. "What I want to know," he said, with considerable

153

heat, "is how such a thing could happen in the middle of the best and most expensive hospital in Dallas."

"That," Detective Simpson said quietly, "is exactly what I'd like to know. If it's all right with you, folks, I'd sure like to talk to each one of you, alone that is."

"Sure," J.R. said. "Start with Sue Ellen. I've got a phone call to make."

At the nurse's station, he found a phone and dialed quickly.

Miss Ellie answered.

"Hello, Momma, it's J.R."

"Oh, J.R., I'm so glad you called. What's happening down there? Dr. Samuels phoned right after you left but refused to tell me anything. Is the baby all right? I hope nothing is wrong."

"He's missing, Momma."

"Missing?"

"He's been kidnapped."

"Oh, my God, no! How can that be?"

"Nobody can answer that question, Momma. The police are all over the place asking questions."

"No, no, I won't believe it. There has to be some kind of mistake. They've got him mixed up with another infant. Something—"

"No, Momma. Kidnapped. He's gone."

"But how?"

"We don't know. Nobody knows anything yet. You'd better tell Daddy and the others. And, Momma, since we don't know why or who or what the kidnappers are actually after, it would be better to be careful out there."

"Yes, yes. Oh, poor Sue Ellen. How is she holding up?"

"That's a good question. She's stunned and acting remote, as if this is all a soap opera on the TV. If she feels anything, I can't tell."

"The poor dear is not well, J.R. Be gentle with her."

"Yes, Momma. Better arrange to have Pam and Lucy brought home by car. I'll get back to you when I can. Bye, Momma."

"Bye, son."

Lieutenant Simpson, hoping that the sight of other people, their nearness, the sound of their voices, would have an affirmative effect on Sue Ellen, had directed her to the waiting room. He had seen other mothers react to the kidnapping of a child, knew the traumatic results that almost always occurred, and believed that Sue Ellen had slipped into shock earlier than most. His human instincts told him to go slow, give her time to snap back; but his police experience told him that in every kidnapping the early hours were precious. The sooner you put your case together the better; as time faded chances of locating the lost child grew progressively dimmer. He got Sue Ellen seated in the waiting room, had coffee brought, and offered her a cigarette. Only then did he begin to question her again, slowly, almost casually, bringing her to the point where she understood exactly what had taken place. But every query drew only worthless replies.

Desperate, he pushed harder. "There must be something you can tell us, Mrs. Ewing. Have you no idea who might have done a thing like this?"

"I haven't been well," she replied lethargically. "I haven't seen my baby in days."

"How long ago did you leave the hospital?"

"I don't know. Two or three days. I'm not sure exactly."

"Did you see anyone suspicious hanging around?"

"Suspicious? Oh, no, no one suspicious."

"Did anything out of the ordinary occur?"

"I don't understand."

"Anyone inquiring about you, your family, about the child?"

Her eyes flickered, and a new light appeared. She brought her attention to the detective. "He's gone, isn't he? Really gone?"

"I'm afraid he is. I know this is difficult for you, but we need all the help we can get."

She leaned back, and her eyes fluttered shut. "It's all my fault."

Simpson, startled, leaned forward eagerly, certain he was on to something. "Exactly how do you mean that, ma'am? About it being your fault?"

Sue Ellen's eyes snapped open, staring past Simpson to where J.R. had entered the waiting room. But she didn't see him, aware only of past sins she had committed.

"I've done terrible things," she moaned. "It's only right that I should be punished for them."

"You believe that something you did is responsible for your child's disappearance?"

J.R., impelled to motion by the fear of exactly which of her sins—or his—Sue Ellen might blurt out, hurried over. He dropped a restraining hand on her shoulder.

"I think that's about enough, lieutenant. My wife has not been herself. You're getting off on the wrong track, in my opinion."

Simpson rose. "If your wife has something to tell us that might help—"

"My wife knows nothing about any of this. If I could have a word with you, privately."

Simpson edged over to the far side of the waiting room, watching Sue Ellen all the time. "I have to advise you, Mr. Ewing, that to obstruct the police in an investigation of this sort is—"

"Why would I do that? Do you think I don't want my son back? I do, more than you can imagine. But I won't have my wife distressed unnecessarily. She was in an automobile accident several weeks ago. As a result our child was born prematurely and almost died. She blames herself for that."

"I didn't know."

"You can understand, then, why I do not want her dwelling on the incident. She is emotional, in a very disturbed condition. I'd be grateful if you'd let me take her home. I assure you neither of us knows anything that could help. I wish we did."

"You know of no one who might want to kidnap your son?"

"No one."

"All right. Go home, Mr. Ewing. Take your wife. I'll send some men with you. We'll want to put a tap on your telephone. I expect you'll get the first call before long."

"First call?"

"Yes, establishing the kidnappers credentials, so to speak.

Next, a demand will be made. A third call will issue instructions, and so on. They all operate more or less the same way."

"Has the F.B.I. been notified?"

"First thing. Their people are involved already. Now, please, Mr. Ewing, don't do anything foolish."

"Meaning what?"

"Meaning that this is work for professionals—the police. If the kidnappers manage to make contact with you or any member of your family directly, bypassing us, you must inform me. We're experienced, and we know much better than you how to deal with them." J.R. started to say something, but Simpson cut him off. "I know—the child is your son, you love him, you want him back. For me, this is only a job. But that is precisely why you must depend on us, because we are pros, because we know how best to function in every situation that may arise."

"Very well, lieutenant. Come on, darlin', we can go home now."

They were almost to the elevator bank when Sue Ellen began to weep. "Oh, J.R., what have I done? It's all my fault—all my fault. But I never meant for anything like this to happen. You have to believe me. . . ."

He put his arm around her and led her into the elevator. It was, he told himself, going to be a rocky trip. For all of them.

Jock drove his horse in toward the herd, working to isolate a steer trying to edge his way in among the cows. Jock loosened his rope as he rode, ready to make his move. The blaring of a car horn set the herd on edge, resulting in considerable lowing and nervous shifting around. Jock swore and reined in his mount, then looked around. A jeep was bouncing across the range in his direction, horn blaring incessantly. It came skidding to a stop a dozen feet away.

"What the hell are you doing!" Jock raged at the driver, one of the barn hands.

"Sorry, Mr. Ewing. Miss Ellie said I was to get out here fast as I could and get you back to the ranch on the double."

157

"What's up?"

"She didn't say nothin' 'ceptin' I was to fetch you and Bobby."

"He's up in Little Horn. Go after him, I'll ride back in."

"Yes, sir."

Jock wheeled his horse, spurring quickly to a gallop, heading for the big house. He knew the sound of trouble when he heard it.

Lucy, laden down with books and her purse, strolled across the campus of Southern Methodist University and into the parking lot. Without warning, a yellow pickup truck with the Southfork emblem on its door came roaring across her path, brakes screeching, tires smoking. A young cowboy named Jimmy hopped out, calling her name.

"Miss Lucy!"

"Jimmy! What in the world's goin' on, drivin' in here like a crazy man?"

"Whatever you say, Lucy. It's your grandma, she wants you home now. And when she's giving orders like she is today, it's best to listen, hands and family alike."

"What's wrong?" Lucy asked, climbing into the pickup.

"She didn't tell me anything, except I was to come and git you. And she said quick." He pressed his foot down on the accelerator, and the pickup leaped ahead.

Jock rode his horse right up to the patio, hitting the ground before the animal stopped running, lunging forward and into the house, calling his wife's name.

Miss Ellie came out of the nursery to the top of the stairs, tears streaming down her face. "Oh, Jock—"

He took the steps three at a time. "What's happened, Miss Ellie? Are you hurt? Damn, anybody laid a hand on you I'll break his body barehanded—"

"No, no, I'm all right."

"Then what is it?"

"It's the baby, Jock. The baby—he's been kidnapped."

The news hit him like a blow to the gut. He staggered and almost fell backwards, gripping the handrail for support. His heart began to pound irregularly, and a gray shadow descended over his eyes.

The yellow pickup came speeding into the parking area, almost colliding with the jeep carrying Bobby in from Little Horn. He jumped out and joined Lucy, hurrying up toward the house.

"What's going on, Bobby?"

"Beats me."

"I was at school. Grandma sent Jimmy after me."

"We'd better get inside."

They found Jock and Miss Ellie waiting in the living room, both seated on a couch, holding hands. Their faces were strained, and it was clear that Miss Ellie had been crying.

"Thank God, you're here," Miss Ellie began.

"What is it, Momma?" Bobby asked.

"What's wrong?" asked Lucy.

"The baby—" Jock's voice was hoarse.

Miss Ellie went on. "J.R. called from the hospital a little while ago."

"The baby," Lucy said in a shocked voice. "He isn't dead?"

"Oh, no," Miss Ellie gasped. "Oh, good God, no."

"Then what?" Bobby pressed.

Jock answered. "He's been kidnapped."

Bobby felt a cold shroud settle over him. Baby John stolen. There was no doubt in his mind as to who had done it. Who had motive enough. Opportunity enough. Who was mean and lowdown enough to do such a terrible thing: Cliff Barnes.

Bobby's voice, when he spoke, was flat and thin. "Where's Pamela? Why isn't she here?"

Miss Ellie shook her head. "I sent Joey into town to find her. He phoned from The Store. She told Liz Craig she had some errands to run this afternoon. Nobody knows just where she is or when she'll get back. I left word for her to call as soon as she does."

Bobby turned it over in his mind. There was only one thing for him to do; get into Dallas and locate his wife and confront that pitiful brother-in-law of his. "I'm going in and wait for her. She'll turn up sooner or later."

Miss Ellie protested. "Bobby, please, let one of the hands do it."

"I'll be all right, Momma, don't you worry. I can't hang

159

around here and do nothing." Before anyone could stop him, he had dashed back outside, and they heard him drive away.

Less than two hours later, Southfork was overrun with reporters and radio and TV newspeople. They wandered around interviewing everyone in sight, and when that didn't get the kind of story they were after, they interviewed each other. As a result, rumor fed off speculation, and stories would appear on the evening news and in the morning papers that bore no relationship to fact. In the frantic search for hard news, Truth was heavily assaulted.

In the living room of the big house sat Jock, Miss Ellie, J.R. and Lucy. With them was another detective, this one named Rollands. He was a slender man in his middle years, with a bitter look to his face but a warm and friendly manner. He was, he had informed the Ewings, the police department's kidnapping expert. He declared his credentials with a touch of embarrassment at his purpose in life.

"With all this news coverage," he announced sadly, "we'll be hearing from every crank in Texas. Try not to get upset at some of the calls that'll be coming through. An event of this sort stimulates the crazies, and they have no regard for anyone's feelings."

"No way of keeping this quiet, I reckon," Jock said heavily.

"No way I know of, sir," Rollands said.

Miss Ellie sat huddled on the couch, looking much older than she had this morning. "What I can't understand is that no one saw anything. How can that be?"

Rollands responded in a gentle, explanatory way. "It may not be, ma'am. It's always like this in the beginning of one of these cases. Nobody saw anything, nobody knows anything. It doesn't mean much, however. Sooner or later things settle down. Somebody remembers something, and it comes to us. A piece of information here, a suggestion of something there; we put it together and move ahead. Always goes that way, I've seen it happen again and again. That's why we keep digging, going over the same points, asking the same questions, checking every statement."

The phone rang, and everyone froze in place.

J.R. looked to Rollands for guidance. "Pick it up and answer. Act normal. I'll listen in on the extension. And talk slowly, make him talk. Remember, everything is being recorded. And a tracer is working to track down the phone being used as of this minute. Now begin."

J.R. reached for the phone as if it were a lethal reptile. "J.R. Ewing here."

"Oh, hello, Mr. Ewing," came a female voice. "This is Muriel, Lucy's friend. Is Lucy there, please?"

J.R. glanced at Rollands. He shook his head. "No, she's not, Muriel. You call back another time, hear. Or better, I'll have Lucy call you just as soon as she gets in." He hung up. "Damn."

"Sorry, J.R.," Lucy said.

"Nobody's fault," Rollands said. "Things like that are gonna happen."

"What now?" Jock asked.

Rollands shrugged. "We wait for the next call. But I have to level with you. It's my guess the contact won't be made by telephone. Any pro will know that we have a tap on your lines by now. He'll find some other way—why take chances?"

Disappointment was apparent in all their faces. But they had no choice. They could wait and hope and pray. And nothing else.

As Pam came running across the street toward the main entrance to The Store, Bobby hailed her. For a split second she failed to recognize him.

"Pam," he said again.

"Oh, Bobby, it's not true. I just heard a radio report. Tell me it's not true."

He embraced her, oblivious to the stares of passers-by. Through the clothing that separated them, he could feel the swift, light beat of her heart. "I'm afraid it is, darling. It happened this morning."

"But how?"

"Nobody knows yet."

"I can't believe it. Do the police have any idea?"

"Apparently nobody saw or heard a thing. Have you talked to Cliff today?"

"Cliff? Why, no. I just stopped by his office, but he wasn't in. His secretary hasn't heard from him all day."

At once she pulled back, exploring her husband's face, struck by the implication of Bobby's questions. Horror and fear were etched on her delicate features.

"Bobby, surely you don't believe that Cliff is responsible."

He answered coldly. "Who else would do a thing like this? Who else hates the Ewings enough? Who else has sworn a personal vendetta against my family?"

"He's my brother."

"I know, which makes it all the worse."

"But that's ridiculous. Anybody, just anybody could have done it. My God—not my brother, not Cliff. Whatever else he might be, he is not a kidnapper."

Bobby wouldn't be dissuaded. "Every time either of us has said that Cliff wouldn't do this or do that in the past, we've been wrong. It seems to me Cliff is capable of anything. Anything at all."

She was filled with fantasies and ambitions that she feared would remain forever unfulfilled. Her woman's body sent powerful waves of desire coursing along her nerves, putting images in her head, ideas that frightened her, made her believe evil of herself. And yet—and yet, it was all her girlfriends talked about: boys and men. What husbands and wives did with each other in the darkness of their bedrooms, what boys and girls managed in parked cars or in rented motel rooms. To the young Pam, it was all talk, but of such intensity that her body tingled with desire, with longing, with the need to know. And to do . . . .

Yet she was scared. But finally the adolescent yearning combined with an insatiable curiosity caused her to overcome her fear, the familial and social taboos, the warnings of father, brother, preacher. Perhaps it would have been different if her mother had been alive to counsel and support her, to guide her lovingly and tenderly. But that could not be.

Desire finally overcame her when Jack Manning asked her out. He was the prototypical high school hero—handsome, strong, star of the football team, already the recipient of a full scholarship at the University of Texas. Every girl's dream of a date, of a lover, of a husband. In fact, he turned out to be far from a dream for Pam Barnes, sweet sixteen and kissed only on the cheek.

Her head told her to refuse Jack Manning's invitation to a hamburger and a movie. But the churning of her blood forced her to accept. Her father was off to Louisiana putting down a well in a new oil field, and Cliff was the man of the house.

"What time you goin' to be home?" he demanded, his voice growing gravelly like Digger's.

"Early."

"Make it ten o'clock, then."

"Oh, Cliff. Maryjane and I need time to study. That hardly gives us three hours."

"Eleven, and that's it."

"You're not my father."

"I know. If Digger was here, he might not let you out at all."

"Don't you trust me?"

He looked her over deliberately. "Not a question of trusting you. A girl looks the way you look, there's nothing but trouble lurking out there. I know. It's my job to protect you. I'm your family, you remember that. Eleven I said, and that is it."

She agreed lest he prohibit her from going at all and tried to work out a scheme that would get her home by eleven without mentioning the childish curfew, certain she could maneuver Jack Manning if she had to. She never had a chance.

They went to Big Top for burgers and malts and, afterward, to the Skyway Drive-In. The movie was a romance.

Afterward, they drove slowly in the direction of Pam's house.

"Know what I've a cravin' for?" Jack asked finally."

"What's that?"

"A stiff drink. How about you, honey?"

Pam had never even tasted liquor, had been warned against it by Cliff, and had her father's example of drinking to excess always before her. "Not this time," she said, smiling vaguely.

"Suit yourself." He pulled the car into a stand of pines and shut off the motor and the lights. He drew a leather-covered flask from the glove compartment. "Here's looking at you, kid."

He sounded a little like Humphrey Bogart, but not much. It was a pretty poor imitation, and she had to keep herself from laughing.

After a long silence, and without any preliminaries, he kissed her. His tongue went into her mouth, and his hand reached for her breast. Forced backward by his great strength, she was immobilized. Her efforts to struggle were futile, and after a moment she gave it up as a bad job. Through the fear and the confusion and the stirred passions that gripped her, she lay still and tried to think. He reached between her legs and began to talk softly to her, misreading her passivity for acceptance and willingness.

"You are gonna love this, beauty. I am gonna put Jack Manning's special on you. Ain't a chick at school hasn't loved it. Any special thing you crave, any special place you got turns you on, you just say so. Like this, like here."

"Let me sit up, Jack," she managed to gasp, not sure what she intended or what she could accomplish. It wasn't supposed to be like this.

He eased himself off her, waiting for her to assume a more comfortable position. A quick glance showed her his face, damp with perspiration, mouth agape, his eyes glazed. It occurred to her that he was less sure of himself than he pretended, perhaps less the great lover than he boasted.

She filled her lungs with air. "Don't touch me again, Jack," she said in a cold, flat voice.

He gazed at her as if struck. "What you talkin' about, honey? I told you, this is the Manning special—"

"I don't want it, not here, not like this."

He wet his lips. "You mean, you'd do it someplace else?"

She watched him closely. "You got enough money for a motel room, Jack?"

He swore under his breath. "I'm almost broke."

"What about where you live?"

"Are you kidding? I got three brothers, two sisters, all sleeping in two tiny rooms. And my old man never sacks out."

164

"In that case, we'll have to go to my place."

"What about your folks?"

"My father's off in Louisiana. My brother is probably out on a date himself."

He gave off a short laugh of triumph and started up the car. "Just point the way, sugar."

"Now I've finally made *the* decision," Pam thought to herself, almost relieved.

They came skidding to a stop in the front yard of the Barnes's house, Jack Manning oblivious to the lights on inside. He jumped out of the car, directing her toward the house, one arm tightly circling her shoulders. Halfway there, he stopped to kiss her again, pressing his body tightly against hers. She was aware of his great size and hardness, and a part of her wished to experience more of him, and of herself. But always there was the fear, the chilling terror of becoming pregnant, of being found out, of being disgraced in front of family and friends. He was pulling her closer now, those great hands of his holding tightly to her trim young buttocks, his middle rotating anxiously.

"No," she whispered, pushing away. "Don't you see—the lights. There's someone home. . . ."

The words made no sense to him. His brain was boiling with passion, and desire, and he heard, saw, and felt only what he at that moment needed and wanted. He reached for her again just as the front door swung open and Cliff stepped out into the night. His voice ripped into the moment like a buzz saw.

"Pam!"

Both heads swung his way. And in that split second both of them were reduced to being children, guilty, susceptible to adult control, and demand. Jack Manning stepped back, boyish, indecisive all of a sudden.

"Get inside!" Cliff ordered.

"Well," Jack said, "guess I'll be going. . . ." He backed toward the car.

"You keep your hands off my sister," Cliff said through clenched teeth, advancing swiftly across the lawn that separated them. "You treat her like you do your own sister, you hear me, boy!"

165

Pam was afraid of what Cliff might do. In the darkness Jack Manning blanched. He braced himself against the onslaught of adult disapproval.

"I didn't mean no harm."

"I see you near Pam one more time, and I'll climb up one side of your head and down the other, you know what I'm talking about, boy?"

Boy. Boy! BOY! The word sliced deep into the youth, rendering him impotent, reducing him in his own eyes and diminishing him before the girl. Brought low and unable to fight back, he gave no answer.

"Speak up!" Cliff demanded. "Answer when I talk to you, dammit!" His rage boiled over, as if his authority had been challenged, his manhood put to the test.

Jack could not respond.

"It's all right, Cliff," Pam cried, suddenly afraid. "He didn't do anything wrong. Nothing happened."

"I told you to get inside, now get. As for you, punk, I'll listen to you apologize for what you've done."

"I didn't do—"

Cliff, half a head shorter but stocky and strong, fearless in his anger, swung without warning. His open hand was like a pistol shot on Jack Manning's cheek. The boy stumbled backward, less in physical pain than shame. He raised his fists automatically.

"No!" Pam screamed.

Cliff launched himself in a two-fisted attack. Jack was overwhelmed, going down onto his back, trying weakly to deflect the rain of blows, bleeding from nose and mouth.

Then he was running for his car. Cliff, stiff, gasping for breath, eyes glazed with fury, watched him go. Then he whirled around and went inside the house.

In the morning he attempted to explain how he had felt, what had caused him to act as he had. Pam listened without interest. His help, she knew, had been unneeded, his anger a sop to his own feelings, not hers. If Jack Manning had been a problem, he was her problem, and she was capable of dealing with it, one way or another. What Cliff had done he had done for himself, to satisfy his own needs, his own self-righteousness, to prove how tough he was. In the name of brotherly love he had embarrassed her and caused her more pain than he had caused Jack Manning.

Pam warned herself that day to beware of Cliff most when he was avowedly trying to help another human being; to support him always with reservations; and to keep a protecting cushion of space between Cliff and herself.

Bobby was right: there was nothing Cliff Barnes wouldn't do to advance his own cause, his own beliefs, his own way of doing things.

Time moved sluggishly for all of them. Tension crept into their faces, into every line of their bodies. The telephone, silent and ominous now, became a focal point of their hopes and their fears. A sense of helplessness permeated their beings as no word came, as nothing happened, as their worst fears were magnified.

"Why?" Miss Ellie burst out, as the afternoon wore on. "Why don't they call?"

"Shouldn't we have heard something by now?" Jock added. Each minute seemed to add years to his face, the lines deepening, his mouth drawn down wearily as if all energy had been drained away.

Rollands answered patiently. "It's hard to say, folks. Sometimes kidnappers move fast, figuring it's the best chance they have of pulling it off. Sometimes they go slow to let the tension and the fear mount."

Lucy, moving aimlessly about the room, unable to remain in place, shuddered and hugged herself in a vain attempt to keep herself warm. The front doorbell rang, and she reacted as if struck an angry blow.

"I'll get it," she said.

Rollands stood up. "Sutton's on the door. He'll take care of it."

Seconds later a policeman appeared. "There's a lady out here, a Mrs. Reeves. Says she's the baby's nurse. Anybody vouch for her?"

Miss Ellie was moving toward the door. "Mrs. Reeves! Oh, heavens, I forgot all about her. Yes, we're expecting her."

Mrs. Reeves, a plump, white-haired woman in her late fifties, was ushered into the living room. She seemed confused by all the excitement attending her arrival.

"That's all right," Miss Ellie said. "Please let her alone. Mrs. Reeves, I'm so sorry."

"Good afternoon, Mrs. Ewing," Mrs. Reeves said uncertainly.

"It hasn't been a very good day, I'm afraid," Miss Ellie said. "You know what's happened?"

"The policeman just told me. I'm so sorry. What can I say—?"

"Let me show you to your room. You can get comfortable and meet the rest of the family later on. If you're hungry I'll have some food sent up."

"That's very kind of you." She turned back at the door, eyes going from one member of the family to another. "Do the police have any suspects yet?"

It was, Rollands remarked to himself, an odd question for a nurse to ask.

Pam hesitated only briefly before inserting the key in the lock and entering Cliff Barnes's apartment. Her brother had wanted her to have a key, intended it as a safety measure back in those days when Digger, their father, had been drinking heavily and living with Cliff.

"Should anything happen," Cliff had advised her, "you won't have to search for me. Just head on over and do what has to be done."

Fortunately, nothing of that dramatic magnitude had ever occurred. The key had never been used and was long forgotten by both of them. Until today. Until now.

The apartment was still, possessing the eerie strangeness of a place not one's own. For a long unsettling interval, Pam had the feeling she had never before been here, never laughed and talked and even cried in these sleek, sophisticated confines. Yet there were the familiar furnishings, the same stereo, the same paintings on the walls. She filled her lungs with air and set to work. Pam hadn't come to wait for Cliff to return. She was there to inspect the premises, perhaps find some random piece of evidence that might incriminate her brother in Baby John's disappearance—or clear him. How odd, she thought bitterly, that first she suspected her own flesh and blood of such a heinous crime. She began the search.

The oppressive silence in the living room at Southfork grew heavier, pervasive pressure that affected everyone equally. Jock stirred and swore under his breath, complained that doing nothing would accomplish nothing.

Lieutenant Rollands tried to explain that there was no method known to modern policemen to expedite the process. Not when the kidnapper held all the cards.

Lucy said she had to get out of there and intended to take a long ride on her favorite horse. Miss Ellie, suddenly afraid for Lucy, objected. But J.R. said there was little danger, especially with the ranch crowded with policemen.

J.R. began to prowl the perimeter of the living room, as if about to burst free of some self-imposed prison. "I don't blame her," he said of Lucy. "All this standing around and doing nothing is getting on my nerves, too. Isn't that damned phone ever gonna ring?"

As if in reply, the phone did ring. It was J.R. who got to it first. "Hello?"

It was a friend of Sue Ellen's.

"Oh, hello, Marilee," J.R. said, visibly sagging. "Yes, we're all taking it kind of hard. No, Sue Ellen's not available to talk, she's lying down. No, that's all right, sugar, appreciate your callin'. Talk to you later." He slammed the phone down, then jerked around to face his parents. "I've got to tell you, I have had it, this hanging around. I can't handle it any more. I am going back into Dallas."

"To do what, Mr. Ewing?" Detective Rollands asked.

"I've got a business to run." The words sounded hollow in J.R.'s own ears.

"J.R.," his father said in warning.

"Don't worry about me, Daddy. I can take care of myself. You need me, I'll be at the office."

"J.R., don't go," Miss Ellie said.

"Let him alone, Ellie," Jock said quietly.

J.R. went up to his room. Sue Ellen turned restlessly on the bed when he entered. "J.R.?" she muttered, half asleep.

"Yes, darlin'?" He removed a .38 police special from the bottom drawer of his bureau, shoved it under his belt, and buttoned his jacket.

"It's all my fault, J.R. I'm to blame."

"It's all right, darlin'. You go back to sleep. You need the rest. Everything's gonna work out okay. I'll see to it. You can depend on me."

"Yes, J.R."

He kept voicing soothing platitudes until she was again asleep. By contrast, there was cold hatred in his far-seeing eyes, and his mouth was a hard, menacing line.

Exactly seventeen minutes after J.R. drove away from Southfork, the telephone rang again. This time it was Jock who answered.

"Hello," he said. "Yes, I'm listening. Yes, go on. Where, where did you say? Now, wait! Wait a minute. I want to ask you—" He dropped the receiver back in its cradle. "She hung up."

"Who was it, Jock?" Miss Ellie asked. "What did she say?"

"Said she took the baby and now she's sorry. Said we'll find him in a carriage by the flagpoles at City Hall."

"What do you think, lieutenant?" Miss Ellie asked Rollands.

He shrugged. "Doesn't sound right, but we've got to check it out. Want to come along, Mr. Ewing?"

"Sure do."

"You go in your car. Some of my boys will follow. I'll have Detective Simpson meet you there. And Mr. Ewing, just one more thing—"

"What is it?" Jock said gruffly.

"Be careful."

Louella was typing and making more mistakes than she had since she first entered business school. Connie was proofreading a report and discovered her concentration faltering, her thoughts far afield. Finally she looked up.

"I can't keep my mind on a thing," she said.

"Neither can I."

The door swung open, and J.R. pushed his way in. They greeted him nervously, fearful of what he might do or say, yet desperate for some information.

"We just heard, J.R.," Connie said. "Is there any news?"

"No. Nothing so far."

"Your mother called, she wants you to call her right away."

J.R. nodded; more trouble, he was sure. "Would you get her on the line for me, please?" He went into his private office as she began to dial. Almost at once, the other phone rang.

As J.R. settled behind his desk, the intercom began to buzz. He answered.

"Jeb Ames is on the line," Connie said.

"Tell him I'm busy," he said with considerable annoyance. He shifted the pistol in his belt around to a more comfortable position.

"He's already called three times this morning. He says it's vital that you talk to him. He says it's about something occupying your attention fully right now."

"Now what in hell is that supposed to—?" He broke off, turning a new thought over in his mind. There was only one thing occupying his attention this day, and that was Baby John's whereabouts; Ames and Garr would know that. Was it possible that those two reprobates had played a role in the infant's kidnapping? He felt his rage blowing up to monumental proportions. "Very well," he said in that deceptively soft voice of his, "put Mr. Ames through." Then, an afterthought: "You ladies go on home. We won't be getting much work done around here today. No sense in your hanging around." He waited briefly before punching the second line on his phone. "J.R. Ewing here. You want to talk to me, Ames?"

"You can be a very hard man to reach, J.R."

"I thought I told you not to bother me again."

"No need to be hard about it, I'm calling to help."

"Help? Help with what, Ames?"

"Why, with your most pressing problem J.R. The press, the radio, the TV, they're filled with the kidnapping of your boy. I'm sure you want him back. Swiftly. Painlessly. And unharmed."

J.R. felt his temper erupt, was incapable of reining it back. "Ames, if anything's happened to that child, I'll whip your ass from one end of Dallas to the other. No matter where you and that scummy partner of yours hide, I'll find you and destroy you. Depend on it. I'll—"

"Slow down, man. Threats won't get you what you want."

"Do you have Baby John?"

Ames laughed, the sound ominous over the wire. "What do you think? Now, I'm going to do you a favor."

"What kind of a favor?"

"I'm going to allow you to hand over one million dollars in used bills to me and Garr—"

"You're insane."

"You want the kid back, J.R.?"

J.R. sucked air into his lungs. "You guarantee his safety, Ames? If anything happens to that child—" He broke off, a sob catching in his throat.

"One million dollars. In fifties and hundreds, J.R."

"How—"

"You'll get additional instructions pretty soon now. And one more thing, J.R.—"

"What is it?"

"Don't run off at the mouth to the cops about this call. Or to anybody else. Not if you want to see that brat of yours again."

Click.

Sue Ellen woke slowly. Reluctantly. Her body gradually unfolded as she came up into a sitting position, blinking against the light. Hesitantly she looked around, afraid of what she might see. A vague and disturbing recollection of something bad stirred her, made her want to weep. She stood up and without knowing why, circled the room, peering into corners, behind chairs, opening and closing drawers. What was she seeking? What had she lost? She went toward the door. It was, she commented absently to herself, a very long way away.

But she made it. She drifted into the nursery. The room was bright and cheerful, a scatter of toys on the shelves and along the walls. A nameless worm of worry nibbled at her conscience, and she advanced cautiously into the center of the room. She stood swaying in the terrible silence, trying to fathom her terrors, struggling to give a name to her concerns. She went to the crib.

It was empty, except for a delicate blue pillow fluffed

perfectly, never used, and a matching sheet tucked and turned tightly. An empty crib.

A crib was for a baby. Her baby. Baby John. It all came flooding back then, everything that had happened. Her eyes filled up with tears as painful memory took hold. She fought back the tears and spoke in a still voice, as if to the room itself.

"I am not going to cry. I won't. No more tears. Too many tears. They've used me. They've hurt me. J.R. and Cliff. But no more. I won't think about it again. I won't be hurt any more. I won't think about them. Or the baby. I won't think of anything. . . ." She banished them—J.R., Cliff Barnes, the missing child—from her consciousness. Wiped away all thoughts of the painful months preceding the child's birth. She would consider none of that any more, allow no one to give her pain again. Her face grew transformed, harder and smoother, the sheen of polished marble chipped into a protective mask. "No one," she murmured, "is ever going to hurt me again." Her eyes went down to the empty crib. "Not even you."

Ewing 1 trailed by an unmarked police car drew up in front of City Hall. Jock and Ray Krebbs climbed out and were soon joined by a pair of policemen in plain clothes. Detective Simpson was waiting for them.

"Hello, Mr. Ewing, I'm Simpson."

"This is my foreman, Ray Krebbs."

The two men shook hands quickly.

"Okay," Simpson said. "You go over to the flags, Mr. Ewing. Krebbs, you stay with me. We'll cover the area. Let's do it."

Miss Ellie answered the telephone. "Oh, J.R., I'm so glad it's you." She told him about the call that had sent Jock into Dallas to City Hall. He heard her out before answering.

"I think it's a hoax, Momma."

"Detective Rollands seemed to think—"

He broke in angrily, his mind elsewhere now. "Then the man is a fool. If the call was genuine, Daddy would be on his way to the bank, not City Hall."

"Not everyone is motivated by greed, J.R." she remonstrated quickly.

"I won't argue the point, Momma. But nothing's going to come of it."

"Maybe you're right—" She stopped short at the sight of Sue Ellen standing in the doorway on unsteady legs, bracing herself against the jam. "Sue Ellen! Lucy, help Sue Ellen!"

Lucy rushed toward the other woman and put her into a chair.

"Momma," J.R. said anxiously, "what is Sue Ellen doing downstairs? She's supposed to be resting."

"I'll take care of it, son. You just get home, as quick as you can. This is a time for family to be together instead of scattered around like a stampeded herd of cattle." She hung up and went to Sue Ellen.

In his office J.R. stared malevolently at the dead receiver. Events seemed to have slipped out of his hands, and he didn't like it. He depressed the button on the phone, waited briefly, then dialed.

"This is J.R. Ewing. Let me talk to Vaughn Leland, please.... Vaughn, J.R. here. I need your help, old buddy. I need it right now. Yes, that's right. I've got to get some money together. Lots of money. That's right, the call came a few minutes ago. Okay. I'm on my way. And, Vaughn, you keep it under your hat. This is important to me, and I don't want any dumb cops interfering." He hurried out of the office.

At City Hall Jock waited. He checked his watch, wiped sweat from his brow, and lit a cigarette. He willed something to happen, anything. Nothing did.

Bobby burst into Cliff Barnes's private office, Cliff's secretary right behind, protesting.

"You have no right to do this. I told you Mr. Barnes wasn't here."

"Where the hell is he?"

"I don't know."

Bobby went to Cliff's desk, examining the papers scattered about.

"You have no right!"

"Where is he?"

She shook her head. "The calls have been coming all day. Even the governor's been trying to get hold of him. I haven't heard from him since yesterday."

"Doesn't he usually tell you where he's going?"

"Usually. Not always."

He began reading through some of the official-looking documents on the desk.

"Don't! You mustn't. That's private."

He held her off, examined Cliff's calendar. "There are no appointments listed for today. Isn't that unusual?"

"It happens."

"Not often, I bet."

"Mr. Ewing, this is an official state office. If you don't leave here at once, I'm going to have to call someone to evict you."

He was on his way out by that time.

"What am I going to tell Mr. Barnes? He'll want to know what you wanted."

"He'll know."

"How did you get in here?"

"I have a key, remember."

"My mistake. Let me have it. You have no right to break in here this way."

"I'm your sister, Cliff. I did not break in."

"This is my apartment. I live here. You seem to have no respect for that fact. Which, I suppose, means you've become a typical Ewing." He dropped down on the edge of the couch, head in his hands. "Oh, damn, Pam, I'm glad you're here. I just heard the reports on the car radio, on my way in from the airport. I was up in Austin all morning. I can't believe it. Pam, do they know anything? Do they have any idea who could have taken the baby?"

"You didn't have anything to do with it, Cliff, did you?"

His head came up. "Me? Are you crazy! He's my son. How low do you think I am?"

"Bobby thinks you are responsible."

"Bobby!" he raged. "That's typical. Your loving husband thinks I've got horns and a tail."

"You can't blame him, can you? I have to warn you—

Bobby will show up here sooner or later, and when he does, you better stay calm and hope he does the same. Let me handle him."

"I'm not afraid of Bobby."

"You would be, if you had any sense. I've never seen him this angry, and when he's this way, he's too much for a half dozen men, let alone one."

Cliff started to respond but thought better of it. "Okay," he said after a moment. "I think you'd better tell me all about it, everything you know."

She began talking and didn't stop until interrupted by an insistent knocking at the door. She jumped up in alarm. "If that's Bobby—let me answer—"

"No. This is my home. I'll see who it is."

He went to the door, hesitated, and opened it. Bobby advanced into the apartment, fists clenched, with an expression to match.

"Take it easy, Bobby," Cliff said. "Before you punch me out, hear what I've got to say."

"You've gone too far this time, you smarmy little bastard. I'm going to break your back and—"

"Bobby!" Pam cried. "Listen to him!"

Bobby turned heavily in her direction. "Did you know he was hiding out here all this time?" he said, voice dripping with disgust.

"Cliff arrived a few minutes ago," she said. "Please listen to him."

"I had nothing to do with this, Bobby," Cliff said.

"Why should I believe that?"

"Because it's true. Dammit, man, don't you think I want my son? And I mean to get him. But kidnapping is not my style. Instead of wasting your time and mine by beating me up, don't you think you should be trying to figure out who did this thing?"

Cliff had maneuvered himself so that a chair separated him from Bobby. Bobby flung it out of the way, the chair shattering against the wall.

"Bobby!" Pam shouted, genuinely afraid now, "for God's sake, listen to what he's saying!"

Bobby, breathing hard, hesitated. "Okay. I'm listening."

176

Cliff breathed a sigh of relief. "I swear. I did not steal Baby John. You can knock me around the room for as long as you like, but it won't change anything. I didn't do it. I couldn't. I wasn't even in Dallas."

"He's telling the truth, Bobby."

Bobby stood without moving, then abruptly lowered himself into a chair. "I believe you. Cliff, I'm sorry."

Cliff shrugged away the apology. "Let's stop wasting time and use our brains for a change. Tomorrow we'll be back at each other's throats, today let's find my son."

Bobby raised his eyes. "All right. Let's do it."

Jock lit another cigarette. It left a foul taste in his mouth, and he let it fall to the ground, then stomped it out. He looked at his watch. Impatience had been replaced by anger and frustration, but he didn't know which way to turn. For a man of action, there was nothing worse than waiting endlessly to no good purpose.

Detective Simpson moved toward him. "I don't think there's any sense in hanging around any more, Mr. Ewing."

Jock set his jaw, reluctant to give in.

"I'm sorry, Mr. Ewing. But these things happen. Some people have a very warped sense of humor."

Jock turned away, starting back toward the car. Ray Krebbs joined him.

"We can do more good at Southfork," the foreman said sympathetically, "than we can here."

Nodding slowly, Jock let himself be led away.

Vaughn Leland's office was designed to inspire trust, confidence, and a willingness to borrow. Money was Leland's passion, banking was his occupation. Dealing with Texas oil and cattle millionaires, he was accustomed to handling large sums. Dollars, pesos, yen, pounds, rubles; these were the daily currencies of his existence. He bought and sold, he lent, he borrowed; what he never did, never, was give anything away. The banker would have considered that a violation of his personal trust, his obligation to the bank, its depositors, and stockholders—not to mention his own sense of correct

177

acquisitive behavior. If anyone had asked Leland what he
wanted most out of life, he would have answered cheerfully
with a single word: "More."

He was a handsome man, a peer of J.R.'s and a friend and
business associate from way back. But such long-standing
connections added up to very little with Vaughn Leland
when a million dollars was on the table. Literally, that is.
Stacked very neatly in a genuine leather attaché case.

"That's a great deal of money, J.R." Leland dropped one
pale banker's hand possessively on the bills.

"Don't I know it? I appreciate what you're doing. Don't
think I don't." He reached for the money.

Leland's hand remained securely in place. "I don't like it,
J.R. I don't like it one bit."

"Don't care for it much myself, Vaughn. Asking for this
kind of money on such short notice is not my way of doing
things. Only thing is, what choice have I got? My boy's been
stolen away on me, and I got to get him back, no matter
what."

"You certain this is going to work?"

"Not certain about a thing. But I got to try, wouldn't you
say?"

"One million dollars."

"That's what the man said."

"You say you know who it is?"

"Oh, I know, all right."

"Why not give him over to the law?"

"Because he's got my boy is why."

"Let the cops put a move on him. They know how to
handle such matters."

"Maybe so. But it's my son, and I got to do what I believe
is right." He lifted Leland's hand off the pile of bills and
snapped the attaché case shut. "I thank you again, Vaughn."

"Thanks is not what I'm in business for, J.R."

"You worried about this money?"

"Wouldn't you be? One million—"

"The Ewings are good for it, you know that."

Leland tugged at his nose, eyes glued to the brown leather
case. "I've prepared a little receipt."

J.R. frowned. "I'm beginning to have doubts about our
friendship, Vaughn."

"I'm a banker J.R." He pushed the receipt and a pen across his desk. "Just put your name right there, will you, please?"

"It's my son's life, Vaughn."

"I know. I understand. But there have to be better ways of dealing with something like this—the F.B.I.?"

"I don't have time for a discussion. I'll sign your damned receipt."

"Just trying to talk sense into you, J.R."

J.R scribbled his name on the receipt. "The ranch is crawling with cops, special agents, Lord only knows what. I figure wherever I go they are on my tail. But the fact is they ain't getting a thing done, Vaughn. Nothing. So I've got to try. My boy's life is on the line."

Leland exhaled noisily and examined the receipt. "The money's yours, J.R. For the time being, that is. The bank expects repayment with interest within ninety days."

J.R. plastered a humorless grin across his wide mouth. "Thanks, Vaughn, old buddy. You always were more heart than the rest of us." The attaché case in hand, he quickly left.

Cliff, Bobby, and Pam entered Dallas Memorial Hospital by a side door, thus avoiding the horde of press people still on the scene. They rode an otherwise empty elevator up to the maternity floor and made their way to the nurse's station. The ward was quiet now, medical business as usual, the police no longer in evidence.

"May I help you?" The duty nurse greeted them with her most professional smile.

"I'm Bobby Ewing."

"Oh, yes, Mr. Ewing, Mrs. Ewing. I'm sorry I didn't recognize you. I'm Paula Barker. We're all so upset about what happened. Is there any news yet?"

"None," Bobby said. "Not yet."

"That's why we're here," Cliff said. "We're trying to get some information. We'd like to talk to the patients, the nurses who were on duty, the doctors, anyone who might have seen something or someone."

Nurse Barker pursed her lips doubtfully. "The police have

been here all day. Everyone's been questioned and then questioned again."

"This won't take long," Bobby said.

A doctor came up to the station. "Is something the matter?" he asked pleasantly. "Can I be of service?"

"Oh, Dr. Freilich. This is Bobby Ewing and his wife. I was just explaining—"

Cliff broke in impatiently. "It's all very simple, doctor. We want to talk to the staff and the patients, take a look at some of your files."

"I don't understand," the doctor said.

"We're trying to find my—the Ewing boy," Cliff said brusquely.

"Who are you?"

"I'm —" Cliff broke off.

"My brother-in-law," Bobby said quickly. "He's helping in the search."

Dr. Freilich ingested the information, weighed it against what he already knew, equated it with his professional obligations. "As I'm sure Nurse Barker has explained to you, the police have been—"

Bobby interrupted. A rising anger gripped him, had pushed him to the edge of his patience. Very little tolerance remained in him for dissembling or procrastination. His voice was tight, words exploding out of him. "Doctor, my nephew was kidnapped from this facility earlier today. Kidnapped. Stolen out of your hospital. There is responsibility to be assessed—legal, moral, and financial."

Freilich blanched. "Are you threatening—"

"I am telling you how it is." Bobby's stiff, strong forefinger beat a tattoo against the doctor's chest. "What I want, what all of us want, is to find out who did it. And how."

"Everyone on the staff is very sorry—"

"Apologies don't add up to a hill of beans."

"We're wasting time," Cliff put in.

"Sympathy," Bobby continued harshly, "does no good. Don't tell me you're sorry, give us your help. You *let* someone walk out of here with a Ewing baby today. It's not too much to expect that you help us get him back."

Freilich ran his tongue over lips that had suddenly gone dry. This young, husky Ewing meant to make trouble and was quite capable of doing so. Trouble for the hospital, trouble for Freilich personally. He wanted very much to avoid both kinds. It was, he decided, more politic to cooperate gracefully now than be forced, perhaps painfully, into greater concessions in the future. He presented his most sincere, most cooperative visage to Bobby.

"We want to help in any way we can, Mr. Ewing. Where would you like to start?"

Cliff responded first. "With the patients. Then I'd like to take a look at your records to see who was on duty and when, what patients were admitted or discharged today, that sort of thing."

"I see how your mind is working," Freilich said. "Nurse, would you get the appropriate records."

"Of course, doctor."

They worked at the nurse's station, examining records, going through files, checking names and addresses. Cliff and Bobby were seated at desks behind the counter; Pam worked standing. Hours went by, and they came up with nothing encouraging.

Cliff threw up his hands finally. "There's nothing here, nothing I can make any sense of. If somebody had taken the baby by mistake, there'd be another baby left behind."

"And no one remembers anything," Pam said. "No one I spoke to."

Bobby shook his head. A weariness had taken hold of him that the hardest day's work had never imposed. He felt close to surrender, to giving it all up. "I don't understand. It's as if Baby John has vanished into thin air."

"There's got to be a clue of some kind," Cliff said desperately. "We've got to keep trying—"

A despirited Pamela turned away from the counter and the hospital records, drifting along the corridor until she came to the nursery window. Inside, a couple of dozen newborns were being attended to by some nurses. They were all so small and helpless, so full of life. One or two were crying, tiny faces screwed up, mouths agape, but no sound coming through the glass.

"Aren't they adorable?" a voice said at Pam's shoulder.

Only partly aware, responding automatically, Pam looked that way. A young woman stood there staring in at the children. Vaguely familiar, yet never before seen by Pam, her presence triggered a mild memory, brought it rushing to the front of her brain. Excited, she hurried back to Bobby and Cliff.

"I think I remembered something!" she cried. They came to their feet, urging her to speak. "There was someone here, every time I visited Baby John. A woman—always at the nursery window—she spent hours here. If she was here this morning, maybe she saw something—"

"A new mother?" Bobby asked hopefully.

"I don't know. But she isn't here now, or I would have recognized her."

"If we only knew her name."

Pam let her eyes close. "I can see her clearly, the way she looked. I could describe her—"

"Nurse!" Bobby called, with hope in his voice for the first time. "Nurse Barker, may we speak to you for a minute?"

Jeb Ames made the call, Willie Joe Garr at his shoulder. "J.R.," he began. "Jeb Ames here."

"I'd know your voice anywhere." There was no humor intended.

Ames laughed uneasily. "Have you got it?"

"I've got it."

"Okay. You stay in your office, we'll drop by."

"When?"

"Don't get itchy, J.R. Soon enough. And, J.R., no tricks, okay. Willie Joe will be with the baby. Try something funny and you'll never see the kid again."

"I hear what you're saying."

Ames dropped the receiver back in its cradle. He grinned maliciously. "The poor sucker went for it all the way. What a stroke of luck. Somebody snatches that kid, and we're gonna get a million bucks out of it. Without doing a damned thing to earn it except make a couple of phone calls."

Willie Joe began to laugh and didn't stop for a very long time.

A growing air of defeat and hopelessness pervaded Southfork. In the living room Sue Ellen slumped in an armchair, eyes dull and seeing nothing. She had refused food and drink, had ignored attempts at conversation. She hadn't cried or even met anyone else's eye.

Mrs. Reeves, the baby's nurse, addressed her as if trying to break through the invisible psychic screen that surrounded Sue Ellen. "We mustn't give up hope, dear."

The words managed to strike some faint responsive chord. Sue Ellen's eyes skittered, and a hint of interest gleamed. "Hope?"

"Yes, hope," Mrs. Reeves said desperately. "I'm sure everything will work out."

"Things happen for the best," Sue Ellen muttered, again picking up some point in space on which to focus.

"Yes, yes. You must keep believing that."

"Yes. Yes, I will." Sue Ellen slumped deeper into the chair.

Miss Ellie and Lucy clung to each other in horror. They understood now without any doubt that Sue Ellen wanted neither her child nor love nor the attentions of any other human being.

And then Jock returned home, an expression of defeat on his rugged face. Miss Ellie embraced and reassured him, glancing past him to the doorway where Detective Rollands stood.

"What do we do now?" she asked plaintively.

He shrugged. "We continue to wait."

It was a simple house on an unpretentious street. The kind of house and the kind of street occupied by hard-working people who keep up their property. Fences were in good repair, gardens green and well-manicured, walks level and straight. This was Priscilla Duncan's house. She was seated comfortably in a neat but slightly worn chair reading a magazine when the knock came. She displayed no surprise, although she wasn't expecting anyone. It was the kind of street where neighbors visited unannounced. Priscilla went to the door and opened it. A very beautiful young woman stood there, an expectant look on her face, a woman Priscilla had seen somewhere before.

"Remember me, Mrs. Duncan?"

Priscilla made an effort to put the face in context; then she smiled. "You're the lady I spoke to at the hospital."

"My name is Pamela Ewing. May I come in?"

Priscilla stepped back unhesitatingly and invited Pam inside.

"I remember you very well now. Would you care for some coffee or something? I have some ice cream in the freezer, if you'd like that?"

"Nothing for me, Mrs. Duncan."

Priscilla led the way toward the sofa, sat down at one end, leaving plenty of room for Pam. "Please," she said, "won't you call me Priscilla? What is it you wanted to see me about? You one of them social workers? They always like to ask a lot of questions, talk a lot."

"I'm not a social worker. Pamela Ewing is the name. It was my nephew who was kidnapped from the hospital this morning. Did you hear about it?"

Priscilla considered the question. "Yes, I saw it on the television. On the news. I saw a picture of the baby's mother. Poor woman. You know, my baby was premature, too. That's how come you saw me at the hospital all those times. I was visiting him."

"That's what I wanted to talk to you about. Nurse Barker told me you were at the hospital this morning. I thought maybe—I mean, I know this has been a terrible day for you, too. But if you saw anything that could help us find my nephew, we'd all be very grateful."

Priscilla frowned. "I wasn't there very long today, you see."

"You didn't see anyone near my nephew during your visit? Someone who looked as though she or he didn't belong?"

"I'm sorry. I don't even know which baby he was. Oh, I am sorry, I wish I could help. What a terrible thing it must be, to lose your baby."

Pam wrote her name and phone number on a scrap of paper and gave it to the other woman. "If you happen to remember anything, would you call me?"

"Oh, yes."

Pam stood up, started to say something else, decided against it, and went to the door. She turned, smiling a little sadly. "It was very kind of you to talk to me, to take the time. I'm sure you'd help if you could."

Priscilla opened the door. "Oh, I would."

Pam started to leave when a baby began to cry from somewhere back in the house. She froze in place.

"What was that?"

"My baby," Priscilla said proudly. "I brought him home this morning. He must be hungry again. What an appetite the little guy has got." The baby cried again. Priscilla was torn between being polite to Pam and attending the child. "Excuse me, just a minute. I'll be right back." She ran toward the rear of the house.

Pam stepped outside. Bobby and Cliff, posted across the street, hurried to meet her.

"Well?" Cliff said impatiently.

"Can she help us?" Bobby asked.

Pam glanced back at the house. "I think—I believe she has Baby John in there right now."

"What!" Bobby almost yelled.

"Where is he?" Cliff said aggressively, starting forward.

Pam stopped him with a hand on his arm. "Easy, Cliff. She thinks Baby John is *her* child."

Bobby set his jaw. "But that's impossible! Her baby is dead. He died this morning. She was there, at the hospital, when it happened. You heard what Nurse Barker said."

"Well, what do we do?" Cliff demanded.

Pam wasn't sure. But it was evident that Cliff and Bobby were close to the breaking point. Neither would continue to be restrained for long.

"Let's go back into the house," she suggested.

They stood in the center of the small living room waiting for Priscilla. When she did appear, the baby in her arms, she was startled to see the two men with Pam.

"Don't be afraid, Priscilla," Pam said. "I'd like you to meet my husband, Bobby Ewing, and my brother, Cliff Barnes. This is Priscilla Duncan."

"Hello, Mrs. Duncan," they said as one.

"Hello," she said tentatively, looking from one to the other apprehensively. "I've already said I don't know any way to help. I'm sorry."

"May I hold the baby?" Cliff asked.

She retreated two quick steps. "No. Oh, no, he's so small—"

Cliff held out his arms. "Just for a little while."

She shook her head adamantly but made no move when he looked down at the infant's face, then gently folded back the blanket. With two fingers he lifted the tiny right fist and read the name engraved on the hospital identification bracelet: John Ross Ewing III.

"It's Baby John," Cliff whispered.

"He's a beautiful child," Pam said.

"Yes." Priscilla was proud of the infant.

"Why don't we all sit down for a moment?" Pam said. "Just for a little while."

"Well," Priscilla said, "for a little while. But I don't have much time. I have to feed him. There's so much to do with a new baby in the house."

"Priscilla," Pam said in her gentlest voice, "we saw the hospital records before we came over here. This baby—he isn't really yours."

"I don't know what you mean. Of course, he's mine. He's mine."

"We're sorry," Bobby said. "We genuinely are. We don't want to hurt you in any way. And we won't."

"He's mine," Priscilla said, beginning to weep. "He really is. Don't take him from me. Please don't take him from me."

"No one will take him," Pam said. "Not yet. Not till you're ready to let him go. To let him be with his real mother, to be home at last."

They sat without speaking, watching Priscilla coo over the infant, rocking gently to and fro, tears coursing down her cheeks. Waiting for her to be ready.

Jeb Ames came to J.R.'s office late in the afternoon. As if to mark his coming, the sun disappeared behind an ominous cloud outside, plunging the office into unsettling shadow. J.R. made no attempt to turn on the lights, remaining in place behind his desk. There was loathing in every line of his face as he studied Ames.

On the desk was the leather attaché case. Ames pointed to it. "Is that the cash?"

"That's it. Where's my boy?"

"Not so fast. Let's see the money."

J.R. gestured. "Nobody's stopping you."

Ames opened the case and scanned the neat piles of bills. "Nice," he said grinning. "Very nice. Shouldn't we have a drink to celebrate?"

J.R. fixed his eyes on Ames. "I said where's my boy?"

Ames grew pale but held his position. There was hatred and menace in his voice, "Willie Joe's taking very good care of him. Did you think I was going to walk in here and let something like this happen and not be prepared? One wrong move out of you and the kid's had it. You know how Willie Joe can be if he gets riled."

J.R. sighed, "Okay, Jeb, you win."

Ames laughed softly, menacingly. "That's the way this game is played." He closed the attaché case. "I'll be going now, J.R. So far you've done everything just right. Don't spoil it for yourself."

J.R. made no reply.

"Soon as I leave here, with the money, Willie Joe will phone you and let you know where to pick up your baby."

The phone rang. J.R. snatched it up. "J.R. Ewing here." He listed carefully, eyes glued to Jeb Ames. "Thank you for calling," he said finally, and hung up.

"I'll be going now, J.R." Ames, the attaché case tucked under one arm, backed toward the door.

J.R. came swiftly around the desk, big hands reaching under his jacket and pulling out a .38. He jabbed it into Jeb Ames' middle. The attaché case fell to the floor, money spilling out.

"What the hell are you doing, J.R.? You gone crazy? Willie Joe, if he doesn't hear from me—"

J.R. slapped Ames across the face. Once, twice, three times, sending the other man reeling. J.R. followed, fist swinging. The blow caught Ames in the solar plexus; he bent double, gasping for air.

"Try to make a fool of me, did you? The baby's okay, Jeb. You never had him. If I had time to clear up the mess, I'd use this on you." J.R. tapped the pistol in his belt. "Now get your filthy ass out of my sight. I ever see you again, I'll bust your back."

"I'll go," Ames said. "But you're not rid of me, of us. You owe us, J.R. Garr and me, and one way or another, we aim to collect."

187

J.R. yanked the pistol out of his belt, and Jeb Ames fled. A relieved expression on his face, J.R. tucked the money back in the attaché case and hurried out of his office.

They were waiting for Priscilla in the living room. Pam cradled Baby John in her arms. "What's going to happen to her?"

It was Cliff who answered, his voice charged with sympathy. "She'll be sent for psychiatric help, probably. Poor kid. Husband running out on her. Baby dying. She's had a rough time."

"Don't worry," Bobby added. "Whatever we can do to help her, we will."

Priscilla entered the room carrying a coat and a hat. "I'm ready."

Bobby shepherded them toward the door, only to discover Cliff hanging back. "What is it, Cliff? You don't expect to stop us now, do you?"

"He's my son." Cliff's voice cracked; he was caught in an enormous emotional struggle.

"He's Sue Ellen's," Pam said. "Please, Cliff, don't make any more trouble. Not now."

Cliff nodded. "I won't. Not now. Not yet," he added, before leaving.

The sun had dropped low in the western sky by the time Bobby's Mercedes drove through the gates of Southfork. He pulled up into the garage area, Pam's Corvette right behind. With Priscilla—now carrying the baby—they went into the big house.

The rest of the family was waiting in the living room, along with Mrs. Reeves and Detective Rollands. They all rose as Bobby, Pam, and Priscilla came forward.

"Is he all right?" J.R. wanted to know.

"He's fine," Bobby reassured them all. "He's been well taken care of."

Miss Ellie moved toward the small group, as if to take the baby. It was Bobby who intercepted her, placing a restraining arm around his mother.

Pam spoke gently. "I'd like you all to meet Priscilla Duncan. This is Sue Ellen, Baby John's mother."

188

Priscilla looked into Sue Ellen's face and began to cry, still clutching the baby. "I'm sorry," she said. "I wanted to tell you myself, how sorry I am. I know I did a terrible thing, what I put you through. When they told me my baby was dead, I couldn't accept it. I just couldn't. I wanted him so much. I loved him so much. What happened after that—how I did what I did—I don't remember very much of it." She handed the baby over to Sue Ellen. "I'm sorry. I thought he must be mine. . . ."

Miss Ellie and Jock stared at Priscilla, all their anger at the kidnapper dissipating in a rush of pity and understanding. Everyone waited for Sue Ellen to respond.

She accepted the infant almost absently, as if her mind were somewhere else. Her eyes were dry and distant. A forced smile faded onto her mouth, was quickly gone.

"Thank you," she said tonelessly.

J.R. put his arm around Sue Ellen and gazed down at his son. For a brief interlude, they were the prototypical portrait of a handsome, happy American family. Sue Ellen shattered the image when she pulled away and handed the baby to Mrs. Reeves, glad to be rid of him. Without a word she marched out of the room, an almost jaunty bounce to her stride. A woman alone and lost.

PART 5

Miss Ellie

11

$\mathcal{I}$t was night, and the only light in the hospital room was a soft reading lamp beneath which sat a private-duty nurse, engrossed in a fashion magazine. On the bed, lying on her back staring sightlessly at the white ceiling, was Miss Ellie. There was no expression on her face, and she made no move. But her eyes were filled with tears.

Early the following morning, Bobby Ewing woke at first light. He shaved and showered and dressed quickly, trying not to wake Pam. It did no good.

She lay in bed watching him as he pulled on a pair of worn brown work boots. "You're up early," she said at last.

"So are you."

"You tossed all night. Were you dreaming?"

"Thinking about Momma. Guess you didn't get much sleep." He went over to her and sat on the edge of the bed. They touched fingers and kissed tenderly.

"I'm so worried about her."

"We all are."

She sat up and embraced him, clinging tightly. "Oh, Bobby, I can't help thinking—something like that could happen to any of us, to me."

"Hush, darling. You're young, you're healthy—"

"But I won't always be."

"I love you, I'll always love you."

She fell back on the pillow, face averted. "All this trouble

193

coming to Miss Ellie at one time—the surgery and learning about Jock's first marriage."

"That surprised us all."

"Have you ever been married before?" She spoke with childish directness.

He laughed. "Nobody'd have me, 'cept you. No, no hidden marriages or any other sinful occurrence."

"I'll bet. How many women have you had before me? Fifty? A hundred?"

He put on a mock scowl. "Hey, give credit where it's due—numbers run into the thousands."

She didn't find that amusing. "You're a very attractive man. Sometimes when I don't see you for a while, when you're in town or up in Austin with all those good-looking government girls, I get pretty damned concerned, I want you to know."

He cupped her face and gazed into her eyes. "I love you, I want only you. And you can depend on that."

"I love you, too."

They kissed lingeringly, and soon his hand moved up onto her breast. She shuddered, and he misunderstood, taking it for passion. He slid his hand under her gown, fingers embracing the firm, warm mound, caressing, aware of her nipple becoming hard and tense.

She broke away.

"What's wrong?"

"My God, Bobby! Your mother's just had a breast removed. How do you think that makes me feel?"

"I'm sorry. I didn't think. It's just that—" The sound of a car pulling into the parking area drew his attention. He went to the window. "It's Jock, he's finally home. I'm going to see if there's anything I can do."

Pam swung up out of bed. "I'll join you in a minute. And Bobby"—he turned her way—"I'm sorry. I love you, I want you. Just give me a little time to get used to what's happened."

He nodded and went out. He met his father coming up the stairs. "How's Momma?"

"She drifts in and out of consciousness. All those damned shots. But I think she understood when the doctors told her what they had to do."

"Did they say if they got all of the cancer?"

Jock's face seemed to melt. "They don't know that yet." He continued on upstairs, a man weary and carrying the years and his burdens heavily. He disappeared inside his room.

The car woke J.R. and Sue Ellen. He began preparing himself for the day at once. She sat up in bed, staring into space, lost in thoughts of Miss Ellie's ordeal.

J.R. came out of the bathroom and began putting on a tie. "You getting up now, Sue Ellen?"

"I was just thinking about Miss Ellie."

"She's going to be all right. She's going to."

"Saying it won't make it happen. Anyway, what are her chances? Really?"

"Don't think that way! Momma's going to live."

Sue Ellen lifted her eyes to his. "Sometimes just living is not enough."

The sound of a car engine starting up brought J.R. to the window. "Well, how about that! It's Daddy. A change of clothes and he's heading back to the hospital. That man hasn't slept at all."

"He loves her very much," Sue Ellen said quietly.

J.R. gave no sign that he'd heard, still looking out the window, his back turned toward his wife.

An hour later they all gathered at the breakfast table. Bobby tried to make conversation and received almost no reactions.

"Lucy, you're not eating much."

"I'm not hungry, Bobby."

"Right. I'll let you know when we leave for the hospital."

"I won't be going. I just can't."

"Why?"

In answer, Lucy fled the room.

"The girl is terrified," Pam said.

"So are we all," Sue Ellen said. She made a gesture. "I keep looking at those empty places—Jock's chair, Miss Ellie's chair, and I keep thinking—"

J.R. stood up angrily. "She's going to be all right, I tell you. Momma's going to be all right."

The words, however, reassured nobody.

An hour later Pam, dressed to go into Dallas and visit Miss Ellie, found Sue Ellen alone in the living room. Sue Ellen was also dressed for town.

"Did Bobby and J.R. leave?" Pam started out.

"Yes."

"And Lucy?"

"Somewhere around, I suppose."

"Why don't we have a little talk with her. The girl needs cheering up."

"Don't we all. You talk to her, if you like, Pam. By yourself."

"I thought you might want to help."

"I can't. Lucy—well, she won't ever listen to me."

"This is different. It's an emergency. The whole family is involved."

"I—just—can't—"

Pam stared at the other woman. "It isn't just Lucy, is it? Something else is bothering you."

"The girl doesn't like me."

Pam shook her head sadly. "You can't handle it any better than the rest of us, though you do pretend."

Sue Ellen drew up her chin. "I'm sure I don't know what you're talking about."

"I'm talking about Miss Ellie. About the operation. About the hard fact that she has had to have a breast removed."

"You're right. I don't want to talk about it, I don't intend to."

"But you must. You have to confront it, for your own sake. For Miss Ellie's sake."

"I can't deal with it."

"None of us likes it, Sue Ellen."

"Are you handling it so well?"

"I don't know."

"If it happened to you?"

"I hope I never have to find out."

Sue Ellen's mouth flattened out, and a spasm twisted her body. A harsh sound ripped out of her, half sob, half ironic laughter. "Do you know why J.R. fell in love with me?"

"You're beautiful, you're intelligent, you're—"

"I was Miss Texas. A beauty queen. Not just another good-looking Texas girl, but *the* Texas beauty. Queen of the

Lone Star State. Miss Perfect in the flesh. No flaws, no blemishes, no deficiencies of any kind. J.R. likes everything he owns to be the best. That was me—top of the line—"

"Love has to do with other things besides beauty."

"Oh, yes, I know about those things. Brains, charm, personality."

"Yes."

"Surely you don't believe that fairy tale for a minute."

"But I do."

"I haven't found a man yet who thinks of brains first when he looks at a woman."

"Sue Ellen, we don't exist just for men. We exist for ourselves first."

"Not if you're married to a Ewing."

"I am married to a Ewing."

"Then open your eyes. Around here, there are no plain but intelligent women. All of us are *beauties!* Blue ribbon winners. Just like the hogs and the steers and the bulls. Anything less won't be tolerated. The Ewing men come first on this ranch. I would have thought you'd learned that by now."

"You forget, I'm married to Bobby, not J.R."

"Bobby, J.R., Jock. All cut from the same bolt of cloth. Give them a couple of years, and they'll see you as one thing, too. Property. Bought and paid for, and you better make sure you're still wrapped in the perfect package!" She started out of the room.

"Sue Ellen—" Pam called.

She spoke over her shoulder, never pausing. "Maybe I'll see you at the hospital. Maybe . . ."

Alone, Pam sank into a chair, her mind reaching back in time early in her relationship with Bobby. It was only their second date, one of those sleek, slick evenings that only money coupled with fundamental good taste could arrange. Cocktails in a lush, dim lounge at the top of the Fairview Hotel; dinner and dancing at Fleur-de-lis, perhaps the best and surely the most expensive restaurant in the Dallas–Fort Worth area, complete with three different wines; and afterwards a nightcap at an after-hours club, with floor show. By the time Bobby took her home, she was tired, slightly lightheaded, and full of fanciful notions about the future. On her couch he kissed her, and for a microsecond she resisted. Then her lips parted to accept his tongue, and soon his hand was at her breast. Her arms went around him, and he opened her blouse and slid his hand over her naked breast. There was a rare, warm pleasure in his touch. Her excitement rose precipitously, and she turned toward him. Then she became aware of his hand under her skirt, and her thighs parted, his fingers sending delightful hot impulses up into her stomach.

She protested slightly.

"You're so beautiful," he had answered. "So incredible, your face, your body. The way you look and feel. You're the most perfect woman I've ever met—I want you so. . . ."

There was no way to stop him. No way she wanted to stop him. She was what he craved, and he was everything she had longed for in a man. Their lovemaking was passionate, bordering on violent, and wildly athletic. He was powerful and insatiable, and he kept telling her how much he desired her.

"You're perfect," he repeated again and again. "Perfect, absolutely perfect."

Now, recalling that night, Pam felt chilled and choked with despair. She knew all at once that too much of what Sue Ellen had said was true. The Ewing men possessed the Ewing women, kept and cherished them, forever and forever —as long as they were *perfect*.

12

By the time Bobby and J.R. reached Dallas Memorial, the heat had taken hold of the city again. Each day it lay over Texas like a thick, invisible pall, cracking the land, drying up the lakes and water holes, destroying livestock and people alike. That afternoon thunderheads would appear in the western sky, and rumbles would be heard, and flashes of lightning would be seen; but no rain would fall. The heat wave went on.

Inside the hospital the air, like everything else, was properly managed. Untroubled by outside reality, the hospital was a contained world of suffering and relief, of emotional upheaval and studied detachment, of life and death; a carefully constructed metaphor for life in all its varieties and shadings, all played out in clean white chambers and gleaming corridors.

Jock was seated on a straight-backed chair next to Miss Ellie's bed; she was asleep. He gave no indication that he was aware when Bobby and J.R. appeared. Bobby came up behind his father, dropping a hand to his slumping shoulder.

"How is she, Daddy?"

Jock shrugged. Look at her, the gesture seemed to say. Your mother, so weak and helpless, so beyond my help. To J.R., his father seemed older, worn down, a man on the verge of giving up. The thought terrified him.

"Daddy, Momma's going to be all right. All of us are."

Jock nodded, but there was nothing affirmative in the movement.

"Have you been able to talk to her yet?" Bobby asked.

This time Jock managed to answer. "She's only been awake for a few seconds at a time, too groggy to speak."

J.R. crouched down beside Jock. "Daddy, let's go out to the waiting room. We'll all be more comfortable there."

Jock looked at him with empty eyes. "Harlan said he'd be by with the lab report."

"He'll find us," Bobby assured the older man and led the way into the corridor. In the brighter light, Jock paused to blow his nose, to wipe his eyes, to struggle with his fear and weakness. He glanced from one son to another. "Boys, I really messed things up with your momma. Just at a time when she needed me most."

"You had no way of knowing. These things happen."

"Bobby, I'm not exactly sure of that. I felt Miss Ellie was fretting over something, something wasn't right. I had that feeling. I even asked her about it a couple of times. Of course she said she was all right, just fine, but I should've known. I wish to God it was me they cut up instead of her."

"Come on, Daddy," J.R. said. "Let's sit down."

Time passed slowly in the waiting room. They drank coffee. They smoked. They made desultory efforts to talk. Nothing worked. Each of them fell back into his worries, his terrors, unable to offer much help to the others.

Sue Ellen arrived, and for a brief interlude the mood was shattered. J.R. took her off to one side and sat with her.

"I was afraid you might not come," he said.

"I almost didn't."

"But you did, I'm glad you did."

"I'm scared, J.R."

"We all are."

She turned those great blue eyes on him, eyes that seemed to draw him inside her, into a dark pool from which there was no escaping, where there was no light or thought, only Sue Ellen's roiled emotions.

"For myself, I mean. What if something like that happened to me?"

"It won't."

She faced front again. "It happens to women regardless of age or shape or social standing. Your mother is the brave one—braver than all the rest of us put together. She shares her courage, gives it to us all. And some of us—the best of us—give back a little bit."

"I know what you mean. This is a difficult time. We have to be more caring, more loving with each other."

The words had a hollow ring in her ears. J.R. seemed capable of being all things to all people at various times, switching his goodness on and off as needed, lapsing back into the old mean, exploitive man that she'd come to know so well. She trusted neither his words nor his reactions. No matter what happened, no matter who was hurt or in danger, he was, after all, still J.R. Ewing.

"Pam talked to Lucy. She can't bring herself to come to the hospital. She's in a constant struggle with her anger. She feels she was lied to—"

"Lied to?"

"She was told it was a cyst, not cancer."

"So were we all."

"Lucy is young, afraid, and has the idea that it may be contagious or genetic, that she could catch—"

"That's ridiculous."

"Is it? What would you do, J.R., if I told you I had the same thing?" She glanced his way; there was a startled expression on his face. "An interesting prospect, isn't it, J.R.? But don't worry. There isn't a thing wrong with me. Not yet, there isn't."

They dropped back into silence. Jock stared off into space. Bobby tried to read a magazine, failed, and tried a newspaper instead. Sue Ellen took out the sweater she was knitting. J.R. went off to the nurse's station to use the telephone. Pam arrived looking trim, lovely, and cool, despite the temperature outside.

"Any news?" she asked Bobby.

"No."

Pam joined the others in silent vigil.

Soon Dr. Danvers entered the waiting room. They all rose, and J.R. hurried to join them.

"Did you get the report?" Jock asked.

"Yes, Mr. Ewing."

"The cancer," J.R. said anxiously. "Did you get it all?"

"Apparently the tumor was localized, and there's no sign that the malignancy has spread. Dr. Andrus also removed

201

twelve lymph nodes. The lab checked those, too. No cancer."

"Thank God," Pam breathed.

Bobby had a question. "Will she need chemotherapy or radiation therapy?"

"That's not indicated at this time. But your mother will have to be observed, naturally. The report is good, people."

Jock felt his knees give way, and he sat back down. He wanted to cry, but it was not something he had ever learned to do.

"I looked in on your wife, Mr. Ewing. She's been sleeping on and off for quite a while. You folks ought to take a break, have some lunch."

"I'll stay with Miss Ellie," Jock said.

"Whatever you wish. I'll talk to you later."

They waited until the doctor was gone before anyone spoke again. "You all get some food in you," Jock said.

"I'll head on back to the office," J.R. said.

"I think lunch is a good idea," Bobby said. "How about you, Pam?"

"Sue Ellen?" Pam asked.

"I want to phone Lucy first, tell her the good news."

"Meet you outside," Bobby said.

Sue Ellen went looking for a pay phone and placed her call. A man answered.

"May I speak to Dusty Farlow?" she asked tentatively.

"He's out just now. Who's callin'?"

"Just tell him a friend."

"You want to leave your name, lady?"

"He'll know. Tell him I'll call back."

"Whatever you say—friend."

Alan Beam came out of Barnes for Congress Headquarters with a couple of volunteer campaign workers, both attractive young women.

"You ladies get out to the plant before lunch time and distribute those flyers. Knock a few up on walls, telephone poles, and the like. Spread the word and keep me informed."

"Will do, Alan," one of the volunteers answered happily. "I just know that Cliff Barnes is going to win."

"It's why we're all here," Alan said softly to their retreating backs. He started back inside when he saw a familiar face coming his way. "Lucy!" he called. "Lucy Ewing, is that you?"

A broad smile split her cheerleader's face. "Hello, Alan Beam. What an unexpected pleasure."

"What are you doing in this neighborhood?"

"Just walking. I've been doing some shopping."

She carried no bags, no packages.

"Shopping?" he said dubiously.

"I said shopping, not buying."

He grinned. "Well, I'm glad you happened by. I've been meaning to call you."

"But you didn't."

He waved a hand to indicate the headquarter's storefront with its posters of Cliff Barnes, its banner and window cards. "This is not designed to give any Ewing pleasure and profit."

"You working for Barnes?"

"You might say I'm the head honcho."

"You're trying to get Cliff Barnes elected to Congress because of J.R.?"

"I don't expect any of the Ewings to approve."

She looked him over admiringly. "Not only did you stand up to J.R. at the rodeo, but now you're backing the man he hates most. Congratulations."

Alan was not quite sure how to take Lucy. Blond and beautiful, voicing hostile sentiments toward her uncle, and apparently making herself very available to him. It was a prospect—and an oppotunity—he found difficult to resist. And decided not to.

"What is it between you and your uncle?" he asked.

She looped her arm through his, breast pressing tightly against his biceps. "Why don't you show me around?"

"A Ewing in Barnes campaign headquarters. Might cause a scandal."

"I can think of a number of different ways to cause a scandal. And any will do, if I can get to feel less like a Ewing."

"If that's what you want."

"Right now, more than anything else."

Miss Ellie very gradually came out of the drugged stupor, not quite fully awake, no longer asleep. Her eyes fluttered open, and she became aware of Jock hovering over her. She said his name.

."Miss Ellie," he said huskily, "we got the report back. They got all the cancer out of you. You are going to be your old self again."

"That can never be true."

He bent to kiss her, and she turned away from him.

— 13 —

The next morning, Pam joined her brother and her father for breakfast in Cliff's apartment. Digger, still wearing his old wool bathrobe, grizzled, unkempt, looking much as he must have looked when he labored as a roustabout in the oil fields, put his fork down and gazed balefully at his two children.

"When did she have the surgery?"

"Day before yesterday," Pam said.

"That's rough," Cliff said.

"Why wasn't I told?" Digger said heatedly.

"I'm telling you now, Daddy."

"I mean right away? Miss Ellie and me, we go back a long time, dammit. I loved that woman, guess I do love her still. You should have let me know."

"The doctors say she's going to be all right," Pam offered.

"She damned well better be." He pushed himself away from the table. "I gotta go see her."

Pam shook her head. "Daddy, I don't think that's a very good idea. Send her a card or maybe some flowers—"

Digger glared down at his daughter. "Dammit, girl. Can't you understand how I feel about Miss Ellie? How I've felt about her for more'n forty years? I'm gonna see her first thing is what I'm gonna do."

He went into the bedroom to change clothes, leaving his children behind. "He really does love her," Pam said.

"He loved Momma, too."

"Did he, Cliff? I don't think I've ever heard him say as

much. When he talks about her, which isn't very often, it's with a kind of reverence, a nostalgia for someone and something pleasant, but hardly overwhelming. He seems to feel a genuine passion for Miss Ellie."

"I suppose. Ellie Ewing was always someone special for Digger. His first love, and he lost her. Don't be too hard on him, Pam. Ever since the Ewing rodeo, he's had a rough time. Seeing Miss Ellie that day had a profound effect on him."

"Cliff, he lives here with you. You should have stopped him from going out to Southfork that day."

"He had a right to see his grandchild."

"Not like that."

"Any way at all."

"You weren't there to see Daddy swallow his pride and allow Jock to go on believing that Baby John is truly a Ewing."

"And who, my dear sister, was all for that cover-up of the truth—you were!"

"I didn't intend for Daddy to be hurt."

"Well, hurt he was. Enough to topple him back off the wagon."

"You mean he's drinking again?"

"I had to pull him out of a saloon last night. Fortunately I got there before he had too much. He's all right today."

"But for how long?"

"Let's face it, Pam, I can't watch him night and day. I have my own life to lead."

"I sometimes wonder about that life, what you're so busy doing. Bobby has picked up information in Austin that you've been getting under-the-table payoffs from some of the other oil companies."

"That's insane."

"Is it? The word is you accept bribes to stay off their backs while you make public points at the expense of Ewing Oil."

"And you believe that!"

"The Ewings have some very valuable leases. If they go under, those leases will be up for grabs. The other companies will be able to snatch them up for next to nothing. That way, you'll—" She broke off when Digger came out of the bedroom dressed in his best suit and tie.

"Hold on a minute," Cliff said.

"Daddy," Pam cried. "You look beautiful, but where do you think you're going?"

"Out. Just out."

"I'll give you a lift," Cliff said.

"I'll take the bus."

"Why are you all dressed up?"

"Say, what is this? I'm a grown man, free to come and go as I like. See you all later."

"You're not going to the hospital, Daddy," Pam said.

"Is that so? And who's going to stop me? Nobody around here, for sure."

"Daddy," Cliff said, "it's not a good idea. You're going to be hurt again."

"Miss Ellie's an old friend. She's sick. I am going to visit her, and there's no sense arguing the point."

Pam stood up. "Jock is bound to be there. He hardly leaves her side."

Digger shook his head doggedly. "Ain't aimin' to cause trouble. Just want to see the lady is all."

"Please don't go," Pam said.

"I am not a child," he replied roughly. "And I don't intend for anybody to run my life for me. And that is a fact of all our lives."

When he was gone, Pam turned to Cliff. "There's going to be trouble."

"I'd stake my life on it."

There were floral arrangements lining the walls of Miss Ellie's room, elaborate and expensive expressions of good will, as well as bouquets, potted plants, and boxes of candy.

"Jock," she murmured.

He came from his chair to stand at her side. "We were talking, and you dozed right off."

"I don't remember."

"It doesn't matter."

"It must be those shots they give me for the pain."

"How are you feeling?"

"I'm not sure. My mind sort of spins around, filled with disbelief that this happened to me, then resentment, anger, a lot of sadness."

207

"You're alive and still with me."

"Am I, Jock?"

" 'Course you are."

She decided not to pursue that line of thought. "My arm feels numb."

"I'll call the nurse, maybe she can give you something to help."

"No."

He took her hand. "Ellie, there's something I've got to say, to clear the air."

"Don't, Jock, not now."

"I never lied to you about anything or anyone else. Believe me. But if I remember back in those old days, I was competing with Digger for you. I was afraid if I told you about Amanda, about being married once before, I'd lose you."

"Jock. Please, no more. I don't want to hear any more. Please, leave me alone now. I need to be alone." She turned her face away, and after a moment, without saying another word, he padded out of the room, wondering what future remained to him and Miss Ellie.

___ 14 ___

They went to lunch at Brennan's in Main Place. It was already crowded when they arrived, but the maitre d' recognized Bobby instantly and led him to a choice table. They ordered drinks and the specialty of the day for lunch.

"Will you have time to go to the hospital after we eat?" Bobby asked Pam.

"Yes. I told them at The Store, I'm taking an extra hour or so off. Now you can fill me in about your conversation with Jock this morning."

The waiter brought their drinks, and Bobby waited until he was gone before answering. "He was in better spirits. Momma's coming along fine, he said. And he thinks maybe their fight is over."

"Maybe?"

"That's what the man said. But you know Daddy. Where Miss Ellie's concerned, he wants things to go smoothly. He really loves that woman."

"Oh, I hope so. Miss Ellie is going to need Jock now. The hardest part is still ahead of her."

"I guess that's so."

"Their marriage has been so good until now. Bobby, do you think he'll stick by her?"

"Of course he will. What are you saying?"

"I mean—really be *there?*"

"That's a hell of a thing to ask, Pam."

"Well, I've been wondering. Worrying is more like it."

"About what?"

She debated whether to give him a straight answer but opted for the truth. "The morning after Miss Ellie was operated on, Sue Ellen said some terrible things about Ewing men."

"That's Sue Ellen."

"Yes. But it made me think. Do you think I'm perfect?"

He grinned. "On a scale of one to one hundred, you're a solid ninety-nine."

"But not perfect?" She was laughing now.

"Not—quite."

She sobered quickly. "What if there were something wrong with me? What if what happened to your mother happened to me? How would you feel about that?"

"That's a dumb question, Pam," he said gently.

"Maybe it is, but I need an answer. At a time like this, I feel kind of unsure."

"You are my wife. I love you. I want you. I will always love and want you, no matter what."

"No matter what?"

"*No matter what.*"

She squeezed his hand across the table.

"Listen to me, Pam, you are married to me, not to J.R. Always remember that. And remember this, my daddy will stick by my momma. Not out of duty or loyalty only, but because he loves her. Theirs was a love match, not a marriage of convenience like your daddy wants to believe."

Pam clamped her eyes shut, and when she opened them again, they were moist. "Digger is going to try and see Miss Ellie today. Cliff and I couldn't talk him out of it."

"That's too bad. But it's something my folks are going to have to deal with. How has Digger been lately?"

"Cliff says he's been drinking again. Not much. But it doesn't take much. Cliff's not much help. He has his head in the clouds over the thought of getting elected to Congress."

"Yes, I heard about the Draft Barnes movement. Is he really going to ride it all the way?"

"He tells me there are some important people putting it to him. People who believe he can be elected. And you know who's running the entire affair? Alan Beam."

Bobby made no effort to conceal his surprise. "I didn't know his trouble with J.R. went that deep."

"There must have been more to that fight at Southfork than we realized."

"Begins to look that way, doesn't it?"

Miss Ellie was sitting up in the bed, pillows puffed softly at her back, wearing a pink satin bed jacket, hand-embroidered with flying doves. She no longer required a private nurse, and a hospital orderly was removing the dinner tray.

"You didn't eat very much, Mrs. Ewing."

"It's hard to work up an appetite for what they call soup around here."

The orderly laughed. "Tomorrow you can have solid food."

"Do I get to order?"

"I bet I know what it would be—a nice juicy T-bone."

"On the money. What do I get?"

"Boiled chicken."

"Yuch," Miss Ellie said, as the orderly withdrew.

Digger entered the still-open door, carrying a small bouquet of flowers. "Hey, is this some kind of a nightclub, all the joking and laughing? It's true what they say—you can't keep a good woman down."

She examined him standing at the foot of the bed with a reaction akin to relief. Those squinty eyes, that wiry gray beard, that rasping voice. "It's so good to see you, Digger."

"Ain't that nice to hear. It's good to see you, Ellie. Your color's high, your eyes are shining—pretty as ever. Can't be much that's wrong with you."

He came down to where she lay and kissed her on the cheek. Chaste, proper, lingering.

"What a nice surprise," she said.

"Would've come around earlier, but nobody tells me what's going on. Here, these are for you. Flowers."

"Wild flowers. Did you pick them yourself?"

"Can't afford no long-stemmed roses."

"They're beautiful."

"I remembered the way you used to look when you picked flowers in the fields, your face all lit up and glowing. Oh, my, Ellie, you were the prettiest thing I ever did see."

She smelled the bouquet. "These mean more to me than all those fancy arrangements."

"You mean that, Ellie?"

"Did you ever know me to say anything I didn't mean?"

"There was one time when I wished you had lied. When you told me you were going to marry Jock Ewing."

"Ah, Digger, when are you going to accept what is and has been for forty years?"

"Never, I reckon. Don't see no reason to accept what causes me grief. Don't you still feel something for me, Ellie?"

"That's not a fair question."

"Don't mean to be fair. But I'll let it go, for now. When you're out of here and feeling sprightly again, I'll ask you again."

"Digger," she began, as if in warning.

He interrupted quickly. "I don't want to tire you out. I'll call you when you're back home."

"I'm glad you came to visit."

"Kids tried to talk me out of it, but I wasn't having any. You're still the most beautiful woman in the world, Ellie."

"You truly believe that, Digger?"

"Always did, always will, and there ain't nothing wrong with my eyes."

"You know," she said softly, "I am not the same any more."

"That's a lot of hogwash. 'Course you are."

"I'm a lot older and—"

"Older means better. Like vintage wine, Ellie. The best parts of you have only gotten better. I'll be in touch, lady, depend on it."

He swung jauntily out of her room and down the corridor, not aware that Jock had been standing just outside the door, privy to every word. Jock, impressed with his own nobility and generosity, pleased that he had allowed Digger this one brief moment with Miss Ellie, went inside.

Miss Ellie, experiencing mixed emotions over Digger's visit, looked up. "Digger was just here. Did you see him?"

"I hope his visit didn't upset you too much."

"Upset me! Why would you think that? And why didn't you come in, if you knew he was here."

"Thought you two would like a little time by your own selves, is why."

"That never stopped you before. What's changed, Jock? Is

it me, that I'm different now? That you care less now that I'm less of a woman?"

"Don't talk that way, Miss Ellie. I love you, I always have. I didn't interrupt because Digger always sets me off with his moaning and groaning about the Ewings. Figured if I didn't talk to him I wouldn't get teed off."

"He only came because he still cares."

"You believe that? If it wasn't me that you married, he would have been out of your life a long time ago."

"Whatever Digger's shortcomings, he was always honest with me. Which is more than you've been, Jock."

He straightened up as if struck. "Digger's a blowhard and a liar and a bull artist from way back. And I don't like you defending him to my face and making me out to be some kind of an evil man."

She stared him straight in the eye. "You can be callous, Jock. Cruel and deceitful. And right now I do not want to be around you very much. So please leave me. At once."

It was an extremely troubled man who left the room. And behind him, an angry woman who wanted very much to cry and couldn't. Sad for a hundred reasons large and small and feeling extremely sorry for herself.

PART 6

Past Imperfect

*I*t was a Tuesday evening, and darkness had begun to envelop Dallas, turning the streets and highways into jewellike strings of slowly advancing lights as the citizens struggled to make their way home. High above the traffic noise, J.R. sat confidently at his office desk, making a phone call.

"That's right, the Golden Horseshoe Restaurant. Just be sure and get there on time. Wouldn't want you to miss any of the festivities. A Ewing party is like no other. See you then."

Kristin Shephard, remarkably pretty and sinuous, with smoldering eyes and a sullen set to her voluptuous mouth, entered his office, placing herself provocatively against the wall, belly outthrust, watching him from under heavy lids. Recently installed as J.R.'s second secretary, Kristin had made herself quickly at home.

But despite her most enthusiastic efforts, in bed and out, Kristin found that she remained outside of J.R.'s most favored circle. Too often he reminded her that her position was second to his family, second to his work, second to his overweening self-interest. Despite all her scheming, Kristin went on accepting the crumbs of his life, financially, sexually, socially. She warned herself not to do anything to jeopardize her tenuous position, but a powerful ambition and need for prestige drove her to take more chances than was wise.

"What time will the party be over?" she asked.

He shrugged into his jacket and adjusted the big white sombrero squarely on his head. "Between ten and eleven, I'd say." He started to leave.

She put a detaining hand on his arm. "Then I'll see you tonight?"

He planted a perfunctory kiss on her cheek. "Sorry, darlin', it'll have to wait. Tonight is family night. First things first."

Kristin, alone in the office, was overwhelmed by a sudden sense of insecurity, of rejection, of loneliness. It occurred to her that despite her best efforts, she belonged nowhere, to no one.

Except herself.

The Golden Horseshoe was one of Dallas's most fashionable, most expensive, and most observed restaurants. If it happened at the Golden Horseshoe, it was bound to find its way into the newspapers or the gossip segments of the nighttime TV news. It was where the richest people in the area were likely to show up, the most notorious—and not always the ones you'd care for the most. It was not the place Jock would have selected, or Bobby; but then it was J.R. who had made all the arrangements.

All the Ewings were in attendance at a great round table strategically placed, with Jock clearly in the seat of honor. Dinner was over, and coffee and brandy had been served. Some were smoking, and all were waiting for Jock to open the pile of festively wrapped packages in front of him.

Bobby was making a toast. "To a man who knows more about life on the range and inside the family than anyone I ever met. To a man of strength and wit and intelligence—to my daddy, one hell of a father!"

There were yips of agreement, applause, and cries of approval. Glasses were raised, and a cake was brought out by a beautiful young woman escorted by a quartet of waiters who sang "Happy Birthday." More cheering followed as Jock blew out the candles and made the first cut.

"Happy birthday," Miss Ellie cried, and they all drank again to that. Jock rose to his feet and looked around.

"Got to thank you all for this first-rate party you've given me tonight. Makes a man feel real good to have his family all around him at a time like this. When I look at you all sitting there, I know I must have done something right with my life."

That evoked a round of good-natured hooting and hollering. Jock went on, unaware that behind him Alan Beam, and a party of friends, had just entered the Golden Horseshoe.

"I'm proud of this family," Jock said, "and expect I always will be. However—" Another burst of laughter.

Alan Beam, a Draft Barnes for Congress button on his lapel, changed course when he spotted the Ewings and made straight for their table.

"However," Jock went on, "don't let it go to your heads. Ain't a Ewing don't have his faults, some worse than others, and that includes this old party, too."

Alan Beam stopped beside Jock. "Sorry to interrupt, Mr. Ewing."

Jock fixed him with a steady glance. "Then don't do it, boy."

Alan went on as if he hadn't heard. "I've been wanting to explain—"

Bobby caught his father's eye; the same thought had occurred to them both—whatever was going on, J.R. surely was behind it.

As if to exonerate himself of any complicity, J.R. stood up and spoke in a loud voice. "This is a private party, Beam. Trot your butt out of here."

"I just want to say," Alan continued blandly, "that I'm still employed by Smithfield and Bennett, Mr. Ewing. They're your lawyers. I wouldn't want any hard feelings—"

J.R. moved toward the young lawyer. "Your presence here is not welcome."

Replied Alan, "What happened that day at the rodeo was a misunderstanding. I—"

J.R. indicated the button on Alan's jacket. "That advertisement for Cliff Barnes tells us where your sentiments lie. Or is that a misunderstanding, too?"

Alan answered stiffly, as if growing angry. "My political beliefs are my own business, J.R. This is still America, and that's the American way."

"Business is just the right word. How much is Barnes paying for your loyalty? It must be plenty. I paid you a fortune and discovered loyalty didn't come with the job."

"Too bad you never learned you can't buy loyalty, J.R. You have to inspire it. You couldn't inspire a dog to sit up and beg."

Tension rippled around the table, everyone embarrassed yet curious. Sue Ellen straightened up so as not to miss anything. Lucy enthralled, silently cheered Alan Beam on, hoping he would do something rash and wonderful. Jock, face screwed up in silent disbelief, vowed to talk about this with J.R.; certainly a charade of this sort could have been performed at a more propitious moment. Bobby was resentful, determined not to get involved and at the same time aware that if things got out of hand, he'd be forced to step in.

J.R. took a long, threatening step toward Alan. "I told you once to get out of here. I am not going to tell you again."

Alan replied with considerable heat, not backing off an inch. "This is a public place. You don't own it, and you don't own me or tell me what to do."

J.R. reached for him. Alan brushed aside his hand and raised his own, as if to throw a punch. J.R. slid ahead, and Alan swung, the blow catching J.R. on the lip. J.R. roared with anger and rushed forward.

Bobby sighed, pushed back his chair, and went to the rescue. He twisted Alan's arm behind his back almost effortlessly, shoving the slender man off to one side and holding him in place. At the same time he restrained J.R. with his other hand.

"That's enough!" he said.

"Damned right it is," Jock growled. "Won't have a couple of bobcats spoiling my birthday party. You want to tangle, do it somewhere else."

Bobby felt the tension go out of Alan's body, and he released him. "My apologies to the rest of you," the lawyer said. "J.R., you haven't heard the last of me, not by a long shot."

"Sorry, Daddy," J.R. said, glaring after Beam's retreating back.

"Agh," Jock muttered, "let's forget it and just go home."

Later that night, watching Miss Ellie remove her jewelry at her night table, Jock was in an expansive mood. He'd put the nastiness between Alan Beam and J.R. out of his mind and was remembering only the good, warm feelings the evening had engendered.

"Seems to me birthdays don't mean much to a man, except when he's very young and getting purty long in the tooth. That was just about a perfect night for me. And being with you, Miss Ellie, didn't hurt a mite. Got to tell you, as usual, you were the best-looking girl in the room." He went up behind her and kissed the back of her neck. She held herself very still, not so much waiting for him to go on as anxious for him to leave her alone. Jock didn't notice the change in her mood. "Here, let me help you get out of that thing."

"I can do it," she said with considerable coolness.

He laughed. "No need for you to exert yourself, when you've got me to wait on you."

"I said I can do it."

He backed off and watched as she awkwardly turned the necklace to the point where she was able to reach the clasp comfortably. He decided to ignore the rebuff.

"Remember when we were first married, Miss Ellie. We'd take a bottle of fine wine up to bed and stay awake half the night talking and the other half making love. Those were good days, great days. I miss you, Ellie. I miss the way we were."

She looked at him as if about to reply when they heard Baby John begin to wail. Ellie rose and started out. He said her name. But she kept going. Jock stood staring at the doorway, empty and more than a little bit frightened.

The following morning J.R. was in an expansive mood. He dressed and left his room without exchanging a single harsh word with Sue Ellen, humming a tune as he descended to a good breakfast. Bobby appeared on the steps behind him.

"That was quite a scene you staged last night, J.R."

J.R. looked back over his shoulder, grinning cheerfully. "Are you so sure it was staged?"

"I ought to know you by now."

"I expect so, little brother. I thought it went off rather well myself. I'm sure it will serve its purpose."

"All that to make an impression on Cliff Barnes?"

"For Alan Beam to impress Cliff Barnes."

"You think he's dumb enough to go for it?"

"Why not? He fell for the rodeo argument. The man is willing and anxious to believe Beam is on his side. He wants power, position, and Alan has him convinced he can get it. With my help he may—come close, that is." Laughing, he snatched the morning paper off the table in the hallway and went out onto the patio, Bobby at his heels.

Breakfast was being served buffet-style, and Pam was already seated and eating. Lucy was at the buffet, heaping scrambled eggs onto a plate. J.R. went directly to the table, filled a cup with hot black coffee, and opened the newspaper.

"Well, what do you know," he gloated. "Seems as if we made the society page."

"That scene in the restaurant last night?" Pam asked.

"You got it, sister-in-law."

Lucy leaned over J.R.'s shoulder. "Picture and all. Now listen to this," she said grinning. "Says here Alan Beam would have wiped J.R. out if Grandpa hadn't stopped him."

J.R. frowned. "That is not exactly how it's put, sugar. Here is a precise and truthful reading—'The timely intervention of Bobby and Jock Ewing saved the patrons of the Golden Horseshoe from witnessing their favorite dining place being laid waste with a brawl between J.R. Ewing and Smithfield and Bennett attorney Alan Beam.'

"There's more, want me to go on?"

"That won't be necessary," Bobby answered. "Since we all witnessed your moment of triumph."

"Personally," Lucy said, eyes glowing, "I thought Alan was super."

"Alan?" J.R. said thoughtfully. "Don't get any ideas about that boy, Lucy. He is not a friend to this family."

She stared him down. "When I require advice on my private life, J.R., you'll be the last to know."

Sue Ellen, wearing a dress that set off her lush figure, took her place at the table. Bobby, his plate loaded with food, joined them.

"Morning, darlin'," J.R. greeted his wife, as if seeing her for the first time. "My, you're up and around early and looking just lovely, I might add. Got yourself someone special to see in town today, honey?"

"Dr. Ellby, as you very well know."

"Lucky man, seeing you at your best. Man's got a reputation as a top-of-the-line headshrinker and a lover of beautiful women."

She frowned. "I see Dr. Ellby four times a week in what is a purely professional relationship, as you well know, J.R."

"Never doubted either one of you for a moment." He

laughed. "Four times a week. Dr. Ellby is Sue Ellen's new medical charity. The contributions are regular and lavish."

"Whatever I pay Dr. Ellby he earns, J.R. Just as you do." Without a backward glance, she left.

Bobby spoke without looking at his brother. "J.R., if anyone ever accuses you of being a sensitive and understanding man, you just punch him out, hear."

"Maybe you like her telling Ewing secrets to strangers," J.R. said sullenly. "I do not."

"Not Ewing secrets," Lucy said with a certain maliciousness. "J.R.'s secrets, and I'll bet some of them make juicy listening, too."

Alan Beam was poring over some books at the Draft Barnes Headquarters when a young boy came in carrying coffee in a plastic cup and a couple of doughnuts in a napkin.

"Here you go, Mr. Beam, breakfast."

Alan found a dollar in his pocket and handed it over. "Thanks, Jimmy. Keep the change. Say, wait a minute! Jimmy, you want to sign up for Mr. Barnes?" He extended a second dollar bill.

"Ain't I too young?"

"Don't ask too many questions and put your name and address on this line."

"That's all?" Jimmy took a proffered pen.

"That's all."

"A dollar a shot, why not?" He signed his name with a ten-year-old flourish. "There!"

"Thanks."

"Any time. For a buck." He skipped out the door. Alone again, Alan entered Jimmy's name into his ledger and added $15.00 after it. This done, he attended his coffee. It was lukewarm, weak, but would have to do. He began studying a computer list of registered voters. From this list he was beginning to compile a roster of "contributors" that would stand up to any cursory inspection Cliff Barnes might care to give it. He was moving along at a good pace when the door to his office opened again. He raised his head and saw Lucy Ewing standing there.

"Lucy! What are you doing here? J.R. send you around?"

She laughed. "If you believe that, you'd believe the moon is made of green cheese. I came to make a contribution to Barnes's campaign."

She dropped a hundred dollar bill on the desk. He eyed it suspiciously.

"This is a lot of money. Are you sure?"

"I'm sure."

"Thank you. Very much. Want to sit down?"

She did, watching him with a faint glint of amusement in her eyes. Blond, petite, and full-bodied, Lucy knew how men felt about her; how much they desired her; and how pleased they were if she permitted them to make love to her. And from the expression on Alan's face, it was clear that he was not much different from the rest.

"This is quite a surprise," he said. "I don't think J.R. would approve."

"There are any number of things I do that J.R. would not approve of. Shall I give you a rundown?"

He wet his lips. "If I knew too much, I might squeal."

"I don't think so," she said speculatively.

"You're right. J.R. and I rarely speak, and never without fighting."

"We seem to have a great deal in common."

He looked her over boldly. This was the second time she had come on to him. Circumstances had prevented him from responding before, but now . . . . "Anything I can get you? Some coffee?"

"I don't have much time. I'm on my way to school. I just wanted to get another look at the man who's giving J.R. so much trouble."

"You could take an even better and longer look over lunch."

"Oh, I can't." She was genuinely disappointed. "I've got cheerleading practice."

"That's what I'd like," he said aggressively, "to get a good look at you in one of those brief costumes."

"Come and see for yourself."

"Maybe we can arrange a private showing."

She hesitated, and he wondered if he'd gone too fast too soon. "All things are possible," she said, standing.

"Since you can't make lunch, what do you say to dinner? Tonight?"

"I say great." Then her face fell. "Oh, shoot! I've been grounded. Three speeding tickets in two weeks. But maybe I can work on my granddaddy."

"You do that and let me know." He handed her his card. "Call me at home around six, if you can make it."

"Oh, I'll make it. I'm very good at handling Granddaddy."

"I'll bet you are. Talk to you later."

"Later," she echoed, making it sound like a promise.

Dr. Ellby was attractive, tweedy, the kind of man women feel safe in confiding to. He was also quiet and withdrawn, not so much sitting in judgment as waiting patiently for life to unfold. His office matched the man: leather and polished wood, books along two walls, sedately curtained windows. He sat at his ease in his Eames lounge chair, sucking on an unlit pipe, a legal pad in his lap, a pen in his hand. Dr. Ellby was at work.

Sue Ellen was angry and let it out. She slammed the arm of her chair. She stamped her foot and changed her position.

"He makes me so mad!" she cried. "He puts down everything I do or want. Do you know what he called you? Well, do you?"

"No way I could know, is there Sue Ellen?"

"He said you were my new medical charity, as if I were your only source of income."

"Does that trouble you?"

"It makes me mad, I told you."

"What else?"

"What else? This—he wanted me to go to a shrink, insisted that I was emotionally unstable, that I required help. When I follow his instructions, he mocks it, makes fun of you and of me."

"How does that make you feel?"

"Are you kidding? Lousy, is how. Rotten. As if I'd like to kill. Wipe that bastard off the face of the earth."

"Would you say you hate your husband?"

225

"Hate is too weak a word. Oh, God, I don't know any more what I feel or what I want. I'm so confused." She leaned forward anxiously. "You're not upset, are you?"

"About what?"

"About being called a medical charity."

"I'm not upset."

"You don't mind that I told you?"

"You're here to tell me whatever you want to tell me. Besides, what J.R. says doesn't matter. What you believe does. For example, do you feel our therapy is working?"

She shuddered. "Besides saving my life, you mean?"

"You feel I've saved your life?"

She lapsed into a long silence, and he waited. "Well," she said at last, "you've helped me see that I'm a person, an independent human being with her own desires and hopes and fears. Not just Mrs. J.R. Ewing."

"Go on," he urged, when she stopped.

"Why do I stay there with him? J.R. and I hardly even speak any more. And I'm a stranger to my baby, poor little thing."

"That will come in time."

"Will it? I hope so. But every time I look at Baby John I think about J.R. and about Cliff and remember how both of them used me. Sometimes I wish neither of them had ever been inside my body, had never been intimate with me. I wish someone else had fathered my child."

"Anyone in particular?"

She felt her cheeks grow warm. "Yes."

"Someone you actually know?"

"Yes."

"Does he have a name?"

"Must I tell you?"

"No, but it would make it easier if we had some polite way of referring to him."

"Dusty."

"His name has come up before."

"Dusty Farlow."

"You've slept with Dusty?"

"Oh, no, nothing like that."

"But you want to?"

"Yes."

"Does he want to sleep with you?"

"I—yes, I'm sure he does."

"What's stopping you?"

"I'm afraid."

"Afraid of what?"

"That he'll be another Cliff Barnes. Another J.R."

"If that's what you think of him, why not simply write him off?"

"Oh, I couldn't. I care about Dusty. I love to be in his company. But I haven't been able to really show him how I feel."

"You don't trust Dusty because you've learned to mistrust men. You're going to have to learn to take chances again, to trust again, to live fully again, Sue Ellen. That takes time and work and courage."

"I don't think I've got either the strength or the courage left, doctor."

"We'll find that out, won't we?"

She didn't answer. She wasn't sure she wanted to find it out. Or anything else about herself.

Cliff Barnes and Alan Beam sat on the couch in Cliff's apartment examining a list of names. Barnes had concluded that it would be a tactical error for them to meet at this point in some public place. "Until I'm a declared candidate," he explained, "it is better for this draft movement to be entirely in the hands of others."

Now Alan was detailing the burgeoning support for Cliff's candidacy. "Here's a letter of support from the Clinton County Ecology Club."

Cliff read it through. "Too bad most of these people are too young to vote."

Alan ducked his head. "Okay, so it's a high-school club. But it's a dramatic indication of the grass-roots support you inspire. They have a subtle and lasting influence on their parents, remember that."

"A good point."

"And high schools being what they are nowadays, some of these kids are over eighteen already."

He indicated the contributors' list he had compiled. "Here's an interesting name. Jimmy Monroe. A black kid, lives in the ghetto. Works as a delivery boy, scratching out a living. Yet he walked all the way over to Barnes Headquarters to sign up for you, make a fifteen-dollar contribution."

"That's very touching," Cliff said, taking the list. He read off some of the names. "Roberto Mendez, $15. Jesus Alvarez, $10. Luiz Romero, $10."

"They're all for you, those and more. All races, all social classes, all economic levels. I tell you this thing is building."

Cliff wanted to believe it, wanted to accept the idea that there was a tide of voter activity in his behalf, that he was the great new hope of the people. "They know only with someone like me representing them do they have any chance at all against the big guys. They know I'll fight for them and win for them. You're doing a great job, Alan."

"Thanks, but I've about reached the outer limits of what's possible. Until you declare, that is. Once you do, I can really get down to work and launch this campaign into outer space."

"I'm not sure yet."

"What are you worried about?"

Cliff answered thoughtfully. "In order to declare, I've got to quit my job at OLM. What if I lose? Then I'm out in the cold with no power base."

"You aren't going to lose."

"Last time I ran for public office I took a whipping."

"Last time. You were caught unaware. No pre-planning. No strong organizing force behind you. No attention to detail. Not enough funding. All that is changed now. This time out you'll have your battle plan prepared, all the logistical problems ironed out up front."

"You are very convincing, Alan."

"Then declare," Alan urged.

Cliff hesitated. "Alan, I'm a human being like any other; with the entire range of personal foibles and quirks. There are things in my past I'm not proud of. A woman I loved died during an illegal abortion. That is a constant prod to my conscience, and on a pragmatic level—well, it's just not going to go away."

"True enough. But don't underestimate the good sense of

the voters. They won't hold you responsible for what happened. Believe me, Cliff, this thing is snowballing. You aren't going to get another chance as good as this one. All the signs are right, all systems are go."

"I'll think about it some more."

"Make it soon, Cliff."

"Don't push me, Alan."

"Urging, not pushing. Advising, not pushing. The field is wide open to you. Pass this by and you pass by what amounts to a sure thing."

"I'll make my decision when I'm ready."

"Of course. As long as it's soon."

"Yes," Cliff said. "Soon."

Alan understood he was being dismissed. He headed for the door. "By the way, I imagine you saw that item about me and J.R. in the papers?"

"I saw it," Cliff said dryly.

Alan spoke with pretended embarrassment. "I suppose I should apologize, to you at least. If you think my behavior last night might reflect badly on your campaign, I'm willing to bow out right now."

"You're my boy, Alan. It's no disgrace to do battle with J.R. Ewing. Or any of the Ewings, for that matter. As far as I'm concerned, it's a badge of honor. Keep up the good work."

Alan gave his most boyish, ingratiating grin. "I'm with you, Cliff. All the way."

Alan returned directly to Barnes Headquarters. Alone in his office, he dialed J.R.'s private wire. That familiar biting voice came on the phone after the first ring.

"J.R. Ewing."

"Alan Beam, J.R."

"I wasn't expecting you to call. Is something wrong?"

"Everything's just fine. Cliff is reaching for the bait."

"I want him on the hook, solidly caught."

"He will be, J.R., I assure you. There's just one thing—"

"There always is. What can I do for you, Alan?"

"For starters, I can use some more money."

"For what this thing has cost so far, I could have had Barnes elected king of the Holy Roman Empire."

"It takes money, J.R. Lunches, dinners, mailings, all the rest. You said it yourself—you've got to spend money to get anywhere in this world."

"I want to see results."

"I'm putting the pressure on. Cliff will be announcing soon."

"I hope so. Did he like what he saw in the papers this morning?"

"Loved it, J.R. Went for it just as you said he would. He trusts me like I was his blood brother."

"Good, good. I knew it would pay off."

Alan slid Lucy's $100 bill out from under the desk blotter and fingered it appreciatively. "It certainly did, J.R. And the rewards have just begun to come this way."

"Oh, damn!"

"I don't want to go."

"Then don't. Don't go to Austin. Stay home with me. A woman doesn't want a husband always traipsing off to other places. How do I know what you do when I'm not around?"

Bobby gazed at his wife with disbelief. They had just left The Store, were strolling along the mall out front, on their way to lunch, when Bobby made his announcement.

"I've got to go on over to Austin again."

That had drawn Pam's ire and had made him uneasy, aware of undercurrents in his wife's emotions that he knew nothing about. "Don't tell me you're jealous, Pam."

"Of course I am. What woman in her right mind isn't? I see the way other women look at you. Give them half a chance, and they'll gobble you up. Well, I won't have it."

He embraced her, laughing. "You haven't got a thing to worry about. It's you I love, you I want. Only you. Why don't you come to Austin with me?"

"You know I can't, Bobby."

"Just take a day off from the job."

"I've done too much of that lately. I like my job, I want to hold on to it."

"We haven't been away together in I don't know how long. It would be good for us, Pam. A night in a plush hotel, a champagne dinner. Make us feel like illicit lovers again."

"Don't try to seduce me, Bobby Ewing."

"It's my pleasure, ma'am."

"Oh, Bobby, I'd love to. But not at this time, okay."

"It would be fun. Neither of us has had a good laugh in weeks."

Her face closed up. "If you want to hear me laugh, you're going to have to take me somewhere other than Austin. Watching you try to destroy my brother isn't my idea of a fun time."

"Do you think I enjoy it?" His voice grew louder, and he removed his arm.

"Then don't do it."

"I would, if Cliff gave me half a chance. I can't sit back and let him ruin us, Pam. Not even for you. I have to talk the legislative people into either removing Cliff from office or disbanding the OLM."

"The only one I see about to be ruined is my brother."

"That's because you don't understand how desperate the situation is. Cliff's using his position as a weapon exclusively against Ewing Oil. He's been able to stop us from digging any new wells and closed down most of our old ones. All our capital is tied up in leases and machinery we can't use. We've got expenses, a payroll to meet, storage facilities, transport, all of that. Money keeps going out, and very little is coming in. I'd have a hard time right now rustling up enough cash to buy you a new car, if you wanted one. I tell you, Pam, one way or another, the Ewings have to stop your brother. And soon."

Her distress was plain. "I sit and listen to Cliff, and he says the same thing about the Ewings, that they have to be stopped. For the good of the people, the land, the State of Texas. I don't know what to believe. What am I supposed to do? I won't help either of you destroy the other."

"If he wasn't taking money under the table to allow other oil companies to drill, I wouldn't be able to touch him."

She shook her head in rejection. She'd heard this painful argument before and refused to accept it. "You don't know that. Not for sure."

"No, no hard evidence. But enough circumstantial to hang Cliff."

231

"Even if he is," she shot back defiantly, "it doesn't make him any worse than all the others who do the same things. And he is my brother. Would you betray your brother?"

It was a telling argument, and he made no reply. They walked on until Pam spoke again, more hopeful and less angry. "Maybe this will end sooner than we think. Cliff's talking about resigning from OLM. Maybe running for Congress."

Bobby, aware of who was behind Cliff's congressional aspirations, aware of the manipulations and conspiratorial arrangements that had been effected, almost blurted out the information to Pam. But troubled as he was by what J.R. was up to, he felt anything done in the constructive interests of his family had to be tolerated and understood in that context. Yet he felt compelled to warn Pam.

"Don't get your heart set on becoming a Congressman's sister."

"Cliff thinks he can win."

Bobby said it flat out. "He doesn't have a chance."

Cliff Barnes and Harry Shaw strolled without urgency, deep in conversation. Shaw was detailing the problems any run for office would present to Cliff.

"I've been through the OLM charter a dozen times, Cliff. It's about as specific as it can get on the subject."

"I have to resign *before* I declare my candidacy?"

"You must."

"Even for Federal office?"

"No exceptions. I've checked it out with a number of election law experts. According to every legal opinion I've been able to get, you stay where you are, or you take off and burn your bridges behind you."

Cliff weighed it without speaking. He felt good as head of OLM, hated risking the loss of that strong position, hated running for office and possibly losing. Yet it was the only way to go, if he wanted a meaningful career in government. "What's the scuttlebutt from Austin, Harry?"

"Not so good. Every time Bobby Ewing makes a trip, ten more legislators line up behind him. That young man is smart and likable—"

"And backed by Ewing power and Ewing money."

"That's the name of the game."

Ahead, coming their way, he saw a familiar face. His eyes on the oncoming woman, his mind wandering, Cliff still spoke deliberately. "I feel as if I'm backed into a corner, Harry. I don't like it a bit."

"It's a corner, all right, but with this difference—it's got a door. You quit OLM and go for Washington, D.C., the big leagues, Cliff. With the support you've got, I don't understand why you're hesitating."

Cliff started to reply but broke off. Six feet in front of him—

"Sue Ellen!"

She stopped as if shot, staring coldly at him. Her jaw flexed. "Mr. Barnes," she said, and tried to move past him.

He touched her arm. "My sister tells me you've recovered entirely from your unfortunate accident."

"I've recovered."

"I'm glad."

"Thank you."

"And the baby?"

There was a perceptible softening of expression, her lips parting. "He's well. Very well. And he's so beautiful."

"Sue Ellen—"

She shrugged away his hand. "Good day, Mr. Barnes." And she walked swiftly away, disappearing into the crowd.

"Lovely woman," Harry Shaw said.

"Yes."

"Does she have a name?"

Cliff kept walking.

The briefcase had a look of elegance to it. Glove-soft black leather crafted in Florence and embossed with Harve Smithfield's initials. It was a briefcase that never failed to impress his many legal clients; it was a briefcase with style and class, the subdued expression of trained craftsmen and considerable money. Even in oil-rich Texas, men were always impressed with large and comparatively unnecessary expenditures.

The briefcase lay open on the polished wood conference table in J.R.'s office. J.R. sat on one side of the table, Harve on the other, passing papers back and forth, exchanging comments, notes, opinions.

"These look okay to me, Harve."

Smithfield, as elegant in his way as the briefcase itself, shook his distinguished head from side to side. "Consider what I'm saying, J.R. Let the lease go. The financial risk as guaranteed in the agreement makes it unseemly at this time. That's a sizable bonus you've agreed to pay."

"I'll find the money. There's oil on that property. And we'll be able to drill for it sooner than you think."

"Not while Cliff Barnes runs OLM you won't."

"Now, Harve, let me take care of Cliff Barnes. Okay with you?"

"Suit yourself. But I'm involved in this too, with young Beam working actively for Barnes's candidacy. I don't want you or your daddy holding that against us. Our companies have done business together for too long. I've spoken to my partners, and we are prepared to fire Alan."

J.R. glowed. "Why, Harve, thank you. We certainly do appreciate that. We surely do. We know how highly you think of young Beam." His brain fed out information, possibilities, probabilities, assessing every prospect from every angle. He smiled graciously, always the charming gentleman. "But how would it look if word got around that the Ewings had a man fired for his political beliefs?"

"It's not just that. He embarrassed a valued client in public."

J.R. produced an easy laugh. "That little set-to at the Golden Horseshoe, you mean? Don't let it get to you. It's all forgotten. No blood, no harm. Wouldn't want it said that J.R. Ewing had someone else fight his battles for him. I can handle Beam, if he needs handling. Besides, I admire a man with a little spunk. Why don't you just let the boy be, Harve?"

"If that's the way you want it, J.R."

"It is exactly the way I want it."

Lucy spoke quietly and urgently on the hallway phone near the entrance of the ranch house. On the other end of the line was her friend, Muriel Gillis.

"Never mind where I am going, Muriel. The question is whether or not you are going to help me."

"But I just hate deceiving people—"

234

"Deceiving is what you do best, Muriel. You are one of my best friends. If I can't depend on you . . ."

"But you can! You know you can, Lucy."

"Then you'll do it. Don't let me down. You just wait ten minutes and call back and—" Her voice became more intimate. "Here he comes now, Muriel. You ready?"

"Oh, Lucy, I don't know."

"I am depending on you." She raised her voice and called out to Jock, descending the stairs. "Hi, Granddaddy, what a coincidence, I was just talking about you to Muriel Gillis on the phone."

"Is that right?" he said.

"I told her what you said about me being grounded and all."

"That's right, grounded. You just have to learn to be more careful with an automobile."

"Muriel was wondering if she could ask you something, just take a minute, she said."

"Well, all right. I have always been fond of Muriel." He took the phone. "Muriel, is that you?"

"Yes, sir, Mr. Ewing."

"Muriel, what can I do for you, sweetheart?"

Muriel struggled to cover up her nervousness. "I just asked Lucy to come over and help me study for our history exam tomorrow. I'm having an awful time, but she said you wouldn't let her drive because of those speeding tickets."

"That's a fact. Lucy's got to learn."

"I know, and you're right. It's just that I do so need her help to cram. Otherwise, I'm bound to fail, I swear I will. Her notes are always much better than mine. Don't you think you could make an exception, just this one time, Mr. Ewing?"

He frowned in that characteristic way of his. "Well, maybe just this once."

"Oh, thank you, Mr. Ewing."

He hung up and turned to Lucy. "Just this once. And you drive carefully, hear."

"Yes, sir, Granddaddy."

He went outside, and the door slammed behind him. Lucy picked up the phone and dialed the number, a number she had already committed to memory.

"Hello," Alan Beam said.

She grinned at the sound of his voice. "It's Lucy," she said. "Tonight's gonna be just fine. Where do you want me to meet you?"

"The Piano Bar all right?"

"I'll be there, eight o'clock. Oh, Alan, I'm looking forward to it so much."

"So," he drawled indolently, "am I."

That evening Cliff stood at the counter in his kitchen, chopping vegetables, preparing a Chinese dinner. He enjoyed cooking, especially when he had guests. A knock at the door brought him out of the kitchen, still wearing his apron, paring knife in hand. Pam grinned at the sight of him.

"Oh," she said broadly, "you shouldn't have dressed."

He laughed, kissed her, and led her into the living room. "I'm the chef tonight. We eat as soon as Digger gets home. There's some wine on the table, help yourself to a drink."

She did so, and he went back to work. She settled onto a tall stool to watch. Cliff spoke after a while.

"I saw Sue Ellen today. By accident, in the street. She looked wonderful, and she said the baby was fine."

"He is." Her eye fell on a Barnes for Congress flyer on the counter. "Have you reached a decision about running yet?"

"Not yet. If I do run, and if I win, I could have Sue Ellen then. She'd leave J.R."

Pam couldn't believe her ears. "If you're counting on that, don't—"

"I just have to prove to her that I'm stronger than he is, that he'll never break me, no matter what."

"Cliff," she said gently. "Sue Ellen does not love you."

"You don't understand."

"I do understand. You are deluding yourself. Anything she ever felt for you is long gone."

"No."

"Has she given you an indication that she still cares for you? Anything at all?" When Cliff did not answer, she went on. "Getting elected isn't easy. Remember what happened last time. I'd hate to see you resign your job because of some fantasy you can't get out of your head, and be disappointed again."

236

He eyed her suspiciously. "Bobby's worried, isn't he? That I'll run and win. Did he tell you to talk me into staying on at OLM? He'd like that. Then he could lobby to strip OLM of its power, while I'm helpless."

"He doesn't even know I'm here."

"Oh. Where is he tonight?"

"In Austin."

"There you are."

"I am sure he would ease up if you would."

"Ease up!" The words exploded angrily out of Cliff. "You can tell him for me there's going to be no easing up. Tell him, if I think I have half a chance of winning, I'll run for Congress. If I'm elected, I'll have the kind of power that will finish him and his family for good."

"What are you saying? Have you forgotten—I'm Bobby's family. What are you talking about?"

"As head of OLM, I decide who drills where in Texas. But what worries Bobby and J.R. is that once I have a Federal office, I'll be able to influence who drills not only in Texas, but anywhere in the world."

"What has that got to do with anything? Ewing Oil isn't planning to drill overseas."

"I have reports that they've leased, secretly leased, oil fields off the coast of Asia. When those fields come in, they'll be so rich no one will be able to touch them."

"But don't foreign leases cost millions and millions of dollars?"

"Yes. But those leases are just the beginning. There's the cost of drilling, salaries, equipment, not to mention the slush funds for bribes—"

Pam cut him off. "Bobby told me you'd tied up all Ewing's capital, that they're close to being broke."

"Sure he said that. How else was he going to excuse what they're trying to do to me? He was lying to you, Pam—"

"No."

"The same way J.R. lies to everyone. Lies designed to make the Ewing family richer and more powerful, no matter who gets hurt along the way."

Pam, horrified at what she was hearing, could do nothing but listen and be afraid.

The Piano Bar was dim, obscure, a scrim of cigarette smoke turning everyone into a distorted blur. Small round tables were lit by red candles. There was a tiny dance floor on which never more than one or two couples swayed languidly, bodies plastered to each other in determined physical resolve against the threat of separation. Waiters glided through the semidarkness with the studied grace of ballet dancers, trays balanced precariously as they swept, dodged, finally faded away. The air was sweet with the scent of good Colombian grass, recently burned.

An ancient, wrinkled black man with long gnarled fingers played New Orleans blues with a dark, heavy left hand at the piano bar. Behind the bar in a high-backed booth, wrapped in shadowed privacy, were Alan Beam and Lucy, knee to knee, hip to hip, shoulder to shoulder. They had been drinking for a long time, talking for a long time, edging closer to each other as the evening wore on.

Lucy had embarked, two or three Scotches earlier, on the story of her life. She wound it up with a laugh.

"When I didn't get married, I thought I would absolutely die. So I went to college instead."

"The lure of higher education," he added.

She grinned. "There seemed to be more of a future in it."

Alan leaned her way. "You are a positive delight."

"Thank you, kind sir."

He kissed her lightly on the mouth.

"What was that for?" she asked with contrived curiosity.

"That was for being so beautiful."

"What you see is what you get." She sounded too glib in her own ears and went on, before he could take her up on such a provocative remark. "I've been talking all evening. You haven't had a chance to get a word in."

"I've enjoyed every moment."

"You mean it?"

He took her hand in his. "Can't you tell?" He kissed the tips of her fingers.

"I can now."

"What would your uncle say if he could see us together?"

"J.R.? He'd have a fit."

"Sometimes I feel my main attraction for you is J.R.'s dislike of me."

She didn't want him thinking that and said so. "It's just that I'm with the one man in all of Dallas who isn't afraid to stand up to him. That makes you a pretty rare bird."

"I've never been afraid of him because he's never had anything I wanted—until now."

"I wish you meant *that*."

"I do." He kissed her again, and this time it was a long kiss. Her lips opened to him, and she accepted his tongue with a compulsive surge of emotion, arms circling his waist. She felt his hand on her breast, and she gasped at the spread of pleasure that went through her. She shifted closer to him.

He pulled back. "This is not wise."

"I think it is."

"Someone could see."

"I don't care."

"There's no point in looking for trouble. Besides, I don't want to do anything to damage you—"

"You mean my reputation?"

"That, too."

She giggled softly. "Oh, Alan, you're so sweet. I have not lived what might be called a celibate life."

"You mean you're not a virgin?" He said it lightly, provocatively.

"Is that a proposition, or are we playing twenty questions?"

In answer, his mouth came down on hers again. His hand was on her knee, moving inexorably along her inner thigh, and she turned to accommodate him, moaning softly in desire, wishing he would go more quickly, his fingers searing every inch of her flesh.

He pushed her away.

"What's wrong?" she whispered, putting her hand to his belt, rubbing gently, reaching.

"No," he said firmly. "Not here. Not like this."

"Then take me somewhere."

"You're so beautiful. So desirable. I don't want to hurt you."

"You—I want you, too. So very much. Please, Alan, don't turn away from me."

For a long frightening interval, he said nothing. Then he jerked his head once in assent. "Let's go home," he said authoritatively. "To my place."

Jock was alone on the patio having his morning coffee when Lucy came out of the house, carrying her schoolbooks. She kissed his cheek.

"'Bye, Granddaddy."

"Don't you forget, young lady. You come right home after school. Last night was an exception. You are still grounded."

The thought of last night, of her time with Alan, came rushing back like a hot flood that made her weak in the knees. She braced herself against the revived passion she felt and put a grateful smile on her mouth. "I sure do thank you for last night, Granddaddy. Muriel's bound to pass that exam now, all that work we put in."

He nodded solemnly. "You just tend to your own studies, hear. Make certain you do well. An education means a hell of a lot, man or woman. More than in my day."

She kissed him again and skipped down to where her car was parked and drove away. Jock was just returning to his newspaper, checking grain futures, when Bobby came out.

Jock put the paper aside. "You got home late last night."

"You were already in bed."

"How'd it go in Austin?"

"About as usual. More promises: people will do what they can, when they can, if they can. The rumors are flying, though. There's talk of a full-scale investigation into OLM's operations, and Cliff's. They say it should get under way soon."

"Sooner the better," Jock grumbled. "I'm tired of empty talk."

"We're making progress, Daddy."

"You're doing fine, boy. You just keep coming at Barnes from the front. Leave J.R. and me to handle the ass end."

"I wish you'd reconsider, Daddy. We can beat Cliff fair and square. No reason for getting mixed up with J.R.'s kind of double dealing."

"J.R. knows what he's about, son."

"But do we?"

Jock set his jaw. "There are some things you refuse to understand, Bobby. Politics is like ranching. It's hard to get anything done without getting a little dirt on your hands."

Bobby looked away. Arguing with his father was akin to talking an enraged bull out of charging; neither listened very much.

"I better get going," he said. "I've got an early meeting in Dallas this morning."

"Have a nice day, son."

Pam drove into town with him. She sat as far away from him as she could get, her profile aloof and distant, excluding him from her thoughts.

"You were asleep when I got home last night," he said finally.

She answered brusquely. "I wasn't asleep."

"I see."

"I didn't want to hear about it."

"About what?"

"About how successful you were in Austin. About how much you accomplished in your crusade to ruin my brother's career."

"Oh, for crying out loud, Pam! I'm not trying to ruin Cliff, I'm trying to salvage the Ewings."

"Is that the way you see it?"

"That's the way it is. I thought we went through all this yesterday."

"Yesterday I didn't know what I know today, what I knew last night. I trusted you, Bobby, and you lied. You lied to me."

He glanced her way in disbelief. "Lied? Lied about what?"

"About Ewing Oil going broke."

"I didn't lie. Cliff has us completely tied up."

"You can't even afford to buy a new car, I remember. Well, if that's so, where is the money coming from to buy foreign oil leases?"

"To do what?"

"Those leases cost millions. Plus the equipment, shipping costs, salaries. Do you think my brother is stupid? That he doesn't know what you're up to? Well, we Barneses may not be as rich as you Ewings, but we're every bit as smart.

241

Cliff knows every move you make. He knows about those fields you've leased off the coast of Asia. He knows your plans. He knows the drilling schedules. He knows—"

But Bobby had stopped listening. One question kept running through his mind: what the hell was going on?

Lucy drove directly from the ranch to Alan's office. Just as she pulled up to the curb, she spotted Alan climbing into his red Thunderbird up ahead. Before she could draw his attention, he'd pulled away, rolling smoothly. A mischievous thought drifted into her brain. She released the brake and trailed after him, keeping a discreet distance behind.

They drove for nearly fifteen minutes, into a section of town consisting of modest working-class homes. The Thunderbird turned down a lane called Fantasia and came to a stop by a public swimming pool behind a wire mesh fence.

A tall man in a white sombrero was standing alongside the fence, deep in conversation. Alan went over to him, shook hands, greeting him warmly. Even from where she was parked, Lucy recognized the man in the white hat—Alan was with J.R.!

Tears blurred her vision as she jerked the car into gear and sped away.

"He greeted me, Dr. Ellby, and my heart stopped beating. His hand came up and seemed to reach out to me. My blood congealed. I could feel him wanting me. But it wasn't me that he wanted. Not me. It was J.R. Ewing's wife. That's all he ever wanted."

"And the child?"

"The boy is mine, only mine."

"If he's the father—do you think he feels anything for your son?"

"I don't know."

"You don't know?"

"Perhaps. I don't know. I don't think Cliff knows, either."

"Can you explain that?"

"He wants whatever J.R. Ewing has: me, my son, Ewing Oil, Ewing money, the ranch, everything."

"Has Cliff told you that?"

"He doesn't have to, I know. He'll do anything to get us, but he won't succeed. I won't let him."

"You're speaking very passionately about someone you say you care nothing about."

"Did I say that?"

"Your exact words."

"But it isn't true!"

"You do care for Cliff?"

"I think I hate him—yes. Yes, I do. I hate him. I want to destroy him."

"And your husband?"

"Oh, yes, more than anything."

"Something is happening, Mrs. Ewing."

"It is?"

"Yes."

"I don't want to know about it."

"The walls are crumbling, Mrs. Ewing."

"The walls?"

"Your defenses are coming down."

"I don't know what you mean."

"See, you're crying."

"I have nothing to cry about."

"You are beginning to feel again—strongly feel again, Mrs. Ewing."

"No. No. That's not what I want. Not ever again!"

Bobby, shirt-sleeves rolled, tie pulled down, sat at his office desk examining a list of companies that leased oil drilling equipment, particularly offshore rigs. About half the names on the list had a line drawn through them. He was crossing out another name when the phone rang.

"Yes?" he said crisply.

The secretary spoke. "Herb Reynolds of Reynolds Equipment and Leasing on one."

"Okay. Line up the next name on the list while I'm on with Reynolds."

"Yes, sir, Bobby."

He punched the appropriate button. "Hello, Herb, that you?"

"Hi, Bobby, how's it goin', man?"

"Good enough."

"Didn't see you at the Cowboys game on Sunday. Not beginning to root for the Oilers, are you? I'd consider that a personal affront."

"No way, Herb. Just been busy out at the ranch."

"Know the feeling, son. Your daddy was there. Lost twenty dollars to him. Man insisted on getting the Rams and points. Too damned many points. But your old man is a bit of a hustler, you know that?"

"There's some information I wanted, Herb."

"Fire away, boy. I'm all ears and mouth. Whatever you want."

"It's about some rigs."

"Well, I'm honest-to-God glad to hear that. Haven't heard word one from J.R. in months."

"You haven't?"

"Well, no. And I hear tell he's buying here and around. Why not me, Bobby-boy? Man gets to feeling left out, you know what I mean. I was thinking J.R. had a mad-on at me, made me feel neglected. Now you got some business we can chin-chin about?"

"Not just yet, Herb. Maybe soon. I'm only checking to see how you'll be set for the full line in a month or so."

"You name it, you've got it."

"Good enough. Be talking to you, Herb."

"*Hasta mañana,* old buddy."

Bobby hung up and ran a line through Reynolds's name. The secretary came back on the line. "Roy Tate of Tidewater waiting for you, Bobby."

He responded at once. "Hello, Roy."

"Howdy, pardner. How goes it?"

"Just fine. Tell you why I'm calling. About those rigs—"

Tate answered too quickly. "What rigs are you talking about, Bobby?"

Bobby followed up swiftly. "Same ones, Roy, the stuff you been kicking around with J.R."

Tate began to laugh. "Had me a little worried there. J.R. swore me to secrecy. Should've known you was in on the deal."

"Family secrets, family business, Roy."

"I hear you loud and clear. Well, you just tell J.R. that right this cotton-picking minute I've got two super rigs on their way down from Japan, be in place before the week is up."

"Thanks, Roy. That's all I wanted to know." He hung up and heaved his booted feet up onto the desk, examining a map of the world that hung on the far wall of his office. J.R. was sure as hell up to something once more; but what?

What? Where? And how in the world did he think he was going to get away with it?

Alan Beam was eating alone. A grilled cheese sandwich, some sliced tomatoes, and Lone Star out of the bottle. He was thinking about Lucy, about the previous night. The girl was a sexual marvel. Inventive, insatiable, willing to try anything more than once, finding and giving pleasure endlessly. He wasn't sure he was up to her pace, but he was willing to make the effort since the rewards were so high. Doing J.R.'s bidding was one thing, becoming a member of the rich and powerful Ewing family was an entirely different and much more profitable affair. Lucy was exactly what he'd been searching for all his life—a genuine one-hundred-percent golden doll.

He reached for the phone, ready to call her, but thought better of it. Keep her anxious, keep her wanting more, keep her on a taut line, gradually drawing her inboard until she would be easy and happy to be caught. The doorbell interrupted his very pleasant ruminations.

It was Lucy. Slightly disheveled, hair a little wild, eyes darting.

"I was just thinking about you," he blurted out. "I was going to phone—"

"You liar."

He misunderstood. "It's true enough." He reached for her hand. "Come inside. You have no idea how good last night was for me. Now that you're here—"

She jerked away. "You filthy bastard!"

"Hey, wait a minute! What's wrong?"

"I thought you were a different kind of man. Straight, courageous, honest. When I saw you stand up to J.R., I honored you for that. What a fool I've been."

"Honey, what are you talking about?"

"Don't call me honey. Last night, I loved last night. All I

could think of today was how it had been. So beautiful, so full of affection and warmth and promise. But now—"

"Will you tell me what's wrong?"

"You bet I will. I saw you today with J.R. Meeting him at the swimming pool. You're still working for him, still together with him in his rotten plans, his awful ways. You're just like him. And all of it—the fight at the rodeo, at the Golden Horseshoe, me—it was all a setup. He owns you, runs you the same as he owns and runs everything else around Dallas."

"Just let me explain."

"Explain! There's nothing to explain! What you did, what you are—that can never be explained!"

Tears were streaming down her cheeks as she ran for the street and her car.

"Lucy!" he cried, reaching out. Then, softly: "I can explain, I know I can explain." He took a step or two after her, realized it was no use, realized he'd blown his big chance. The golden doll was gone.

Kristin wondered why it was that she always felt used and debased whenever she and J.R. made love. There was never a sense of completeness to the act, as if some essential but unnamed fragment had been removed. Or never put into place.

They never spoke of love, of course. Unless Kristin initiated it, and then their exchanges were brief, perfunctory, something to be done with. There was never any afterplay, no affection, no cuddling, no good humor or joy over what had just been experienced. Rather, an abrupt dismissal, as if J.R. had to get on to more important matters. And he almost always did.

They went at it like two half-angry creatures desperate to get somewhere, seldom taking real pleasure in what they did, always peering ahead to some ultimate and ultimately unsatisfying goal. And every time Kristin found herself in an inferior position—physically, spiritually, emotionally.

Now, both of them had dined and drunk a bottle of champagne, and now both of them were naked, Kristin kneeling in front of J.R., gazing up at him, pleading for some recognition of her humanity.

"Do what I want," he commanded.

"It's always that way, what you want."

"If you have any complaints, sugar, we can always terminate the relationship."

"Oh, J.R., must you always act like the bastard you are?"

He stood up. "I'll leave."

She flung her arms around his strong thighs. "No, not like this. I'll do whatever you say."

He sat back down again. "I thought you might."

"Once," she murmured, head going down between his thighs, "just once I would like you to make me feel like a whole person instead of just the various parts of me."

"Do it." His voice grated, and he held her head between his powerful hands, squeezing hard. "Do what you're told, Kristin, like a nice girl."

Then the private phone he'd had installed in her apartment with the unlisted number began to ring. He swore softly. Only a very few trusted associates had the number, along with instructions to never call unless it was an emergency.

"Shall I get it, darling?" she said against his flesh.

"Bring the phone to me."

She did and went off to open another bottle of champagne.

He lifted the receiver. "J.R. Ewing here."

"J.R., it's Alan Beam."

J.R. broke in gruffly. "I sincerely hope the reasons for this call are sound and solid, Alan. It comes at a most unpropitious moment."

"This may be very important, J.R."

"I'm listening."

"I ran into your niece—Lucy, I believe her name is."

"You believe?" Alan was pretending to only a casual interest in Lucy. Why? It made no sense. A shard of information to be filed away and considered at another time.

"Yes, Lucy. Apparently she was driving past when we were talking, out on Fantasia today."

"Damn."

"I've been thinking about it. It could be serious. If it should get back to Cliff, if he got suspicious, it could blow the entire operation."

Annoyance rose in J.R. like a gray cloud. There was no reason for such things to happen, yet they did. Nor should he be expected to deal with such minor irritants; yet he was. And always did. It was the price one paid for power and competence and the desire for more of each. "All right, I'll handle it. I'll think of something."

"I hope so, J.R. Otherwise, everything could go right down the tubes."

"Goodbye, Alan," J.R. said coldly, and slammed the phone down.

"Trouble?" Kristin said, returning with a glass of champagne for each of them. She'd donned a multicolored caftan and looked quite lovely, a beautiful young hostess offering refreshments to her guest.

"Nothing I can't handle. What do you think you're doing?" She offered him a glass.

"Put them down on the table." She did so. "Now take that damned thing off. And get back down here and finish the job you started like the good working girl you are."

And once again, she did as she had been told, beginning to hate herself almost as much as she hated him.

Neither one was able to sleep. Or even to consider sleep. Their bodies were taut with apprehension, with uncertainty, with a pervasive sense of guilt. Until finally Pam sat up and turned on the light.

"Dammit, Bobby, I hate this. I can't stand it any more, and I won't. Talk to me."

He wanted to take her in his arms, but a lingering resentment hung on, the way a vine does to a wall, lest a sudden shift might bring disaster to both. "What do you want to talk about?"

"What is happening? You tell me one thing, Cliff tells me another. My feelings are in a state of flux, not on one side or another, wanting to believe both of you and to go on loving both of you."

"Will you believe what I say?"

"I'll try. I will truly try."

He reached out. finding her warm thigh, and held on. The contact was helpful, encouraging, but not quite enough. He let his eyes close.

248

"Don't, Bobby," she pleaded. "Don't turn away from me. Tell me the truth, whatever it is, and I'll believe you."

He rolled toward her. "The truth is I don't know what's going on. But something sure as hell is. Those Asian leases, the rigs; I don't understand where the money came to pay for all that. I don't know, but I intend to find out. Do you believe that?"

She sighed and nodded, leaned over him, mouth settling down on his. Soon his arms went around her, familiar and strong, reliable. Their kisses deepened, and she felt the first breaking waves of arousal stirring low in her belly. She pressed herself against him, hand reaching until she found what she wanted, pleased to discover that he desired her as much as she did him.

Bobby discovered J.R. standing at the downstairs hall telephone in the morning. The brothers greeted each other affably, if not with warmth.

"I've been wanting to talk to you," Bobby said.

"Any time, little brother."

"I'll catch you in the office this morning."

"At your convenience."

Bobby went into the dining room, and J.R. glanced up the stairs and began running through the morning mail. After a while, he picked up the phone, but didn't dial. He waited patiently, eyes returning to the staircase frequently, obviously looking for someone. Then Lucy appeared, carrying her schoolbooks, looking very unhappy. J.R. began talking into the dead instrument.

"Excuse me just a minute, Harve." Then, brightly, to Lucy, "Mornin', sugar."

She nodded curtly and started past him.

He continued into the phone. "As I was saying, Harve, about Alan Beam . . ."

Lucy dropped her books and knelt to retrieve them, listening closely.

"I tried to talk to him again yesterday," J.R. went on. "Tried to talk some sense into the boy. I was just as nice and gentle as could be, but the young fool won't listen to reason. He's in the Barnes camp solid and plans on staying there. Much as I hate to say this, Harve, I think you're gonna have to get rid of that young fella. That's what I mean—fire the little bastard."

Lucy stood up, books cradled in both arms. For a moment she felt confusion and there was skepticism in her face. Then it drained quickly away, replaced by a wide, pleased smile. She believed every word she'd heard, she had to. She wanted to.

J.R. watched her leave, having done a good morning's work before his first cup of coffee.

When he arrived in his office, J.R. made one quick call.

"J.R. Ewing, here. That you Alan?"

"Yes, sir. What can I do for you?"

"Try not to screw up this time. With my niece, that is. I fixed up the damage you caused, letting her see us together—"

"But J.R.—"

"—And I expect you to make certain it doesn't happen again."

"Whatever you say, J.R."

"Remember that. You just get in touch with Lucy soonest you can. Maybe even sooner than that, y'hear? Be all soft and friendly and get it straight with her."

"What if she—?"

"I fixed it up, I told you. She can't wait to tell you how sorry she is. So put a good move on, boy, and let's keep the old ball rolling."

"You're the boss, J.R." Alan was delighted with this sudden turn of events. "I'll phone Lucy at once."

"She's off to school. Trot your butt over to the campus and dig her out, show her how much you care. And next time, Alan, be smarter."

"Yes, J.R."

That done, J.R. decided to deal with Brother Bobby. He found Bobby in his office, slumped into a seat at one side of his desk.

"Here I am, Bobby. You said you wanted to see me. What's so all-fired important this early in the morning?"

Bobby decided to plunge right in. "I want to know more about the Asian oil leases Ewing Oil has been buying."

J.R. kept his face stolid, eyes holding steady on Bobby. "What leases are those, brother?"

"Don't try to snow me, J.R. I *know*."

"How did you find out?"

"That's not important."

"It is to me."

Bobby stood up, walked around his desk, then settled into a chair within arm's length of J.R. "I don't intend to allow you to evade the issue, J.R. The point about those leases is this—there is no record of any such deal in the books. I knew nothing about it, and I suspect Daddy knows nothing about it."

J.R. held his hands apart in a gesture of dismissal. His manner, his tone of voice, all said this was much ado about nothing. "With Momma sick and all, I didn't see any sense in worrying Daddy about this affair. You know how it is—there is a substantial risk to the venture. What the hell, Bobby, in the oil business, nothing is for sure."

"Exactly. And you know as well as I do that right now we can't afford to drill overseas."

"We can't afford not to. Look, your damned brother-in-law has us tied up in Texas. But overseas—well, hell's bells, he can't lay a glove on us there. And then there's all that oil just waiting for us to bring it up."

"What if the wells come up dry?"

That was something J.R. chose not to consider for very long. "I'll take the risk, I'll take the responsibility. Look, Bobby, I'm trying to save the company for all of us."

"One question—where is the money coming from, J.R.?"

J.R. looked away. "Leverage. Loans."

The more he heard, the less Bobby liked it. J.R. was being evasive, saying much less than he knew. "Leverage on what?" Bobby said. "Who's lending us money, with things as they are?"

"Now don't you fret about such things, little brother. It is a very complicated deal, I admit, but I have every itty-bitty detail indelibly inscribed in my head." He laughed shortly. "The J.R. computer bank, I like to think of the old brain."

"Never mind the itty-bitty details, just give me the broad strokes of the deal."

"I've been able to raise the required capital. That should be enough for you."

"No way it's gonna be enough. Not for me, not for Daddy. Level with me. Have you been lying? How close to broke are we?"

J.R. rose quickly. "You know as well as I do we've had serious financial setbacks. And you know why."

"Okay. What I want to know is where in God's name is the money coming from?"

"I raised it. That's enough for you to know. Now get off my back." He strode toward the door, then turned around, face flushed with anger. "And stop spying on me. I don't take kindly to people checking me out."

Bobby, also on his feet, body leaning as if to spring ahead, answered in kind. "That's too damned bad, because I intend to find out what's going on. If it's the last thing I do."

It was evident to each of them that the battle lines were drawn, and there was no turning back. One of them was going to get hurt. And badly.

Alan located Lucy coming out of the library on the S.M.U. campus. At the sight of him, she stopped dead in her tracks.

"Lucy—"

She didn't move, waiting shyly, until he stood near her. "Good morning, Alan. What are you doing here?"

"I came to see you. I had to explain about yesterday."

"No, don't. Don't say anything. I was the one who was wrong. Jumping to conclusions, getting angry. I have no right to judge you."

Alan silently complimented J.R. Whatever had been done or said, it had certainly resulted in the desired effect. Lucy was soft putty in his hands. He arranged his features solemnly.

"Frankly, Lucy, I respect you for it."

"You do?"

"You're a woman of honor, of conviction."

"Oh, Alan, I could kiss you, I'm so glad to see you again."

"Here?"

"Someplace quiet, someplace private, might be more fun."

"I know just the place," he said, taking her elbow. "My apartment."

"There go my class cuts for the month, but it's in a good cause." She smiled up at him.

His arm went around her. "I want you to know—no one matters more to me now than you do. Nothing matters more to me now than you do. I want you in my life for as long as I can have you."

It sounded like the warm declaration she had yearned for. It was, in fact, a statement of cold ambition, a public relations release carefully structured and sculptured for maximum results. She had become the most vital rung in Alan Beam's determined ascent up the ladder of business success. He saw her as a vessel overflowing with power and profit; she viewed him a chivalric hero, glossy and pure. He wanted the great authority and wealth and prestige she was heir to. Lucy wanted only to be loved. It was a match contrived and executed in the darkest circles of purgatory.

Or in the devious mind of J.R. Ewing.

PART 7

Miss Ellie

15

J.R. glanced at his watch.

Bobby, reading a newspaper, looked up and went back to reading.

Pam went to the window and peered out, turned back, glanced again over her shoulder.

Sue Ellen, seated stiffly on a straight-backed chair, crossed her legs, and recrossed them almost immediately.

J.R. checked his watch, listened to make sure it was still going.

"They should be here any minute," Bobby said.

J.R. grunted. "We should have gone to the hospital with Daddy."

"He said no, J.R. Daddy's been toughing it out this past week, all those visits alone with Momma. He's giving it a real shot, trying to heal things between them."

"Everything was going fine until that father-in-law of yours showed up that night. Man has a piddling little romance with a woman more'n forty years ago and can't put it out of his mind. I don't make any kind of a connection with that kind of a mentality."

"Romance has never been your long suit," Sue Ellen said with elaborate sweetness.

"Digger loves Miss Ellie still," Pam said. "Why is that so difficult to understand?"

"Love for J.R. is a twenty-four hour virus," Sue Ellen said. "A good dose of salts and it'll go away."

"That's enough of that," J.R. barked at his wife.

She bowed her head in mock assent.

"What time is it?" Pam asked.

Bobby answered quickly. "I guess it took a little longer to check out than expected."

J.R. examined the face of his watch again. No more than a minute or two had expired. "What happened to your appointment with the eminent Dr. Ellby, Sue Ellen? Giving up on that little habit?"

Sue Ellen turned luminous eyes his way, all cold marble and suppressed rage. "I wanted to greet your mother when she returned, if that doesn't offend you."

At that moment the sound of a car in the driveway brought them all to the windows. "It's them!" Bobby cried, heading for the door. He led the way outside.

Behind them, on the staircase, Lucy descended uncertainly. During all the time her grandmother was in the hospital, she had not paid a visit. Now Miss Ellie was home, and Lucy faced that fact with mixed and frightening feelings. She heard the joyful sounds of the family greeting each other and commanded herself to join them. Her legs refused to function. She stood rooted on the third step up, waiting. Just waiting.

Miss Ellie entered the house, Jock a discreet distance behind her, as if their emotional differences still kept them apart. Lucy held her position, aching to run to her grandmother, to beg forgiveness, wanting to hide in shame and embarrassment, wishing the earth would open up and devour her.

Miss Ellie paused a few feet away, eyes examining the young blond girl. "My, Lucy, you are a lovely little thing."

"Oh, Grandma—"

"I missed you at the hospital, Lucy."

"I'm sorry. I couldn't come, I just couldn't."

"I understand. I hope I understand."

"I'm happy you're home, Grandma, real happy."

"Well, so am I. I'm certainly glad to be back. I'm a little tired from the drive, and I think I could do with a little rest, if nobody objects. I'd like to go upstairs now." She started up the stairs going past Lucy, then swung halfway back, and smiled wanly. "But I would surely appreciate some company later on this evening."

Jock, his wife's suitcase in hand, followed her upstairs.

Inside her room, Miss Ellie inspected the walls, the corners, each item in the chamber and said in a still voice, as if to herself: "It's so good to be alive."

Night, still and hot, giving no relief to the land, the people, the animals of the southwest, descended on Southfork. Pam, in a loose-fitting cotton dress, was sitting on the patio nursing a tall, well-iced drink when Bobby appeared, breaking into her drifting thoughts.

"Momma's been asking for Lucy," he started out. "Have you seen her?"

Pam drew the thick, warm air into her lungs, then exhaled between pursed lips as if trying to cool the night itself. "She left a little while ago. She said she wouldn't be home for dinner. Something about studying with Muriel Gillis."

"Been doing an awful lot of studying with Muriel lately, it appears. I wish there was something we could say to Lucy, something that would bring her around."

"I tried, but reaching her right now is just about impossible. She informs me, politely, of course, that I don't know what I'm talking about."

"She's scared, Pam. Trying to cover up."

"We, all of us, are scared. This thing that Miss Ellie is going through—it's every woman's nightmare. Lucy—the only thing we can do is give her time."

"Time, that's what everybody needs a lot of. Only right now she's fighting more battles than anyone should have to fight. She doesn't need Lucy adding an extra hurt to her burdens."

"I know. But what can we do about it?"

Try as he could, Bobby was able to find no suitable answer.

Miss Ellie sat in a chair, feet resting on an embroidered footstool her grandmother had made. She wore a soft robe, and her hair was neatly arranged to make her look quite young. A little lipstick lent a touch of color to her still pale face. On the edge of the bed, also dressed for the night, was Sue Ellen. Slightly tense, anxious, sitting forward as if prepared to make a quick move.

"Your spirits seemed good today, Miss Ellie."

A faint, almost apologetic, smile touched Miss Ellie's mouth. When she answered, it was after a reflective interval. "I'm grateful to be alive and to be back on this ranch I love so much."

"Well, you have a full life. You've always had. That must make it easier to accept what you went through."

The older woman assessed her daughter-in-law gravely. Sue Ellen seemed preoccupied with her own problems, her own life, rather than interested in Miss Ellie's tribulations. She was dwelling on her answer when Pam appeared, closing the door behind her. Glad of the interruption, Miss Ellie saw that she was installed in a comfortable chair. She was pleased by the visit; it was becoming increasingly difficult to hold a conversation with only Sue Ellen.

"We're all so pleased to have you home," Pam said.

"Everyone except Lucy," Miss Ellie pointed out.

Pam frowned. "She's taken it very hard. She'll come around in time."

"I hope so."

"Are you going to go through reconstructive surgery?"

Miss Ellie put her eyes around to Pam, surprised by the bluntness of the question and pleased that the younger woman respected her sufficiently to deal honestly and directly with her problem. "I have six months to think about it. There's no way to duplicate my own breast, but it makes you feel kind of put-back-together-again, or so they tell me." She smiled.

Sue Ellen shuddered. "Has Jock said anything?"

"About what?"

"About how he feels about the surgery."

"No. He hasn't."

Pam leaned forward. "But he has told you that he loves you."

"Yes."

"You sound as if you don't believe him."

"I'm just not sure any more."

"I don't understand."

"I don't know if I can ever be sure of Jock again."

The words seemed to sting Sue Ellen into action. She rose hurriedly, edging toward the door. "I'll see you all in the morning," she said, one hand rising and falling as if out of control. "Good night, Pam. Good night, Miss Ellie."

"Good night, dear."

She hurried back to her own room, mixed and frightening emotions surging through her body. Her heart beat oddly, and her throat was dry. The room was empty, and she went right to the telephone, dialed, and waited.

"Hello. Oh, I'm so glad it was you who answered. I know it's been quite a while. But with Miss Ellie not well. . . . If you still want, I'll see you. Is tomorrow all right?"

Dusty Farlow cleared his throat. "Tomorrow's not soon enough."

"Where?"

"There's a hotel in Fort Worth. The Regent—"

"A hotel! I don't think so."

"The Regent. I'll be there at one o'clock. If you're not there, I'll understand."

"But Dusty—" The connection had been broken. The decision was hers alone to make. This time she could get no help anywhere. A great, warm longing suffused her torso, an almost insatiable need, a hunger. She tried to clear her mind, to think, to decide whether she could handle this relationship at this time. Whether she wanted to.

J.R. was at his desk the next morning when Bobby came barging in, a pugnacious expression on his usually good-natured face. His shoulders were hunched, the powerful muscles gathered together as if preparatory to striking out, and he moved on the balls of his feet with the practiced grace of an athlete, which he had been and still was.

"Well," J.R. said at once, as usual getting in the first words, "didn' expect to see you in here today. Figured you'd hang around at the ranch, keep Momma company, like that."

"I'm part of this family, part of this business."

"Never said no different, little brother. Daddy and I are going to break for lunch by 'n' by. Care to take potluck with us?"

261

"No, J.R., I do not. I came into town expressly to talk to you."

J.R. rocked back in his chair, fingers laced, chin resting lightly on them. "Talk away, Bobby. I'm all ears."

"I didn't want to bring it up while Momma was in the hospital."

"Bring what up?"

"Alan Beam."

"What's the little sneak done now?"

"I figured you might be able to answer that question better than any of us."

"Meaning what?"

The door opened, and Jock followed it inside. "Well, wasn't expecting to see you in town today, Bobby. Care to join us for lunch?"

J.R. grinned, waved his father to a chair. "Bobby's back is up about something or other."

Jock settled down. "Got a burr under your saddle, son? Spit it out, make you feel better."

Bobby jerked his head once. "Okay, J.R. Days after Alan Beam has a fight with you at the rodeo, he opens a headquarters for the Draft Barnes for Congress movement."

"Guess that tells us something about Beam."

"Fill me in," Jock said. "What are you two carrying on about?"

"I didn't want to rope you into this, Daddy, but as long as you're here—I have reason to believe J.R. has cooked up a scheme that we ought to squash right now."

"This is none of your business, Bobby."

"The hell you say! Just so happens it is as much my business as yours, it's family business. I have been busting my butt down in Austin trying to get an investigation committee to look into Cliff Barnes and the OLM, and you go out and rig up a stunt like this. Why? Everything we wanted done was going to get done. Legally. Without any dirty tricks."

"Hold on," Jock broke in. "What are you up to, J.R.? Spit it out, son."

All his impulses were to attack Bobby, but J.R. reined them in. He'd been forced into a corner, and he didn't like

that one bit. With his father present, there was only one
course to follow—strike out straight down the middle.

"I'm behind the movement to draft Cliff Barnes for Congress. You could say that I *am* the movement. I planted Alan
Beam in that office, and I am footing the bill for the
campaign."

Jock snorted angrily. "That's crazy!"

"As the saying goes, 'Crazy like a fox.' Daddy, in order for
Barnes to run for Congress, he has to resign from the OLM.
That is the law. Once he's out, he's off our back. We can
open our wells and start drilling again."

Jock seemed to puff up, eyes narrow and penetrating, his
voice hard, edged with threat. "J.R., a man like that, getting
into Congress, he could do us a lot of harm."

"That's the whole point, Daddy, for him not to get to
Washington."

"Run that by me one more time, son."

"Barnes is never even going to get the nomination. I'm just
working him up to the point where he *commits*, declares his
candidacy. As soon as he resigns from OLM, I pull the plug
on the sonofabitch. His funds dry up, and he's left out in the
cold."

Bobby swore softly. "I can't go along with that kind of
politics. It's dirty pool, and I don't like it at all. Once the
State Senate Investigating Committee tunes in on Cliff, he'll
be thrown out of office. There's a strong belief in Austin that
he's taking payoffs."

"Wouldn't be the first," Jock muttered.

"We don't have that kind of time, little brother. Those
committees move like snails on a dry trail. That man is
bleeding us bad."

"I'm all for getting rid of Cliff, but not that way."

Jock stood up and began pacing the room, his sons watching. "I want that smarmy little bastard stopped. I want him
stopped soon; any way we can do it. Barnes has used every
trick to try and break us Ewings, and I have a belly full of it.
I don't see that what J.R. is doing is any worse than the stuff
Barnes has pulled. On this one, Bobby, I am going to stand
one hundred percent alongside of J.R."

"In that case," Bobby said, "count me out."

"To hell with that, boy! We don't count out anybody in this family. This is a Ewing company, and you are part of it, now and forever. And another thing, I don't want this discussed outside of this office. If Barnes finds out what's going on, we will never get rid of the shifty critter."

Nobody spoke for a while, each of them weighing and assessing. Finally Bobby said what was on his mind. "I don't understand the rush. It seems to me this family has money enough to hold out for whatever extra time it takes to get rid of Barnes legally."

Jock began to grumble.

Bobby went on. "I'll respect your wishes, Daddy. I'll keep my mouth shut."

J.R. and Jock followed him out of the office, the door swinging silently shut behind him. Jock was concerned; J.R. was delighted.

____ 16 ____

They gathered at the dining table, all the Ewings currently living at Southfork: Lucy, Sue Ellen, J.R., Bobby, Pam, Jock, and Miss Ellie. At the head of the table, Jock raised his glass.

"Miss Ellie," he declared, his voice thick with emotion, "it's been a long time, too long, since you've graced this table. And we are all honored by your presence. I think a few words from you are in order in honor of the occasion."

There was a cheerful smattering of applause, Jock's call echoed and approved.

Miss Ellie's gaze went deliberately from one face to another, around the table. "I'm so glad that we're all together again. You know how important that is to me. For me, the family is everything, the center of the nation, of life on this planet. For me, everything good and worth having grows out of a strong and sound family life." She smiled a faint, rueful smile. "I don't have anything else to say except . . . J.R., will you please pass the rolls."

They laughed, and J.R. responded. "Glad to have you back, Momma."

"Glad to have you back, Miss Ellie."

"Glad to have you back—"

Miss Ellie swung around to face Lucy. "Is that the way you feel, dear?"

"Of course." She spoke too quickly.

"You've hardly talked to me since I came home."

"I guess I've been really busy."

265

Miss Ellie nodded agreeably, her eyes shifting to J.R. "I noticed you and Bobby didn't have very much to say to each other during cocktail hour."

J.R. gave a casual shrug. "Nothing to it, Momma. A little business dispute is all. Ain't that a fact, little brother?"

"Not little at all," Bobby said, angrily shaking his head.

"Bobby!" Jock cried in warning, his face darkening.

J.R. said, "Bobby's got an exaggerated view of business dealings. Kind of dramatizes everything."

"The hell you say!" Bobby burst out.

His mother smiled quickly and wryly. "It's wonderful . . . to be back home . . . for a normal evening with the Ewings. All this peace and tranquillity, all this harmony and good feelings. Will somebody please pass the butter?"

Jock drove his car as close to the ranch house as he could and parked. He helped Miss Ellie out and trailed her up onto the patio.

"Slow down," he cautioned.

"I'm doing just fine."

"Just because the doctor took off the bandages is no reason for you to start exerting yourself."

"It is time to stop acting like an invalid, which I'm not any more."

"Don't overdo it."

"Jock, I am feeling so well that when Merilee and Linda called, I invited them over for lunch. I'm going upstairs and change."

He hesitated at the foot of the stairs, then went after her to their room. Miss Ellie took off her coat and carried it to the closet, hung it up, and examined the garments hanging neatly on the rod before making her choice for the afternoon. She selected a dress—a brightly colored print, one of her favorites—and placed herself in front of the full-length mirror. One glance told her that the cut of the dress was all wrong. There was no way it would conceal the scars of her operation.

She went back to the closet and hung up the dress. She repeated the process twice more, each time with identical results. Panic took hold of her, and the dress she was holding slipped out of her fingers. She began to tremble, and her knees grew weak; she collapsed to the floor next to the dress.

Jock hurried to her. "Miss Ellie, what's wrong?"

"Please go away."

"I can't do that. I can't leave you like this."

"Nothing fits," she moaned.

"It doesn't matter. We'll go shopping. All you want, whatever you want—"

"It does matter. You think it doesn't matter because I'm not a young woman any more? Well, you're wrong. Don't you understand that I still care how I look?"

"I care for you, Ellie. *You.* I love you. I'm grateful you're alive. Nothing else matters."

"Don't you see, I'm deformed, Jock! Deformed. Don't tell me that doesn't matter."

"No, no. You're not deformed. Ellie, if you lost an arm or a leg, I would feel that loss with you. But it wouldn't change anything between us."

"I'm not talking about an arm or a leg. I am talking about my *breast.* My femaleness. What do you know about that? What could you possibly know?"

"Ellie, how do I explain how I feel for you? You haven't changed for me."

"Do you think I don't know that you still have an eye for a pretty woman?"

"Ellie—I am telling you—it doesn't matter."

She stared up at him, eyes polished and icy, and spoke in a voice to match. "Just the way it didn't matter for Amanda!"

___ 17 ___

$\mathcal{M}$iss Ellie lay on her bed, eyes closed, trying to think, fighting to exclude all feeling, all sentiment. It was impossible to do. Memories kept crowding in on her, memories of happier times. Of her young womanhood when her days and nights were filled with parties and suppers and handsome, attentive young men clamoring for her attention. She had been a beauty in face and figure, and the most modest dress was unable to disguise her lush femaleness. The years had made the memories and the feelings no less vivid than if they were the result of yesterday's happenings.

The jangling telephone beside the bed jarred her back to the present.

"Hello."

A familiar voice, gravelly, larded with memories of its own, edged with half-forgotten innuendo. Digger Barnes.

"Hello, Ellie."

She sat up, fluffing a pillow at her back. "Digger!" Her spirits soared, and her voice took on a youthful lilt. "How nice of you to call."

"I said I would, and I always keep my promises."

"Always?" she prodded, with a flirtatiousness that startled her.

"Almost always." He laughed a laugh that was pure evil. "Anyway, this promise was a snap to keep. I wanted to speak to you."

"I'm glad to hear from an old friend because right now I feel as if my whole world has about caved in."

"Well, to hell with that kind of talk. Old Digger knows just the remedy for that."

"And what remedy is that?"

"You meet me someplace, and we have a good old-fashioned talk. Are you up to getting off that ranch of yours and going out with an old flame?"

"That's a prescription that suits me from top to bottom. Name the time and the place, Digger."

"Curtis Park okay with you?"

"Perfect."

"In about an hour?"

"Make it an hour and a half."

"I'll be waiting."

"See you later."

Dusty Farlow looked neat, slender, and incredibly handsome in his hand-tailored Western suit of tan gabardine and boots from Cutter Bill's. Handsome and nervous. He glanced at the champagne cooling in an ice bucket near the serving table, complete with two glasses, some black caviar, cream cheese, chopped onions, and English water wafers. He put a cigarette between his lips and fired a match, blew smoke in quick, edgy clouds, and ground the cigarette out. He picked up the phone.

"Get my bill ready, will you? That's right—Farlow, in seven twenty-one. Guess I'll be checking out." A tentative knock at the door brought him up short. "Hold on there, just cancel that. I'm gonna hang around for a spell." He went to the door and opened it. Sue Ellen stood there, immense eyes gazing up at him uncertainly, a weak, fading smile on her voluptuous mouth.

"I almost didn't come," she offered.

"But here you are." He took her hand and brought her inside. "And I was never so glad to see anyone. I'd just about given up on you."

"I'm very frightened," she said.

"That makes two of us."

"Frightened. Nervous. Skittish." She gave a small, fluttery

laugh. "You'd think I was a naive little virgin on her first date."

He saw her seated in a comfortable chair and opened the champagne.

"Not for me," she said quickly.

"It's genuine French bubbly, best in the world, they claim."

"I can't drink."

"If you can't, I won't." He pulled a chair around to face her, straddled it, and stared into her face. "You are the purtiest thing I ever did lay eyes on."

"Don't you want to know why?"

"Why? Why what?"

"Why I can't drink."

"If you want to tell me."

"I'm an alcoholic. Or maybe I'm not quite. Either way, I can't handle the stuff. I can't take the chance on even one sip. When I was pregnant, I was drinking and got into a bad accident. I almost killed myself and my baby."

"I'm sorry."

"I've tried to shut out everything, all my feelings. I wrapped myself in my own little cocoon."

He rose and took a single long stride that brought him in front of her. He drew her to her feet, hands at her waist. "No need for you to do that any more."

"I don't know. . . ."

"I know," he said, his mouth seeking out hers. His lips were incredibly soft and pliant, moving subtly against hers. She sighed and pressed up against him. His hands moved down to the rise of her round, firm bottom. For an extended moment, she gave herself to the embrace, then pulled away, moving deliberately around the room.

"Very elegant," she said, the words putting cool distance between them. "You have style."

"It's easy when you're rich."

"Oh, yes, you are rich. But you walked away from all that money. You said you didn't want to be tied to it. You wanted to be free."

"I think I've changed my mind."

"Why?"

270

"Because," he said in a vibrant low voice, "I want you."

She came around to face him. "I can't—don't you see, I can't."

He went to her, took her by the shoulders, and kissed her again. Gently, briefly, but very effectively. She shuddered and put her head against his chest. "Why not?" he asked. "There's nothing more for you at Southfork."

"Yes. But it's a way of life I'm afraid to change. I know the problems I have to confront there, I'm used to them, I believe I can deal with them. Anything else, a new life, a new way—I don't believe I have that kind of strength."

"I'm offering you my strength."

"It's so soon. . . ."

"What did you think, that I wanted only to get you into bed?"

"I don't know what I thought. I tried not to think. Can you understand? You are a very attractive man. A very kind man. I find you desirable. I wanted to find out if I could take one step out of that cocoon. Just one step, do you understand that?"

"Yes. But there's one tiny problem we have."

"What is that?"

"I have fallen in love with you."

Her hand went to her breast. "Oh, my God. What am I supposed to do about that!"

"Whatever you want to do. Or nothing."

"I need more time."

"We don't have much time, Sue Ellen. I'm going home. Back to the Southern Cross Ranch."

"Will I ever see you again?"

"If you want me, you know where to reach me. I will always want to see you."

"Yes," she murmured softly.

He kissed her again. Without passion, without provocation. An affectionate touching of lips. Then she hurried away, leaving behind a disappointed and concerned cowboy.

Miss Ellie and Digger Barnes strolled aimlessly through Curtis Park, speaking only occasionally, careful not to touch, pausing once in a while to watch a squirrel foraging for nuts, to listen to a flock of pigeons sensuously cooing. She carried a small bouquet of wildflowers, which she brought up to her face now and then.

"No one's given me wildflowers in years, Digger."

"Ah, it's nothing."

"It's a great deal. And you've done it twice."

"Hey. Come on, those were supposed to make you smile. No tears, hear."

She sniffled and smiled briefly in his direction. They walked on.

"You getting tired?" he asked presently.

"A bit."

He guided her toward an unoccupied bench. Bringing out a large red-and-blue kerchief, he dusted the seat. "Can't have you messing up that pretty dress. Go ahead, sit down."

She stared out into the sunshine, young people sitting on the grass or walking hand in hand, the vibrant life of the park. "The dress is old, Digger. I feel old, too."

"Are you kidding! You hardly look any different than you did when we were going out together."

"I'd like to be able to believe that."

"It's true, all right. You wouldn't believe it of an old boozer like me, but I got a memory like a steel trap. Sometimes, that is. I can remember every day we spent together. You recall the time you tried to teach me to ride a horse?"

She laughed. "You were hopeless."

"Guess I was at that. Big Palomino, he was. Fine-looking animal, name of—Buckwheat."

"You're right."

"Sure. The old brain still clicks away real fine from time to time." He chuckled, thinking back. "I had oil on my boots. . . ."

She swung around to face him. "It took me hours to clean off that horse."

"Sure did," he said with considerable satisfaction. "That horse treated me super rough, if you recollect."

"He put you down into the only spot of mud in the corral. What a mess you were!"

"Got to admit it, I wasn't much of a horseman."

"No, you weren't. But it didn't matter, Digger. You never

let people find out how really gentle you were underneath that roughneck exterior of yours. But I knew."

"Agh," he growled. "Don't let anybody hear you say that. Kept folks intimidated for years with my temper. Still do."

She took his hand, and they sat without speaking for a long time.

"I wish—" she began.

"Yes?"

"Nothing."

"I'll tell you what *I* wish, Ellie. I wish things had worked out differently. We were good for each other."

"For a while, Digger."

"I think we still are." She turned her face to him, waiting for him to go on. Suddenly she understood how much she needed to hear such words, needed the reassurance they gave, the reaffirmation of her attractiveness, her femaleness. "You know how much I always loved you, Ellie. Still do, if the truth be known."

She patted his hand and released it. "Digger—Willard Barnes, always the romantic."

He hawked his throat clear. "Don't let it get around, ruin a man's reputation."

"Trust me."

"Always have."

"Oh, Digger, this is so nice. Makes me wish I could blank out the last few weeks, become the girl you remember once again."

"You can, with me. We could travel, get out of Texas for a while. You've been stuck in one place for too damned long."

"I belong at Southfork," she answered quietly.

"With Jock? Hell, you don't need him, Ellie, not any more. That man's hard, and he's mean, and he stole you away from me, the way he stole my oil." The old rasping edge came into his voice, and his grizzled face clenched with long-nurtured rage.

To Ellie's surprise she felt a strong need to spring to Jock's defense. "He didn't steal me, Digger. Jock may be a lot of things, some not so nice, but he's no thief, never has been."

His anger erupted, and the words came flooding out of

273

him, one stumbling over another. "If it wasn't for Jock Ewing, you'd be married to me now, and we'd both be sitting on top of the world. I'd be rich with my own oil company. I'd be respected and powerful. I'd never have become a drunk, if it hadn't been for Jock Ewing and what he did to me. He ruined it for both of us!"

Miss Ellie shook her head in dismay. The same old complaints, the same excuses for failure, the same angry distortions of past history. The same old Digger. "No, Digger. You wouldn't have changed, and neither would I. I'd still be the way I am. Right now. No different. I wanted to pretend I could turn back the clock. I tried. To forget what has happened, to imagine things were as they used to be. That won't work. It can't. And time can't be stopped, can't be reversed. I'm fond of you, Digger, I always have been, always will be." She kissed him on the cheek. "I'm sorry." She stood up. "I have to get home now."

He reached for her. "What did I say?"

"It's all right. We'll always be friends. But you have just helped me to put things into perspective. You've helped me put my life in order. I can see clearly again. And for that, Digger, I will always be beholden—goodbye."

She strode off across the park, her step remarkably spry and girlish, the best-looking woman Digger had ever seen, the most desirable. He stood up and watched her go. But he made no attempt to follow her.

18

*B*obby was helping several of the ranchhands unload irrigation pipe from the back of a flatbed truck, hauling them into place, when Jock came driving up in one of Southfork's many jeeps. He lurched to a stop, and Bobby went over to him, drawing off his heavy work gloves.

"What are you doing out here, Daddy?"

"I want to go over those feed orders with you. Enough time's passed." His tone was gruff, almost cavalier.

"If you think back, I tried to get you to look at those a couple of weeks ago. More'n once. You were always too busy with something else. I took care of the matter, Daddy."

Jock rolled his shoulders in obvious displeasure. "Well, I want to see them now."

"I've got work to do here."

"Those hands can deal with it. Don't need you wrastling pipe when there are more important things to do."

Bobby climbed into the jeep beside his father. "Let's get this settled right now, Daddy."

"Nothing to settle."

"The hell you say."

"Just want to see the orders. I'm still running this ranch."

"Then maybe you better damn well run it without me."

An uncomfortable silence followed, and when Jock spoke, it was in a small, hurt voice.

"Bobby—"

"J.R.'s making all the decisions around here these days. Talk to him."

"Bobby," Jock said in a calm manner, "I don't give a damn about Cliff Barnes and the OLM, or anything else, for that matter. It's your momma."

All resentment drained swiftly out of Bobby. "Daddy, you can't drop a bombshell the way you did, and when you did, and expect her to turn around right away and be sweet and loving again."

"I don't know. I've really tried with that woman. When I think everything is okay, suddenly it isn't any more. I've tried every way I know to let her know how much I love her. That what happened between Amanda and me has nothing to do with us."

"I wish I could help you, but I don't know how."

"I didn't expect you would, son. Just had to talk to someone, and the only one I could think of was you."

Bobby reached over and dropped his hand on his father's arm, and the two men sat that way without speaking for a very long time.

When Miss Ellie arrived back at the ranch after her meeting with Digger, she found Lucy sitting on the patio, sunning herself. As soon as her grandmother appeared, the girl sprang to her feet, a guilty expression suffusing her pretty face.

"Lucy," Miss Ellie said, with a certain amount of force, "I have been wanting to have a little talk with you."

"I have to get back to the books, Grandma. I've got an awful lot of studying to do."

"It will keep. What I want to know is why you have been avoiding me."

"I haven't—"

"Don't fudge, Lucy. You didn't come see me in the hospital. And since I've been back, you've avoided me, except at meals when the others are around."

"Grandma, I really have to go now."

"Have I done something to hurt you, Lucy?"

"Oh, no."

"I do not believe you are being entirely truthful with me."

"I don't know what you're talking about."

"I had cancer, girl," Miss Ellie said without emphasis.

"You are my granddaughter. Are you concerned lest you catch it from me? Is that what's on your mind?"

Lucy started to turn away.

"Come back here, girl."

"I don't want to talk about it."

"Doesn't matter one bit whether you do or you don't. You are going to talk about it. We have to talk about it."

"Why? There's nothing I can do about it. Talking is not going to make it go away."

"Which means, I suppose, you are going to go on hating me because I got sick."

"Is that what you think? I don't hate you."

"I believe you do."

The cool, defensive mask dropped away, and Lucy began to tremble. Her voice cracked.

"Grandma, stop it! I feel terrible about what happened to you, but I don't know what good this is doing. I don't want to talk about it. I do hate you for getting sick, for having the same blood in you as I have in me, for making me so afraid. Why me? Why me, Grandma?" She began to cry.

"Why *me*, Lucy? Why anyone? Do you think anybody wants this to happen to them? Fate plays funny tricks on people, and never asks permission. God's ways are unfathomable to us ordinary folk. We Ewings have acquired a lot of the good things of this world, a lot of profit and pleasure, perhaps an inordinate amount of rewards, maybe more than we deserve. So why not some of the bad, as well? I'm not a philosopher, Lucy. I'm not a prophet. I can't explain much of life to myself, let alone to somebody else. I just know that we all have to play the cards we're dealt, live out our destinies as best and as bravely as we can. None of us is perfect, nothing is. But I am not going to allow my granddaughter, who is precious and unique and whom I love very dearly, to go on avoiding me. I couldn't stand that, Lucy, not for one more day, hear." She extended her hand, and Lucy took it.

"Oh, Grandma, I'm so scared. I don't want to go through what you've been through."

"Lucy, because it happened to me doesn't mean it will inevitably happen to you. But I don't want you to avoid learning about your own body because you're scared."

"Self-examination didn't stop you from getting it."

"I discovered the disease in time, and here I am, still alive and full of life."

"I can see that."

"Better believe it."

"But I don't know if I could live—that way."

"Would you rather I had died?"

"Oh, my God, no!"

"Then, Lucy, I don't think there is anything more to say about it."

"Maybe so. But how do I handle the fear?"

"We all live with fear some of the time. You learn to deal with it and get on with the business of living."

"Grandma, I'm not sure I can."

"Can you try?"

"Yes. I can try."

"Good enough. You try, and you will."

"I'll try," Lucy said, before burying her face against her grandmother's breast. "I'll try, I surely will try."

By late afternoon the clouds began to form—dark, swirling masses that blotted out the sun and shadowed the landscape, bringing on an early nightfall. Thunder rumbled in the southeast, lightning stabbed through the sky, and the thick scent of moisture hung in the air. Soon rain began to fall. Droplets at first, then welcome fat blobs of water that disappeared thirstily into the parched land. All over Texas great shouts of joy went up, and men and beasts alike stood out in the open to welcome the end of the drought. The heat wave was over, life would soon return to normal.

By the time Jock and Bobby made it back to the ranch house in the open jeep, they were drenched, but uncomplaining. Laughing and joking, they went inside and started up the stairs, intending to change clothes.

Miss Ellie, coming out of the den, stopped them. "Jock," she said sternly, "I want to talk to you."

"Let me get out of these wet clothes," he replied.

"No, now." She disappeared into the den.

Jock and Bobby exchanged a puzzled glance, then husband followed wife, closing the door behind him. She was waiting in the center of the room, unsmiling, her gaze level.

278

Jock mopped at his face, wondering what new blow was about to take its toll.

"Jock," she began without preamble, "when I found out you'd lied to me all those years, I was hurt. Damned hurt."

"I never meant for you to be hurt."

"I know that now." Her manner softened perceptibly. "If you hadn't told me about Amanda, I reckon I'd've found some other excuse to try and drive you away."

"Drive me away?"

"Exactly."

"But why?"

"Because I was so afraid of losing you after the operation. I'm not happy that there was an Amanda, but I finally realized I had used her as an excuse so that if you did leave me, I could pretend it was because of her, and not because you couldn't stand to look at me, to touch me."

"Oh, Ellie, never. Never."

"I'm still afraid I'll lose you," she said. "And I don't know how to change that. But if you'll be patient with me—and strong—maybe we can make it work again. Will you try, Jock?"

"You know I will."

"So will I, Jock."

He took two quick strides, closing the space that separated them, taking her in his arms. "Damn," he muttered thickly. "I'm gonna get you all wet."

"Oh, I don't care, Jock, I don't care."

He caressed her gently. "I love you, Miss Ellie. I truly do."

"And I love you, Jock."

They stood there rocking for a very long time, darkness closing in outside and the rain falling, life returning to the land each had loved for so long and so very much.

ABOUT THE AUTHOR

BURT HIRSCHFELD was born in Manhattan and raised in the Bronx. He left school at the age of seventeen and took a series of menial jobs. Immediately after Pearl Harbor he enlisted, and spent three of his four years in service overseas. After the war, he attended a southern college for several years. For the next fifteen years he worked on and off for movie companies and also did some radio and acting work. Burt Hirschfeld did not write his first novel until he was in his early thirties. He worked on it for three years and, when it only earned $1,500, he abandoned writing for several years. At thirty-seven, he decided to find out once and for all whether he had the makings of a successful writer and began to freelance. He wrote everything—from comic books to movie reviews. He also wrote numerous paperback novels under various pseudonyms and eleven nonfiction books for teenagers which were very well received. *Fire Island* was his first major success. His recent novels include *Key West, Aspen, Provincetown* and *Why Not Everything?* Burt Hirschfeld lives in Westport, Connecticut.

COMING NEXT

The amazing third novel in the new series about
television's most notorious family

THE MEN OF DALLAS
By Burt Hirschfeld

*A different breed of men. Larger than
life. Struggling for money, power and sex.
Some of them will stop at nothing.*

J.R. He plays the game according to his own rules
in business—and in love.

BOBBY. He lives in his brother's shadow, but
how long can that last. Will the ties of blood be
strong enough to keep the two brothers together?

GARY. The lost brother. He's searching for a new
life away from Southfork.

CLIFF BARNES. Related to the Ewings by marriage, his greatest desire is to destroy the family.
But they are determined to destroy him first.

DIGGER BARNES. Will he ever be able to
accept the fact that Jock got what he wanted so
desperately—Miss Ellie and the oil?

JOCK EWING. His blood and sweat built the
Ewing empire and he's determined not to let anyone take it away from him.

THE EWINGS OF DALLAS

The Ewings of Dallas—the most closely watched family of America. Now, you can follow TV's most fascinating family in these three new titles from Bantam. You'll want to complete your own set and order additional copies as gifts for fellow Dallas addicts.

THE DALLAS FAMILY ALBUM   (01289-4) $6.95

This large format (8⅜"x10⅞") book contains over 150 photographs (many in color), narrative captions, and star biographies which bring the illustrious Ewing family to life.

THE EWINGS OF DALLAS   (14439-1) $2.75
Burt Hirschfeld

Follow the escapades of the Ewings—the oil barons of Texas who love, hate, and wheel and deal their way to fortune.

THE QUOTATIONS OF J.R. EWING   (14440-5) $1.50

The pithy sayings of America's favorite villain. "Not since John Milton gave Satan all the good lines in *Paradise Lost* has a villain so appalled—and fascinated—the world."—*People Magazine*

To order indicate title and number of each book(s). Include check or money order (plus $1.00 for postage and handling).
Send to: **BANTAM BOOKS**, DEPT. EW, 666 FIFTH AVENUE, NEW YORK, NEW YORK 10103.

THE LATEST BOOKS
IN THE BANTAM
BESTSELLING TRADITION

Bantam Book Catalog

Here's your up-to-the-minute listing of over 1,400 titles by your favorite authors.

This illustrated, large format catalog gives a description of each title. For your convenience, it is divided into categories in fiction and non-fiction—gothics, science fiction, westerns, mysteries, cookbooks, mysticism and occult, biographies, history, family living, health, psychology, art.

So don't delay—take advantage of this special opportunity to increase your reading pleasure.

Just send us your name and address and 50¢ (to help defray postage and handling costs).